PRAISE FOR *DESIGNATED DAUGHTERS* AND MARGARET MARON

"Maron knows how to adorn a solid murder mystery with plenty of ancillary entertainments. But her broader theme involves the way families flourish when they work together for the common good...the clan members Maron really cherishes are those who devote themselves to caring for the elders of the family. Living saints they are, every last one of them."

—*New York Times Book Review*

"Maron weaves family threads together with current events that leave the reader wanting to know more about the Knott family tree...[*Designated Daughters*] offers loyal fans a fresh look at [Deborah's] expansive family and community. Readers will savor the slow-paced Southern culture and layered story."

—*Library Journal* (starred review)

"In MWA Grand Master Maron's outstanding 19th mystery featuring judge Deborah Knott of North Carolina's Colleton County (after 2012's *The Buzzard Table*), Deborah's elderly aunt, Rachel Morton, lies near death in a hospice...Maron achieves a delicate balance as she explores differences between mistakes, sins, and crimes, and shows that justice is not always arrived at by conventional means. Humor (e.g., Deborah outfoxes an unscrupulous auctioneer) and social issues (e.g., the difficult role of caregivers to the elderly) add to the warmth of a large family with all its foibles, squabbles, and quirks."

—*Publishers Weekly* (starred review)

"There's nobody better."

—*Chicago Tribune*

"Maron writes with wit and sophistication."

—*USA Today*

"As always, Maron skillfully layers an absorbing plot with the doings of Deborah's large extended family."

—*Booklist*

"Opening a new Margaret Maron is like unwrapping a Christmas gift."

—*Cleveland Plain Dealer*

"Of today's series writers none has been more successful at weaving the bond between star and audience than Margaret Maron."

—*San Diego Union-Tribune*

"Maron has a pleasant, easygoing style that's smooth, generous, and perceptive...a delightful, thoughtful, good-natured series."

—*Providence Journal*

"Always a writer gifted with the ability to convey an enthralling sense of time and place...Reading Maron is like sipping a Carolina cooler—solid comfort together with fascinating sensations."

—*Greensboro News & Record* (NC)

DESIGNATED
DAUGHTERS

DESIGNATED DAUGHTERS

MARGARET MARON

GC

GRAND CENTRAL
PUBLISHING

NEW YORK   BOSTON

Copyright © 2014 by Margaret Maron
Preview of *Long Upon the Land* copyright © 2015 by Margaret Maron
All rights reserved. In accordance with the U.S. Copyright Act of 1976, the scanning, uploading, and electronic sharing of any part of this book without the permission of the publisher constitutes unlawful piracy and theft of the author's intellectual property. If you would like to use material from the book (other than for review purposes), prior written permission must be obtained by contacting the publisher at permissions@hbgusa.com. Thank you for your support of the author's rights.

Grand Central Publishing
Hachette Book Group
1290 Avenue of the Americas
New York, NY 10104
www.HachetteBookGroup.com

Grand Central Publishing is a division of Hachette Book Group, Inc.
The Grand Central Publishing name and logo are trademarks of Hachette Book Group, Inc.

The Hachette Speakers Bureau provides a wide range of authors for speaking events. To find out more, go to www.hachettespeakersbureau.com or call (866) 376-6591.

The publisher is not responsible for websites (or their content) that are not owned by the publisher.

Printed in the United States of America

Originally published in hardcover by Hachette Book Group
First mass market edition: May 2015

10 9 8 7 6 5 4 3 2 1
OPM

For
John and Andrea,
With so very much love

ACKNOWLEDGMENTS

My continuing gratitude to the three who have been my go-to sources almost from the very beginning: District Court Judges Shelly S. Holt and Rebecca W. Blackmore and John W. Smith, director of the Administrative Office of the Court (NCAOC). District Court Judge Shelley Desvousges has become their local backup. Thanks also to Patricia Sprinkle, Joan Hess, Larry Doran, Katy Munger, and especially Sarah Farris Smith for sharing their stories.

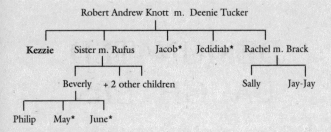

Robert Andrew Knott m. Deenie Tucker

Kezzie   Sister m. Rufus   Jacob*   Jedidiah*   Rachel m. Brack

Beverly   + 2 other children   Sally   Jay-Jay

Philip   May*   June*

DEBORAH KNOTT'S FAMILY TREE

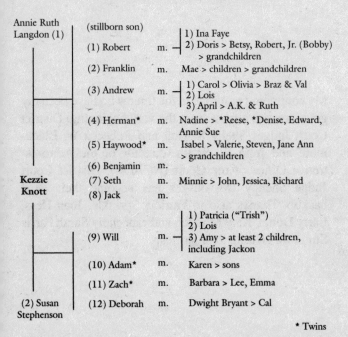

Annie Ruth Langdon (1)

(stillborn son)

(1) Robert   m.   1) Ina Faye
2) Doris > Betsy, Robert, Jr. (Bobby) > grandchildren

(2) Franklin   m.   Mae > children > grandchildren

(3) Andrew   m.   1) Carol > Olivia > Braz & Val
2) Lois
3) April > A.K. & Ruth

(4) Herman*   m.   Nadine > *Reese, *Denise, Edward, Annie Sue

(5) Haywood*   m.   Isabel > Valerie, Steven, Jane Ann > grandchildren

(6) Benjamin   m.

(7) Seth   m.   Minnie > John, Jessica, Richard

(8) Jack   m.

Kezzie Knott

(9) Will   m.   1) Patricia ("Trish")
2) Lois
3) Amy > at least 2 children, including Jackon

(10) Adam*   m.   Karen > sons

(11) Zach*   m.   Barbara > Lee, Emma

(2) Susan Stephenson

(12) Deborah   m.   Dwight Bryant > Cal

* Twins

DESIGNATED
DAUGHTERS

CHAPTER
1

What shall we say of lawyers?

— Cicero

Wednesday morning, and we were nearing the end of jury selection for a civil case when the rear door of my courtroom opened and several people entered. In the quietness of the courtroom, as they took seats in an empty bench to the left of the jury pool, I heard a faint squeaking sound, but I couldn't determine its source. The latecomers ranged in age from late teens to a wizened old man in a wheelchair. I recognized only one of the group—Marillyn Mulholland, who owns a printing company here in town. She had printed up my business cards back when I was still in private practice and, although semiretired now, she had personally overseen our wedding invitations when Dwight and I were married Christmas before last.

Taking the seat beside her was an unfamiliar young woman. She was slender and wore trendy turquoise-blue leggings, an off-the-shoulder purple jersey, and matching purple hair.

Then I did a double take. Young woman? Like hell! Her slender figure and push-up bra may have fooled me momentarily, but the face beneath the purple hair would have looked at least twenty years older than mine except that I knew for a fact she'd had a second face-lift last year. The purple hair was new, though, and must be a wig, because her own hair had never come back in properly after the chemo.

Sally Crenshaw.

My cousin. The sixty-two-year-old daughter of my daddy's sister Rachel.

Now what had brought her to my courtroom this morning? At first I wondered if she'd come to personally tell me that Aunt Rachel had finally died, but she studiously avoided my eyes and seemed caught up in the jury examination being conducted by the two attorneys at the front of the room. I turned my attention back to counsel for the plaintiff, who asked that I excuse the next prospective juror because she had just said she knew the sister of the defendant.

I nodded and we moved on. This was our second day of voir dire, a tedious, time-consuming process. Some people are eager to serve, usually for the wrong reasons, but most would rather not spend the time listening to legal jousting when they had planned to spend the week doing other, more interesting things.

"Your Honor, I have a hair appointment for this afternoon," a blonde woman said.

"Color?" I asked, noticing a thin line of dark roots at the hairline of her forehead.

"Just shampoo and cut," she said brightly.

I denied her request. Color appointments aren't all that easy to get, but there was no reason she couldn't reschedule a simple cut.

I had already excused several from the pool because they had personal connections with some of the participants and I was again reminding them about their need to keep an open mind, fairness, etcetera, etcetera, when I noticed that an older man in the second row of the jury box seemed to be having trouble hearing me. He leaned forward intently, turning what was probably his good ear toward me and frowning in concentration.

I glanced down at the diagram I'd filled in of the current occupants. "Mr. Ogburn?" I said, speaking more loudly and clearly than usual. "Is there a problem with your hearing?"

"Yes, ma'am, Your Honor. I don't do so good without my hearing aid." He held up a small flesh-colored device.

"Is your battery dead?"

"No, ma'am, but there was a sign outside that said to turn off all electronic devices."

I tried not to laugh. "That doesn't apply to hearing aids," I told him; and when he had put it back in his ear, I let the two attorneys have their turn. Thankfully, the last two jurors were acceptable to both sides.

Today's case was a civil action: Bruce Connolly versus Dotty Connolly Morefield, a middle-aged brother suing his middle-aged sister over their late mother's possessions. The woman had died without a will, so the clerk of the court had appointed Mrs. Morefield the administratrix for the estate. Well before her death, the mother had given Mrs. Morefield her power of attorney and that was good enough for our clerk. After receiving her account of all the assets, he had split everything equally between Mr. Connolly and his three sisters, "everything" being her bank account and whatever possessions were in her house at the time of death.

Mr. Connolly's suit alleged that the sisters had removed certain valuable items from the house before the mother's death and he claimed he was owed money for conversions of those possessions.

A sour-faced man with receding gray hair and glasses that he kept taking on and off to polish, he asserted that Mrs. Morefield, a motherly looking woman with soft white hair, had not listed all the assets.

His attorney quickly established that Mrs. Morefield had been the mother's main caregiver. She had sold the family home as the mother wished and used the money to rent a smaller house near the three sisters.

Mr. Connolly, who lived out in the mountains four hours away, had agreed to the arrangement.

"My wife and I would've been glad to have Mother come live with us," he testified in a pious tone as he polished his glasses for the fourth or fifth time, "but her church and all her friends were here and she said two women didn't need to be sharing a kitchen. Dotty'll say that moving Mother was mostly on her, but the whole family helped. I drove all the way over here in my truck and almost threw my back out getting her stuff moved. Mother only lived there two years before she passed, so there should have been a lot more cash."

He had a copy of the check from the sale of the house, and copies of rent receipts were also entered as evidence.

When I looked up from those documents, I saw that my cousin Sally was leaving the courtroom, her telephone to her ear, and I realized I'd missed my chance to tell my bailiff I wanted to speak to her.

Too late. I gave a mental shrug as Connolly's attorney said, "No further questions, Your Honor."

By now it was almost twelve, but before I could adjourn for lunch, Mr. Connolly, still in the witness-box, said, "It's not just the money, Your Honor. It's her silverware and her Hummel figurines. She spent a fortune on those things and Dotty never listed them. I just want my fair share."

Fair is such a slippery term, and my definition of fair seldom satisfies both sides.

CHAPTER
2

*As in the case of berries on the trees and the
fruits of the earth, there must be that which in
its season of full ripeness is ready to wither and
fall.*

— Cicero

MIDMORNING, WEDNESDAY

The old woman lay motionless against the pillows
that supported her head and upper body and helped
her breathe more easily. The ventilator had been removed two days earlier, as had the IV that had kept her
hydrated and nourished. Neither food nor water had
passed her lips in the seven days since her last stroke.
Nor had she spoken in all that time.

Nevertheless, the gray-haired aide hired by the
woman's family to supplement the nursing staff here
kept up a running stream of cheerful chatter as she
sponged that frail body and smoothed on sweet-

smelling lotion. She swabbed her patient's mouth with a wet gauze pad, checked the pad beneath those withered hips—*still clean and dry, poor thing*—and gently dressed her in a fresh nightgown that was now two sizes too large.

"We're gonna have to get you a new gown, Miss Rachel. This one's real pretty with all the lace around the neck, but it keeps on slipping down, don't it?"

Not that Miss Rachel had much to be modest about anymore, the aide thought to herself, pitying the flaccid breasts that had nursed two children in their prime and now lay flatter than an empty purse on that emaciated chest.

Like her children, like her siblings, like her parents before her, Rachel Morton had been tall and big-boned, a country woman who had worked in the fields alongside her husband, who had cooked and cleaned and kept her vegetable garden as free of weeds as her house was free of dust. Until her husband died and the farm acreage was sold, she had worked at their roadside vegetable stand long past any real financial need, dispensing friendly conversation, country wisdom, and girlhood anecdotes along with her tomatoes, corn, butter beans, or whatever else was in season.

Customers who pulled up to the open-sided shelter, intending to grab a cucumber or melon and be on their busy way, often wound up staying much longer. Insatiably interested in people, Rachel remembered the smallest details and would inquire about children and grandchildren by name, ask if someone's rheumatism was better now that warm weather was here, and want to know how that luncheon turned out that another customer was planning when she stopped by last week for a half-dozen identical tomatoes to serve as chicken salad cups. Lonely retirees would sit down in one of her slat-backed chairs to talk of bygone days when they were active and needed; and young stay-at-home moms, hungry for adult conversation, would watch their barefooted toddlers build hoppy-toad houses in the warm dirt. She was a natural storyteller and could turn even the most prosaic event into an amusing story.

"Rachel could talk the ears off a mule," her husband used to say with a fond smile.

Her white hair was still as thick as in her youth, and the aide brushed the soft curls into place murmuring, "Sure wish I had your pretty hair, Miss Rachel."

The old woman lay quiet and unresponsive and no emotion touched that finely wrinkled face. When the aide first came to help care for her, those eyelids had occasionally fluttered open and those lips had curled in a smile.

No more.

According to her doctor, she was in no pain and the end was expected soon. Indeed, death had been expected as soon as they took her off all the machines and brought her over here to the hospice wing of the hospital, but that hadn't happened yet and her vital signs were as steady as ever.

Her midmorning ministrations completed, the aide sat down in the recliner next to the window, uncapped the cup of coffee one of the staff had brought her, and reached for the worn King James Bible that had been the old woman's comfort when she moved into her daughter's home after the first bad stroke. She had tried to accommodate herself to the modern version, but it was the old familiar phrases that spoke to her heart most deeply. Before the last stroke, she had wanted someone to read it aloud and the aide enjoyed it as well. Psalms and Proverbs were the old woman's favorites, and the aide turned to the page she had left off at the evening before, because it was said that people could hear and understand, even when in a vegetative state.

> *"He that goeth about as a talebearer revealeth secrets...An inheritance may be gotten hastily at the beginning, but the end thereof shall not be blessed."*

The aide paused to take a sip of the hot, fragrant coffee and glanced over at her patient. The old woman's eyes were open wide and her clear blue eyes bored into the aide's.

"...secrets," she whispered. "...not an inheritance...was a debt he never paid...But it *was* blessed, wasn't it? All those babies saved?"

The aide was so startled that coffee splashed across the Bible's thin pages.

"Miss Rachel?"

"I didn't tell Jacob. You know I didn't, Jed...you have to tell him...you need to stop or tell him yourself."

Those first words came out thin and raspy but her voice strengthened with each new syllable.

The aide mopped up the worst of the spilled coffee and laid aside the Bible, then went to bend over that newly animated face. "Miss Rachel? Miss Rachel, honey?"

The old woman paused as if listening, then smiled up into eyes only she could see. "Did you see the way Ransom looked at me in church? You reckon he likes me?"

The aide patted her cheek and said, "I'm sure he does, honey."

"Well, it's about time you answered me! Where'd Jacob get to? The cow's got out again and I can't find her and it's almost two hours past milking time. Kezzie's gonna skin y'all alive if he comes home and sees y'all didn't mend the fence. Mammy said..."

Moving over to the window with her cell phone, the aide touched one of the numbers on her call list and waited until someone finally answered. "Sally? This is Lois. You know how you and Jay-Jay were grieving that you'd never hear your mama's sweet voice again? Both of y'all need to get back over here right away, honey. She's talking a blue streak."

CHAPTER
3

When you have no basis, abuse the plaintiff.
— Cicero

So who died?" I asked Portland Brewer when she joined me for a late lunch at Bright Leaf Restaurant, a block from the Colleton County courthouse.

Her uncle Ash is married to my Aunt Zell and we've been best friends ever since we got kicked out of the junior girls' Sunday school class for reducing prissy little Caroline Atherton to tears two Sundays in a row. Black does nothing for her olive skin or dark curly hair or even for her figure now that she's back to her pre-pregnancy shape, so the only reason she has a good black suit is because she still believes red isn't suitable for funerals.

"Laurel McElveen's niece," she said, and when she saw my blank look, she elucidated. "You know...the woman that came to live with her after the accident?"

Mrs. McElveen is one of Portland's blue-chip clients and a mover and shaker here in Dobbs. The widow of a wealthy cardiologist, she sits on several boards, including the library and the hospital. Two or three years ago, she was crippled in a car crash. I heard about the accident at the time, of course, but I'd never met the companion and her name wasn't familiar.

"What happened?"

"Heart attack, apparently. Same thing that killed her mother. Mrs. McElveen blames herself for not realizing Evelyn might've had a weak heart, too. In a weird way, though, it seems to have put the starch back in her."

"Starch?"

"She used to be so opinionated and decisive before the accident, and no rubber stamp for any of the board members she worked with."

"I've heard Barbara on the subject," I said dryly. My brother Zach's wife is Colleton County's library director. "Mrs. McElveen browbeat the county commissioners into keeping the libraries funded."

"Don't I know it? For a while there, I was afraid she was going to make me take the whole board to court, but ever since Christmas, it was like she was drifting into a fog or something. She stopped going to board meetings, stopped her therapy, just didn't seem to care about anything."

"Depression?"

"Maybe. She worked really hard to get the use of her legs back, but she still can't walk more than a few steps, so maybe she did get depressed. But she called me last week and when I saw her right after the funeral today, it's as if she's decided to rejoin the living. All piss and vinegar again. Wants to rewrite her will now that her niece has died. You having wine?"

She'd been totally conscientious about alcohol while carrying and then nursing the baby, but she'd missed her occasional glass of wine with our lunches.

I shook my head. "You go ahead, though. I have to be back in court this afternoon."

The waitress had already brought me a glass of iced tea, and when she came back with Portland's wine, she asked if we wanted to split the shrimp salad, our usual choice when we eat here. Bright Leaf serves the same gigantic portions that made it popular back when farmers came to town on Saturdays after a week of heavy manual labor in the tobacco fields that used to surround Dobbs; and while I have a healthy appetite, I do try to keep it reined in.

Now that we're both working mothers, we don't hang out together as much as we used to, so there was a lot of news to catch up on. Her baby, Carolyn Deborah, was seventeen months old now and talking like an iPod left on autoplay, while my stepson—no, not my stepson, I happily reminded myself, not since the adoption went through last month—my *son*. Cal turned ten last month and would be playing Little League baseball again this summer.

Three years ago, neither Portland nor I had seen this coming.

She and Avery had been married for fourteen years

and had almost given up hope of ever having children, while Dwight wasn't even on my radar except as a longtime family friend who furnished a handy shoulder to cry on whenever my love life turned sour. Then suddenly we were married. A month later, his ex-wife was murdered and his son Cal came to live with us. Happily, we've all managed to adjust and now it's hard for Portland to remember what her life was like before Carolyn. Same for me. I can't begin to imagine mine without Dwight and Cal in it.

"Did I tell you that we're finally building the pond shed?" I asked as I speared the last grape tomato on my plate. "Seth and Haywood are going to help Dwight pour the slab this weekend."

Portland laughed. "When are you going to show him the pig?"

My brother Will runs an auction house and he'd given me a good deal on a large pink metal sign that was pig-shaped, measured about five feet long by three feet tall, and spelled out BAR-B-CUE & SPARE RIBS in bright pink neon. The metal was rusty and dented, and the pink tubing on the back side was too broken to be repaired, but my brother Herman, Haywood's twin, is an electrician, as are his daughter and son. Together they've done a great job of getting the front side working so that when it's switched on, the feet look as if they're running. Cal giggles every time he sees it. When the shed is built and the front sides screened in, that pig should look great on the back wall.

I'm crazy about neon, the lit tubes and bright colors

rev me up, but Dwight thinks the signs I've collected are white-trash tacky. I still have hopes of converting him, but I need to choose the right moment. "I'm going to let Cal give it to him for Father's Day."

"Sneaky," said Portland. "Be sure you let Avery and me know when you plan to unveil it. We want to see Dwight's face."

We moved on to courthouse gossip. There was a rumor going round that one of the magistrates was sleeping with her husband's business partner and that her husband might be embezzling from the firm, so was it true passion or a safety play on the wife's part? Stay tuned, folks.

As we walked back to the courthouse together, the sun burned down from a cloudless blue sky and made us grateful for the fully-leafed crepe myrtles and acanthus trees that shaded the sidewalks. Middle of May and almost every tree had a ring of colorful petunias, impatiens, or coleus around its base, and bright red geraniums bloomed in the concrete urns on either side of the courthouse door.

I don't hear too many jury cases, but when I do, I give a slightly longer than usual lunch break so that people don't have to bolt their food, which was why Portland and I could take our time.

"All rise," said the bailiff as I entered the nearly empty courtroom. Except for a couple of gray-haired courtroom buffs who attend jury trials as a form of cheap entertainment, the other eight or ten seemed to be partisans of the combatants, and that included the group that had come in with my cousin earlier.

I took my place behind my nameplate, a gift from Barbara McCrory, a Wisconsin friend who made it to the bench before me. My name is on the front, but the back reads: REMEMBER: THIS IS NOT ALL ABOUT YOU.

"Oyez, oyez, oyez," the bailiff intoned. "This court is now back in session, the Honorable Deborah Knott present and presiding."

With Mr. Connolly back on the stand, Joyce Mitchell, the attorney hired by Connolly's sister, was ready to cross-examine. Joyce is a quiet, soft-spoken woman who looks at least fifteen years younger than I know her to be.

She adjusted her glasses, tucked a strand of dark hair behind one ear, and smiled pleasantly. "Mr. Connolly, were you aware that your mother sold her house at the bottom of the market?"

"I know she got a lot less than the house was worth, but her rent wasn't all that much either."

"You also know that she needed round-the-clock nursing care the last three months of her life?"

Mr. Connolly gave an indignant snort. "And that was a waste of good money when she had three daughters living here who could've taken turns sitting by her bed."

"And you, too, of course?" Joyce asked with sympathetic interest.

"Objection," his attorney said. "What bearing does this have on my client's claim?"

"It goes to show why there was considerably less money than he expected, Your Honor," Joyce said.

"Overruled," I agreed. "Continue."

"Anyhow, I live four hours away." He removed his glasses and polished them with his handkerchief. "All of them are just minutes."

Joyce glanced at the jury box and I followed her eyes. A woman sitting in the front row had pressed her lips into a tight line.

Moving on, Joyce said, "I gather your mother was quite a collector, Mr. Connolly? Had a lot of valuable possessions?"

"She sure did. And I want to know what happened to them, because when my wife and I went to help clean out her house after the funeral, it'd been picked clean."

"You're sure she had a good eye for things of value?"

"Absolutely." He slid his glasses back on and gave a firm jerk of his head to emphasize his point.

"Like those figurines for instance?"

He shrugged. "They might not've been to my taste, but I've looked on eBay and they're asking eight or ten times what she would've paid for them."

"Asking or getting? I daresay your attorney here could ask a thousand dollars an hour to represent you, but would you pay it?"

Smiles and laughter from the spectators.

Joyce allowed a dubious frown to cross her pretty face. "But maybe her furniture wasn't as valuable?"

"Oh, yes, it was!" he said quickly. "Some of it—"

He suddenly realized where Joyce was headed and tried to backtrack. "I mean, some of it was good, but most of it was just ordinary furniture store stuff."

"When you drove over in your pickup truck to help move your mother into a smaller house, did you take any of her furniture home with you?"

"Well, I might've taken— I mean, Mother might've *given* me some things she didn't have room for."

Joyce pulled a list from her files. "Did those things include a Chippendale piecrust table, a mahogany sleigh bed, an 1830 blanket chest, a Queen Anne chair, and a Hepplewhite mirror?"

A juror seated in the second row leaned forward to listen with bright-eyed interest. There was something familiar about her.

Mr. Connolly glared at Joyce. "Mother wanted me to have them."

The juror raised a skeptical eyebrow and I realized that she was a picker for my brother Will's auction house. I glanced at the seating chart. Jody Munger. I might not know what a Hepplewhite mirror was, but I bet Jody Munger did.

"Even though those six pieces are worth many times what the figurines would actually bring?" Joyce asked.

Mr. Connolly finally had the good sense to hush and let his attorney speak for him.

"Objection. Is there any proof that she owned those pieces or what they're worth?"

Joyce held out copies of the document from which she had been reading, one for him and one for the court. "Your Honor, I'd like to enter as evidence this appraisal from her insurance company."

I nodded and she reeled off values for the benefit of the jury, then turned back to Mr. Connolly. "At that same time, did you also take a twelve-gauge shotgun that had been appraised at around a thousand dollars?"

He could not let that go unchallenged. "That shotgun belonged to my daddy's daddy and I'm the only Connolly male. Mother knew they wanted it to come to me."

While the men on the jury might have agreed with that sentiment, two of the women exchanged glances that did not bode well for Mr. Connolly.

"No further questions," Joyce said.

The only other witness for the plaintiff's side was an antiques dealer from Raleigh who was presented as a specialist in Hummel figurines. She explained that they began as drawings by a German nun and were turned into ceramics in the 1930s.

"Mr. Connolly thinks that his mother began collecting them in the mid-fifties, so she might well have had some early examples worth several hundred dollars."

An enlargement of an out-of-focus snapshot taken a few years earlier was entered into evidence. It pictured the late Mrs. Connolly standing in front of several shelves crammed with the knickknacks. The dealer pointed to one of the clearer items. "That looks like an *Apple Tree Boy* from the early seventies. Even though it's comparatively late, it could fetch up to five or six hundred, depending on condition."

Upon cross-examination, however, the dealer admitted that she had never actually seen the collection, only this picture. "Some of these do look like rare pieces, but without actually seeing them, I can't be one hundred percent sure."

She also grudgingly agreed when Joyce suggested that prices had dropped dramatically in the last few years.

With no further witnesses for Mr. Connolly's side, Joyce Mitchell called a Peggy Clontz to the stand.

Mrs. Clontz was a cousin who had known the siblings from birth—"He was always a greedy little boy"—and she was present when the late Mrs. Connolly expressed dismay at what her son had taken. "She said she had told the girls to keep whatever was left for themselves."

"Objection, hearsay, and self-interest," said Connolly's attorney.

Before I could rule, Joyce Mitchell quickly said, "Were you one of her heirs, Mrs. Clontz?"

The woman looked confused. "I thought she didn't leave a will."

"Let me rephrase that. Did you benefit in any way by her death?"

Mrs. Clontz shook her head.

"Did you expect some of the silver or the figurines?"

"Absolutely not. About three months before she died, we were looking at her collection. That's when she gave me *Feeding Time*."

"*Feeding Time*?"

"It's a little farm girl feeding the chickens, like when we were children."

I smiled at that, having a soft spot for chickens myself.

There being no questions from the plaintiff, Joyce called the sisters to the stand, beginning with Mrs. Morefield, whose blue eyes flashed with indignation at being accused of acting unfairly.

The two younger sisters confirmed what Mrs. Clontz had said and one added, "Dotty could have emptied Mother's bank account, but she didn't want to bust up the family over money."

Her voice broke and she searched in her bag for a tissue. "He's our brother, yet that's all he seems to care about—money."

(Or, as one of my law professors was fond of quoting, "Never say you really know someone till you've divided an inheritance with him.")

Despite stringent cross-examination, all three sisters were clear about their mother's wishes. Plaintiff's attorney argued for the letter of the law, which was that when someone died intestate, the assets should be equally shared. "The furniture Mr. Connolly took should not be figured in, since his mother gave it to him before her death."

"By that argument," Joyce said, "there were no figurines and no silverware to share, because she gave everything else to her daughters before she died."

The jury was out less than half an hour. They found

for the defendant and wanted to know if they could compel Mr. Connolly to pay her legal fees.

I suppressed a smile, thanked them for their service, service that would exempt them from jury duty for the next two years, and said, "At this point, I will entertain motions from counsel."

Mr. Connolly polished his glasses so vigorously that I expected to see the lens crumble to dust, and his attorney sat glumly while Joyce Mitchell made a formal motion to have me do exactly what the jury had suggested. She presented her figures and her fee was quite reasonable, so I signed the order that would require Mr. Connolly to reimburse his sister.

Marillyn Mulholland and some of the others seated near her had broad smiles on their faces as they surged toward Mrs. Morefield to congratulate her.

I rapped my gavel for silence and told them to take their celebration out to the hall. With order restored, I was looking at the documents for the one civil matter that remained on my calendar when my clerk whispered that my brother Seth's wife had called and asked her to relay a message about my Aunt Rachel, my daddy's younger sister.

"She died?" I asked, thinking that this was why Sally had left so abruptly. I was sad for her and for Daddy and Aunt Sister, too, but Aunt Rachel's death had been expected for several days now.

The clerk shook her head. "Miss Minnie says she's talking again and you might want to be there."

By now it was after four o'clock, but rather than

have me continue a simple uncontested divorce to a later date, the woman's attorney swore we could get it done in fifteen minutes. I'm a fast reader. Ten minutes later, all the papers were signed, the marriage was formally dissolved, and I was out of there.

CHAPTER
4

Yet there is a certain musical quality of the voice which becomes—I know not how—even more melodious in old age.

— Cicero

As soon as I turned into the hospice wing that afternoon, the usual hospital smells of antiseptics and germicidal floor cleaners gave way to a warm yeasty aroma of cinnamon, nutmeg, and honey. Right away I knew Aunt Sister's twin granddaughters must have driven down from the mountains with a hamper of the signature sweet rolls they make for the tea room they run up in Cedar Gap. I was holding court up there in the mountains a couple of years ago when they lied to their parents about being enrolled in Tanser-McLeod College and used their tuition money to buy a half interest in the business.* It was only open for lunch and

_____
*High Country Fall

afternoon tea, but the twins shared such a talent for melt-in-your mouth baked goods that the place was usually jammed. I hoped I'd be able to snag one of their buttery caramel buns before they disappeared.

Knotts old and young spilled out into the hall from Aunt Rachel's room. Mostly they were the younger generation: my cousins, nephews, and nieces. They sipped from plastic water bottles and munched on sugary rolls, talking in the low voices you always hear when death is near. The older ones had crowded into Aunt Rachel's room to cluster around her bed.

Hospice rooms are fairly big and visiting rules are more relaxed so that friends and family don't have to take turns saying goodbye. Nevertheless, mine is such a large family that the room couldn't hold all of us at one time. Still, I managed to eel my way past some of my brothers and cousins and their spouses to get close enough to see and hear.

My brother Herman's wheelchair occupied the space normally allotted to a nightstand, and Daddy and Aunt Sister sat on the other side. Aunt Rachel's son Jay-Jay and her purple-haired daughter Sally sat shoulder to shoulder. The bed had been lowered almost to the floor, which made it easy for them to reach out and stroke her arms or hold her hands.

Daddy and I had visited here as soon as Jay-Jay called to say that he and Sally had agreed to have Aunt Rachel's life-support system turned off, but Sally had gone home to shower and change, so I hadn't seen her in several weeks. How I'd missed hearing about her new wig was a mystery since Doris and Isabel, my most judgmental sisters-in-law, took great pleasure in starting phone calls with "You will *not* believe what that flaky Sally's gone and done now."

I myself thought they should cut her a little slack considering that she had beaten the big C and had even taken Aunt Rachel into her home after the stroke. They thought that cancer should have sobered her and they were a little miffed that Aunt Rachel thought the multicolored wigs were cute.

Tears ran down Jay-Jay's face as he held one of his mother's restless hands. As quiet and self-effacing as Sally was loud and flamboyant, he was sixty years old but had remained her baby boy despite a receding hairline, an expanding waistline, two failed marriages, and three children of his own. While he and Sally and everyone else had begun grieving last month when it became clear that Aunt Rachel would never regain consciousness, hearing her voice again had triggered another outpouring of emotions.

Earlier, when I returned Minnie's call, my favorite sister-in-law had described how Aunt Rachel seemed to be back in her girlhood, talking to people long dead. "Your daddy and Aunt Sister had almost forgotten some of the names. One minute it's like Jay-Jay's just been born. The next minute, she'll start talking about Jacob and Jed like they were still alive and cutting monkeyshines."

Jacob and Jedidiah. Not that I or any of my brothers had ever known them.

Twins run in our family—Aunt Sister has twin granddaughters and Daddy has two sets of twin boys: Herman and Haywood from his first wife, Adam and Zach from my mother. But there had been twins in his generation, too.

At nineteen, Daddy had been the man of the house for more than four years when they died.

Aunt Sister was eighteen.

Aunt Rachel, the baby of the family, was fourteen and just getting interested in boys.

Jacob and Jed were halfway between them. The summer they turned sixteen, Jacob hit his head on a rock and drowned in Possum Creek. Jed was so devastated that he ran away from home, lied about his age, and joined the army. He was killed in a training exercise at Fort Bragg before he even finished basic.

Aunt Rachel loved Daddy and Aunt Sister, but she had idolized Jed and Jacob. When her own son was born, she had named him Jacob Jedidiah, Jay-Jay for short, and now that she was wandering back in time, she seemed to be caught in a sort of loop where one name summoned up the others.

"Jed says her name's Annie Ruth…Letha says she may not be pretty but she's a real hard worker. Mammy likes her, Sister, even if you don't. If they was to get married…"

I didn't know who Letha was but, hearing the name of his first wife, I glanced at Daddy and saw him raise an eyebrow at Aunt Sister, who's a bit of a snob. Not that she had anything to be snobbish about back then.

Through the years, though, I've always had the impression that maybe she looked down on Annie Ruth, who was indeed a hard worker if my older brothers' dim memories of their mother could be trusted.

Daddy couldn't have been such a great catch himself. The son of a moonshiner? A grade-school dropout with four younger siblings and a widowed mother to support? But they did own a house and a hundred acres of rich bottom land, which was a hundred acres more than Annie Ruth's family ever held title to. And Daddy's mother read to them from the Bible every night. I'm not real sure Annie Ruth could read all that good.

"I'm so sorry, Richard." Grief laced Aunt Rachel's voice. "Those poor little babies and Jannie! That house was a tinderbox, just waiting for a match...Her husband...How could he hit her and then stand up in church like that? But the deacons put the fear of God in him, didn't they?"

A moment later, her lips twitched with sudden amusement. "And one of 'em's a cowbird egg, Brack. He still don't know and he could eat that pretty little goldfinch with a spoon...Love's blind, ain't it?" Abruptly, her brow furrowed. "It ain't love, Jed. Sister says y'all are like two hound dogs after a bitch in heat...So hot, so hot. All that work and that last batch of soup ruined...Mammy just set and cried till dark. Oh, Jacob, Jacob, Jacob!"

Distressed, Jay-Jay grasped her hand. "It's okay, Mama. It's okay."

"Annie Ruth always did want a lot of babies...babies. Annie said...Oh, those precious baby girls! He signed a note, but I'm sure he never paid it."

Here in May, the days were still getting longer, but as shadows lengthened across the grounds outside, Aunt Rachel talked on and on, gesturing with her hands and half rising up from the pillows, her blue eyes flashing. She talked of babies, fires, and unpaid debts, of someone who beat his wife and of cowbirds and vegetables and broken jars. She relived the grief of Jacob's death over and over, the joy of Jay-Jay's birth, and whether someone named Ransom might like her as much as she liked him.

Unlike Aunt Sister, who could be chary with her words, Aunt Rachel had a gift for mimicry and dramatic narratives. As a child, I loved it when the adults got together to play and sing and amuse each other with community news and gossip. Aunt Rachel seldom named names even though she lived some twenty-five miles away at the other end of the county from us and it was unlikely that we would know who she was talking about. Mother's theory was that she liberally embellished her tales, and certainly it was true that she could make crossing the road to mail a letter sound funny.

Aunt Sister's wit was as dry as Daddy's but more caustic and usually at someone else's expense, while Aunt Rachel's was warm and self-deprecating, which was probably why such a cross section of the wider community had gathered. Family members, church friends, longtime neighbors, and former customers came and went as word spread through the community that she was talking again. Several of the younger cousins were using their cell phones to catch her ramblings.

"Annie worried that he wouldn't amount to much if she didn't help him, but she made him promise...He kept it all, though, didn't he? Just like her Easter basket. Ate all his chocolates and hers, too. Always wanted what he wanted, didn't he?...I'm real glad she never had to know...break her heart right in two. She said my tomatoes held their flavor the best... Mammy's seeds. So hot to be canning, no wonder Jacob went to the creek, and not just for Letha neither. Corn...okra..." A smile curled Aunt Rachel's lips. "Remember when Sally put a tomato in Brack's chair and he sat down on it and Jay-Jay..." Her voice trailed off into hoarseness and Sally leaned over with a spoonful of crushed ice to moisten her mother's mouth.

Aunt Rachel swallowed and said, "Jay-Jay?"

My cousin leaned forward, clasping her bony hands even tighter. "I'm here, Mama. It's okay. I'm here."

"Where's Jacob? Won't y'all supposed to be helping Kezzie?" She paused as if listening. "Yeah, she come by but leave her be, Jed. Jacob saw her first. She's too fast for y'all anyhow. That bathing suit!" She began to giggle. "Hazel was so proud of that fancy new bathing suit...Six dollars for it at Hudson-Belk's but soon as it got wet, it showed everything she had. She said Rufus's eyes like to've popped out of his head 'fore she could get a towel..."

The words came with more difficulty as if rasped from raw vocal cords.

Sally looked at the aide. "Shouldn't she ought to rest now? She's been talking for hours."

"Since about noon," the aide agreed.

Her minister stepped forward with a worn leather Bible in his hand. "Maybe if we pray?"

He was a young man, but his voice held pulpit phrasing and we all automatically bowed our heads. "Lord God, who healed the lame and gave sight to the blind, we thank you for the precious gift of words that you have bestowed on this family—"

"...and if it's a boy, we'll name him Jacob Jedidiah," Aunt Rachel croaked. "Oh, Sister, why? Where was Billy? Or Ransom? Why'd he sneak off to the creek like that? You reckon Letha told him she'd be there? Be just like her, wouldn't it? Stirring up trouble?"

So much grief laced her words that the minister fell silent.

"Sing," Daddy said suddenly. "Remember that time when she was so sick with the whooping cough we thought she was gonna cough herself to death and Mammy made her easy by singing to her? Remember, Sister?"

With tears in her eyes, Aunt Sister took a swallow from the Pepsi can in her hand and began to sing in a soft low voice.

Sleep, Rachel, sleep.
Just count your daddy's sheep.

Her daughter Beverly joined in. We've always made music together and over the years, made-up lyrics have replaced some of the original ones. Soon a half-dozen voices or more added harmony to that old lullaby.

Now mammy shakes them sleeping trees
And dreams drift softly down like leaves.
Sleep, Rachel, sleep.

After two more verses, Aunt Rachel's hoarse voice dwindled into silence. Her lips continued to move, but no sounds came out. When her clear blue eyes closed, we automatically began to step back quietly. Seth stretched out a hand to help Daddy to his feet and her son-in-law did the same for Aunt Sister.

Both are in their eighties now but still straight of back and steady on their feet once they're actually standing.

"How'd we get so old, Kezzie?" she whispered. "Set too long and everything wants to seize up."

As she turned to follow him, someone bumped her arm and her Pepsi went flying, landing in the middle of the bed. Brown liquid fizzed from the can and soaked into the sheet covering that frail body.

"Oh, dear Lord!" Aunt Sister gasped.

We all held our breath, expecting Aunt Rachel to waken, but she lay motionless except for her lips, which still formed silent words.

"Don't you worry," said the aide. She stepped forward to raise the bed to working level. "Why don't y'all go get some supper? I'll change her sheets and freshen her up a bit."

Even Jay-Jay realized that *freshen her up a bit* meant she was going to change his mother's gown, and he joined the general exodus.

I realized I could use some "freshening up" myself, but by now there would be a line in the public restroom. Although there were several rooms on this floor, Aunt Rachel's was the only one being used, so I ducked into the darkened room across the hall and tried the bathroom door. It was locked.

"Just a minute," said a female voice from within and a moment later, I heard a flush and the rush of running water, then a very pretty young woman stepped out, one arm in a pale green summer cardigan.

"Sorry," she said and held the door for me. As she put her other arm through the sleeve of her sweater, a button caught in her necklace and pearls went flying everywhere.

"Oh *no*!" she cried and immediately began picking them up. "I *knew* I should have had them restrung."

I helped her finish picking them up, then she left and I went on into the bathroom. As I was washing my hands afterwards, I spotted a gleaming pearl that had bounced onto this tiled floor. I retrieved it from where it had landed between the wastebasket and the wall, then walked toward the elevator and staircase, which lay around the corner at the end of the hall. There was no sign of the girl, so I dropped her pearl in my purse and joined the others. People were voicing their regrets as they left, all telling Sally and Jay-Jay to be sure and let them know if there was anything they could do to help in the coming days.

Sally almost looked her real age and Daddy and Aunt Sister were clearly tired, but they didn't want to go home. An open wooden staircase led down to the hospice family room on the next floor, part of the original main core of the hospital before new wings were built, and they did agree to go that far when the preacher said that some of Aunt Rachel's prayer group had set up a makeshift buffet of cold cuts and salads.

"I believe I could eat a ham biscuit if anybody's brought some," Aunt Sister said, and Daddy allowed as how a deviled egg might taste right good.

The minister paused at the bottom of the worn oak steps and assured them that the funeral service would include all the hymns and readings that Aunt Rachel had requested when she gave him instructions after her first stroke back last winter.

"Although I'll be glad to stay with y'all tonight if you want me to," he said.

"That's okay," Sally said. "We'll be fine."

After sitting so long on hard straight chairs, though, they were glad for the overstuffed chairs and couches and Aunt Sister gave a sigh of pure pleasure as she settled into a soft leather sofa.

While grandchildren and cousins gave them goodbye hugs, I fixed them both plates and then went back for one of my own, stopping to say a word here and there to the church women, who gave me sympathetic smiles.

"Poor Sister," said one of the older women. "First Rufus and now Rachel."

"At least she's back home now and got all y'all," said another.

Uncle Rufus retired some twenty years ago. The children were grown and off on their own, so he and Aunt Sister had sold their house, bought an RV, and turned into gypsies. With relatives scattered from California to Florida, there was always a friendly driveway where they could park for a few days and even a few weeks when they came through Colleton County. The high price of gasoline and his tricky heart had brought them home for good two years ago. They traded their last Winnebago in on a used doublewide, and Daddy let them put it on a piece of land he owned a few miles west of the farm, over towards Fuquay. While Uncle Rufus was out picking butter beans in their garden last summer, his heart stopped beating. A neighbor saw him fall, but he was gone before the rescue truck could get there.

My two aunts had talked about moving in together now that both were widowed, but before they could decide which home to give up, Aunt Rachel's stroke had made that moot.

"At least Rufus didn't linger like Rachel," said another of their friends. "It's awful hard on the family if it takes so long."

Someone vaguely familiar was talking to Minnie,

someone I seemed to connect with politics since Minnie acts as my campaign manager and has always been active in the party. She waved me over.

"Deborah, I don't believe you've met James Collins?"

"Please. Call me Jim. Both of you." He was short and solidly built, with a bald head and the largest nose I'd ever seen on a face that small, but his friendly smile soon made me forget his looks. Especially when Minnie reminded me that he had donated to my campaign last fall.

"I hope I thanked you properly," I said. As a judicial candidate, my donor base is so small it doesn't take long to send each of them a personal note of thanks.

His smile broadened. "You did," he said. "In fact, yours was the only handwritten thank-you I got. Refreshing."

When I got back to Daddy and Aunt Sister, the aide was there. A cheerful little butterball, she said Aunt Rachel's breathing seemed to be shallow, but otherwise she was resting easy, so Sally encouraged her to go get something to eat. They themselves had almost finished and were back to talking about Aunt Rachel's amazing burst of speech.

"Such a gift," said Sally as she accepted another plastic cup of sweet iced tea. "Right before y'all got here, she was talking to Dad like he was still alive and they'd just got married. It was so sweet. I just wish she could have stayed at that part of her life instead of going back to when the twins died."

"Funny," said Jay-Jay. "I've been hearing that story all my life about somebody who bought a bathing suit that got transparent when it got wet, but Mama never said who it was, so I didn't know that it was Hazel Upchurch or that Uncle Rufus was one of the men who saw her."

Daddy grinned. "Me neither. Rufus ever talk about it, Sister?"

Aunt Sister rolled her eyes, but her daughter Beverly laughed. "He did to me. Told me to always wet a new bathing suit before I wore it in public."

Aunt Sister chose to ignore that and gave a disapproving frown as she reached out to adjust Sally's purple jersey top, which was in danger of slipping off her shoulder entirely.

We're all used to Aunt Sister's prudery and Sally just smiled.

"What was that about cowbirds and goldfinches?" I asked.

Aunt Sister frowned and shook her head and Sally didn't seem to know either.

Daddy gave a half smile. "Cowbirds don't build a nest or raise their own chicks. They just lay their eggs in somebody else's nest. Sounds like she knew somebody that was raising a cowbird."

"What I want to know is who was Letha?" asked Sally. "I don't ever remember hearing that name."

"And who was Ransom?" asked Jay-Jay, equally curious.

Although both had worked alongside their parents on the truck farm and at the vegetable stand, both had left for easier office jobs in Raleigh as soon as they finished high school.

"Ransom?" Aunt Sister's wrinkled face softened with a smile. "Your mama had such a crush on him. What was his last name, Kezzie?"

Daddy cast his mind back over the years. "Barber? Barton? I can't rightly remember. His people came from Georgia and they moved back after a few years. Barkley?"

"Barley!" Aunt Sister exclaimed, delighted to have retrieved the name. "And he had a brother named Donald. Nice-looking boys, both of them. I believe their daddy worked as a lineman for the power company so he got moved around right much."

Sally spread some chicken salad on a cracker and handed it to her brother. "He was Mama's boyfriend?"

"Not really. Rachel was only fourteen that summer and Mammy wouldn't let us go off in cars till we was sixteen. And then it had to be at least two couples."

"Really?" Sally was amused. "Bet if I know Mama, she bent that rule a time or two."

"And Mammy bent a peach switch across her legs, but that didn't stop her from sneaking down to the creek to meet him once in a while."

Daddy smiled at Jay-Jay. "If he hadn't moved back to Georgia, I'm thinking your last name might be Barley now."

Aunt Sister shook her head. "Naw, now, don't you

remember? After Jacob drowned, she wouldn't have nothing to do with any of them boys."

"That's right." Daddy's smile faded. "She blamed them 'cause they didn't save him. Blamed Jed, too, didn't she?"

"Blamed who for what, Mr. Kezzie?"

I turned and saw that Dwight had come in unnoticed.

"Where's Cal?" I asked, half expecting to see our son with him.

"He and Mama went to pick strawberries over at Smith's Nursery." Then to the others, "She sent y'all her regards."

"You eat yet, Dwight?" asked one of the church women who's known him since childhood and doesn't stand on ceremony even though Dwight is now Sheriff Bo Poole's second-in-command.

"No, ma'am."

"Then you need to let me get you some of my turkey casserole."

She bustled off to the buffet and Sally said, "What happened with Dotty Morefield and her brother, Deborah? Did he win?"

I shook my head and she gave a triumphant fist pump.

"Why were you and Marillyn Mulholland there? Are y'all friends with Mrs. Morefield?"

She nodded. "I don't know her as well as Marillyn and the others do. Her mother died last year before I joined the Daughters, but she still comes by once in a while."

"Daughters?" I asked.

"Designated Daughters," she said, licking a fleck of chicken salad from fingers that sported bright turquoise nails that matched her leggings.

She smiled at my look of puzzlement. "They got the name when the first members began meeting at the senior center at least twenty or thirty years ago. It's stayed the same even though Charles is a man and Kaitlyn, the one pushing the wheelchair, is a grand-daughter and JoAnn's a niece. Everybody's a caregiver and we meet to bitch or cry or share ways to cope with the lemons life's handed some of us." She patted Jay-Jay's hand. "Not that this has been a lemon for me. Jay-Jay's been over every week since Mama's moved in with me after her first stroke. But some of them—like in court today? Some people don't want to do any-thing for their loved one and yet they're right there with the U-Haul when it's time to clean out the house. You wouldn't believe the stories I've heard."

"Want to bet?" I said, totally jaded after five years on the bench.

Before either of us could start citing chapter and verse, the aide stopped to tell Sally she would be with Aunt Rachel if they wanted her. She had a piece of pecan pie on a paper plate and took it with her around the corner of the staircase to where the elevator was.

Sally and I had just seated ourselves near Daddy and Aunt Sister—she with pie, me with a steaming cup of coffee—when we saw the aide reappear at the top of the stairs. She hurried down them, almost stumbling in her haste. Her round face white with shock, she leaned into our group and spoke to my cousins in low urgent tones. "Sally! Jay-Jay! Come quick. Miss Rachel's dead!"

"Dead?"

For a moment, we sat stunned. Less than forty minutes ago, we'd seen her in animated conversation, talking and laughing. True, it was with friends and family long gone, but still...to slip away that quickly?

Sally grasped my hand to come with them and Daddy rose to his feet to follow, too.

When we got up to the room, Aunt Rachel's head lay back against the pillow as if she were still sleeping. Her lips were still now, but there was something odd about her face.

"What happened to her nose?" asked Sally. "Is that blood?"

It was as if Aunt Rachel's nose had slightly collapsed to one side. A hairline trickle of red had seeped from her left nostril and collected in the wrinkles at the base of her nose.

"Let me get a washcloth," said the aide and raised the bed up from its position near the floor before stepping into the bathroom.

Sorrow welled up within me as Jay-Jay put one arm around his tearful sister and, with his other hand, smoothed back his mother's tousled hair. I linked my arm through Daddy's and was leaning against his shoulder when I noticed that one of the pillows had fallen on the floor under the bed. I stooped to retrieve it and a cold chill ran through me as my brain tried to make sense of what I was seeing on the pillow's underside.

A small patch of bright red.

"Where'd that come from?" asked the aide. She looked at my aunt's lifeless form, bewildered. "I left her with two pillows under her head. No way could Miss Rachel pull one out and throw it on the floor. And where's her pillow slip?"

"Somebody go get Dwight," I said and stopped her before she could wipe the blood from Aunt Rachel's nose.

"Dwight?" asked Sally, bewildered.

"Noses don't break by theirselves," Daddy said grimly. "Somebody put that pillow on her face and mashed down real hard, so yeah, we need Dwight up here right now."

CHAPTER 5

*No one is so old that he does not expect to live
a year longer.*

— Cicero

As soon as he saw the blood-spotted pillow in my hands and took in the situation, Dwight phoned for reinforcements, then asked Daddy and my cousins to wait downstairs. I laid the pillow on the bed and started to follow, but he held me back and closed the door to the hall. "You okay, shug?"

I nodded even though there was a lump of grief in my throat that I couldn't quite swallow. "This is so weird, Dwight. We knew she was dying, and if she'd gone like we expected, we'd be sad, but we'd also be feeling a bit of relief that it was finally over. But to go like this? To be smothered so hard it broke her nose?" I tried to blink away the sudden tears that blurred his face.

He took me in his arms and gently stroked my hair. "I know, shug. I know."

He didn't rush me, but when I was able to talk again, he said, "What went on here today, Deb'rah?"

I understood his need to switch from husband to lawman, and I tried to match his professionalism, but it was hard with Aunt Rachel lying there so still and silent, her bright blue eyes forever closed.

"They say she started talking a little before noon and she was still talking when I got here after work," I said. "She talked till she was hoarse. Not to us. She didn't know we were here. She thought she was a girl again and that Jacob had just drowned. She used names I've never heard and it was like one name would call up another. She switched from Jacob and Jed to when Jay-Jay was born and then back to the twins again."

Dwight's been a virtual member of our family since before I was born, so he knows most of our family stories and I didn't have to explain who Jacob and Jed were.

"She finally went to sleep about thirty or forty minutes ago, then Aunt Sister accidentally spilled a drink on the bed so we all cleared out of her room and went downstairs while the aide changed the linens. You got here about ten minutes after that."

"Everybody left?"

"I think so. I didn't count heads but I'm pretty sure nobody stayed behind. The aide—I think her name is Lois—she can tell you."

There was a tap on the door, and as one of his

deputies poked his head in, Dwight gave me a quick hug and asked me to go wait with the others.

As I walked downstairs, I passed a tearful Lois, who was being escorted up by one of Dwight's officers.

By eight o'clock, I was getting antsy about Cal. When I called Dwight's mother to let her know what was happening, Miss Emily assured me it would be no trouble for him to stay overnight, but Wednesday was a school day for them both. She's told the school board that she'll finally be retiring in June, and even though they had already announced that my brother Zach would succeed her as principal, I knew she was trying to get through a lot of work so as not to hand him any unfinished business.

At that point, only a few of us remained in the family waiting room. The church women had packed up their casseroles and jugs of tea and left after giving Sally and Jay-Jay their sympathies. Jay-Jay is divorced, with no one to go home to, and he'd told Sally's husband that he'd see she got home safely.

Aunt Sister was physically and emotionally exhausted and her daughter tried to take her home, but she wouldn't leave. Seth and Minnie were still there, too, because they had driven Daddy over from the farm and he didn't want to go till he'd heard whatever Dwight could tell us. I told them he could ride back with me, but Seth, who's five brothers up from me, said, "Naw, honey. We'll sit a while longer."

"We're fine," Minnie said, and went back to texting on her phone.

All our phones kept chirping as those who had left earlier heard the bad news and called to see what was going on. When you have eleven older brothers, it doesn't take long for all the dots in the family network to connect. Barely an hour since Aunt Rachel died and both brothers out in California had already checked in.

"Sounds like a bunch of spring peepers in here," Daddy said sourly. He doesn't hold with landline phones all that much and he certainly doesn't see the point of walking around with a phone in his pocket.

Out of respect, we either turned ours off completely or put them on vibrate, except for Minnie, whose thumbs kept flying across the screen. She and Seth are the hub of our family and our first go-to in times of crisis, but this seemed a lot of traffic, even for her.

Jay-Jay put his phone in his pocket. "Did you get all the stuff she was saying, Sal?"

Sally stuck out one thin but still shapely leg and smoothed down the turquoise leggings, which had bunched up below her knee. "Some of it. The burned babies? That was Jannie Mayer and her little girls."

"Such a horrible thing," said Aunt Sister. "You reckon thinking about Jacob called up Jannie?"

"Who's Jannie?" I asked.

"You must've heard about that," said Sally. "Richard Howell's sister? Their parents were killed in a car wreck when they were teenagers, and their grandmother finished raising them. Jannie was married and

Richard was in med school when she died so the house sat empty for a year or two till Jannie's husband left her with two baby girls. She had to move back to that old tumbledown house where she could live for free."

"So the Richard she kept talking to was Dr. Howell?" I asked.

Sally nodded. "He was in his first year of residency when the house burned with his sister Jannie and her two babies in it."

"Now I remember," said Aunt Sister. "He never quit blaming himself, did he?"

"Not his fault," Sally said. "You heard Mama. The house was a tinderbox, but Jannie had no place else to go after her husband left her without a penny to even buy fuel oil instead of that old woodstove."

"Rachel said they thought a log fell out of that heater in the kitchen," said Daddy, "and it went up like a Roman candle. Pure lightwood."

"And Rachel had to stand there a-watching it burn," said Aunt Sister, "knowing they was inside and there won't a blessed thing she could do."

"Mama was the one who had to call and tell Richard," said Jay-Jay. "The only good part, if you can call it good, is that they found the baby in her cradle and Jannie and the other baby in bed, like they'd laid down for a nap, so they probably died from smoke inhalation and never knew the house was on fire."

"Jay-Jay and me, we were coming home on the school bus that day," Sally said. "It was winter and we could see the black smoke rising way above the trees. I knew it was either our house or Jannie's or Miss Kitty's. I felt guilty for years."

"You?" I said. "Why?"

"Because I knew Mama had already bought our Christmas presents and I was going to get a twin sweater set and some black satin sheets I'd been wanting. So I was glad it wasn't our house till I heard about Jannie and those babies. And of course, Richard blamed himself 'cause he was away doing his residency and not there to save them. I got over it. Got over those satin sheets, too, about the third time I slid out of bed. But he never did, did he?"

"You always did have outlandish tastes," Aunt Sister said. "Whoever heard of giving a sixteen-year-old girl black satin sheets?"

I had to smile at Aunt Sister's predictable comments even as I now remembered hearing my mother read aloud the story that was rehashed in the *Dobbs Register* when Dr. Howell funded the Jannie Howell Mayer Memorial Burn Unit for our hospital back when I was a teenager. Mother approved of civic-minded citizens who gave back to their communities, and now I realized why he was visiting Aunt Rachel this afternoon even though he wasn't her doctor. Out on a back-country farm road, he would have known her, and she and his grandmother would surely have been friends.

Jay-Jay wasn't distracted by satin sheets. "But the way Mama kept talking about the twins?" He leaned back heavily in the chair and his belly strained against his khaki pants. He was as plump as Sally was skinny and that extra layer gave him a face that was almost as wrinkle free as hers. He rolled down the sleeves of his blue checked shirt and buttoned the cuffs. "I just don't get it. She almost never talked about them when we were growing up, did she, Sal?"

"Not really." Sally frowned as she tried to remember. Like Jay-Jay, like her mother, like most of the rest of us, her eyes were the same forget-me-not blue as Jay-Jay's shirt. "I mean, it's not like it was a forbidden subject or something we weren't supposed to mention. She'd look a little sad whenever it came up, but now that I think about it, she never brought it up or talked much about that day itself—who was there or how it happened."

"And I never saw her cry or carry on about them like she did today," said Jay-Jay. "She always warned us to watch out for each other if we wanted to go swimming, but she never stopped us from going."

Sally smoothed the short straight bangs of her purple wig and turned to Daddy and Aunt Sister. "What really happened, Uncle Kezzie? How could Jacob have drowned in a place where he must have been swimming his whole life? And why would Jedidiah run away like that?"

"I won't there," Daddy said gruffly, and I realized he never talked much about them either. "I was down in the woods that day and didn't get back there till atter they'd pulled him out of the creek."

Seth gave me a discreet wink. Daddy didn't have to say what sort of work took him to the woods back then. We could guess.

He seldom alluded to those years after his father died when he was actively making moonshine himself, dodging patrol cars and delivering untaxed white whiskey to local shot houses as a way of providing for his mother and his siblings. Later, after he was married to his first wife, his mother dead and his sisters married, after the baby boys started coming and there was a little more money, he would supply the equipment, the sugar, and the grain for a much larger operation. He hired others to make it for him and they hired men to haul trunkloads of full half-gallon Mason jars all up and down the eastern seaboard. He was never arrested for running a still, but he did do eighteen months in a federal prison for income tax evasion when the feds tied him to a little crossroads store that bought a lot more sugar than he could prove that the store sold.

My mother's father was a prominent attorney in Dobbs, and when he grudgingly accepted that she was determined to marry a bootlegging ex-con come hell or high water, he somehow managed to get Daddy's prison record expunged as his wedding present.

"Them boys was supposed to be suckering tobacco that day, not larking in the creek," he said.

"Jed stuck with the suckering," Aunt Sister said sharply. "You know he did, Kezzie. I was right out there in the field with him. It won't his fault what happened to Jacob."

"Wish you could've made Jed know that," Daddy said. "I sure couldn't."

Before we could get back on that carousel of ques-

tions that might never be answered, Dwight finally
came downstairs from Aunt Rachel's room.

"Dr. Singh's already examined her," he told us,
speaking to Sally and Jay-Jay.

Our current medical examiner is a pathologist and
keeps an office there at the hospital.

"As we thought, she was smothered with that pillow.
It's her blood. If it's any help, he says that it would
have been so quick that in her condition, she couldn't
have suffered more than a few seconds. There's so
little blood, her heart couldn't have beat more than a
time or two, and if she was unconscious instead of just
sleeping…"

Sally nodded numbly.

"Was there anything special about her pillow case?"

"Pillow case?"

"The aide said one's missing. She says she put a
fresh one on that pillow and now it's gone. She also
swears there was no blood on that pillow when she
changed it."

Sally frowned. "Was it linen? With a lacy edging? I
brought four of them over when she came to hospice.
Mama never had many fancy things but she took a lik-
ing to linen a few years back. Remember, Jay-Jay?"

"Five hundred dollars for a set of bed sheets? Damn
right, I remember."

"We went in with Dad and bought them for her
sixty-fifth birthday," Sally said. "Then she went out
and bought another set of matching pillow cases because they both slept on two pillows. She just loved the

way linen got so silky feeling when it's ironed, the way it felt against her face. I thought it would comfort her to have them here. Why would somebody steal one?"

Even Aunt Sister, who clearly categorized linen sheets with black satin, had no answer for that.

"Anybody have a grudge against her?" Dwight asked.

The question was meant for my cousins, but we all shook our heads automatically.

"Who inherits?"

Jay-Jay gave an exasperated snort. "*Inherits?* This is Mama, Dwight, not Doris Duke. What the heck did she have for anybody to inherit? Most of what they got for the farm went to the hospital when Dad got sick. There might be a few thousand left after we pay all of Mama's bills, but it'll take that to get the house fixed up good enough to sell."

Sally glared at Dwight. "And before you start thinking Jay-Jay and me are ready to sail off to the Caribbean—"

He held up his hands to stop her attack. "Whoa, Sally. I don't think that either of you could do that to your mother." He gave a placating smile. "Besides, everyone says you two came downstairs here and didn't leave, but what about the aide?"

"Lois? You thinking Lois—?" Sally shook her head. "Never in this world, Dwight."

"She had the most opportunity and I'm hearing that y'all left her alone in the room with Miss Rachel right before it happened."

"She's been alone with Mama off and on for the last two months," Sally said. "If she was going to hurt her, why would she wait till so many people were here?"

"To maybe spread suspicion around?"

"Never!"

"Then who else was here this evening who'd have a reason to do this?" Dwight asked. "And don't tell me nobody, because that pillow didn't wind up pressed against her face all by itself."

He looked at each of us in turn and then sighed. "Okay. We do it the hard way."

He turned to Mayleen Richards, one of his deputies who had joined us. "Get as many of the names as they can remember."

Practical-minded Minnie reached out and touched his sleeve. "I've already got the kids working on it, Dwight. They were all taking pictures and videos on their cell phones and they'll forward those to you with a list of all the names they know as soon as you tell me where."

I should have realized.

"God bless technology," Dwight said.

CHAPTER
6

*Nor was he great only in public and in the eyes
of the community; but he was even more excel-
lent in private and domestic life.*

— Cicero

Aunt Rachel was buried Friday morning next to Uncle Brack at Bethany, his family church down near
Makely, amid his Morton kinfolks. Even though her
death was officially declared a homicide, Dr. Singh had
decided that the state could dispense with an autopsy.
Not just because Aunt Rachel was Dwight's aunt by
marriage but because, in his experienced opinion as
both a doctor and the county's medical examiner, the
immediate cause of death was a pillow held forcibly
over her nose until she quit breathing.

Had it not been for those few drops of blood—
"Sheer carelessness," he'd said disapprovingly—her
death would have gone down as a long-expected and
natural ending.

"Who the hell kills a dying woman?" he'd asked angrily. "And how stupid was it to think no one would notice that pillow under her bed?"

He and Dwight had hypothesized that the killer must have acted on the spur of the moment and in such haste that he was too afraid of being seen to risk taking the pillow away.

("*Or she*," said my cynical mental pragmatist as he listened to them speculate.)

"Maybe he thought that no one would see it till after Aunt Rachel was moved and the bed was being stripped," I said. "The pillow case could go out in a purse or pocket but by the time the pillow was found, a little blood in a hospital room might not have seemed important."

"I doubt if he was thinking that far ahead," said Dr. Singh, pausing to shake hands with Dr. Howell, Aunt Rachel's one-time neighbor, as he was opening the door of the car parked a few feet on the other side of ours. It was a mid-range Toyota and not the Cadillac or Porsche most successful doctors of his age usually drove.

Between private practice and shrewd investments, Richard Howell could have retired to some tropical island by the time he was my age. Instead, he continued to head the burn unit at the hospital and was one of Dobbs's most generous benefactors. In addition to the hospital wing and a state-of-the-art burn unit, he had established a couple of scholarships for physician assistants at Colleton Community College in memory of his nieces. He's had just about every civic honor that could be bestowed on someone not in public office and had been Dobbs's "Citizen of the Year" twice. His name is mentioned in the local papers almost every month. Gray haired, with slightly rounded shoulders and rimless half-glasses that kept slipping down his thin nose, he was now hailed by an elderly couple who had approached from the other side. I remembered that they had been in Aunt Rachel's room, too. They moved with the careful attention the very old give to their fragile bodies.

The old woman called to Dwight. "I'm Rachel's friend Kitty Byrd," she said and fumbled in her purse for some papers. "They say you were asking for people to write down the names of everyone they saw in Rachel's room Wednesday? I'm afraid I don't know all the names, but I did the best I could."

Family members were streaming from the church's graveyard now and I was swept up by several of my brothers and their families.

I looked back and saw that Daddy and Seth had lingered at the grave with Jay-Jay and Sally and Aunt Rachel's grandchildren. Sally's husband Buzz had his arm around her and Jay-Jay's daughters were clinging to him, too.

As is usual at the funeral of an older relative whose death had been expected, once we were away from the grave, the day began to take on the aspect of a family reunion rather than an occasion of real grief. True, there was anger and puzzlement over the way Aunt

Rachel had died, but some were beginning to question whether it really was murder.

My oldest brother Robert stopped Dwight to say, "We was talking on the way down here, Dwight. You reckon a little blood vessel might've popped in her nose and that's what killed her? Wouldn't take much for somebody that sick."

His wife Doris lit a cigarette and nodded. "That's what I think, too. Almost every winter, my nose'll bleed a little if I blow it too hard."

"For the last time, Doris, it's not winter and she won't blowing her nose," said Haywood's wife Isabel. "And them cigarettes are probably what's making your nose bleed." The four of them had ridden over together and Bel won't let anybody smoke in their new car. "Besides, how'd that pillow get up under the bed and where'd the pillow slip go?"

Doris shrugged and took another deep drag on her cigarette. Knowing she was going to have to put it out as soon as the others were ready to go, she looked around for something to delay the inevitable.

"At least Sally wore a black wig today," she said, "but that red dress!"

"And them red heels!" said Isabel, taking the bait. "They had to be at least five inches high. It's a wonder she didn't sink down to her ankles walking out to the graveyard."

Haywood was the only one of the four that had been at the hospital when Aunt Rachel died, and he, too, had a list for Dwight. "I reckon you can read my writing," he said, handing over a crumpled piece of lined note-book paper. "You still gonna pour that slab tomorrow?"

"The foundation's ready," Dwight said. "The gravel truck's supposed to come around nine o'clock and they'll bring the concrete as soon as it's level. I'd like to get it all done before lunch so I could go by work before Cal's ball game."

"I'll put the pusher blade on the Cub," Robert said. "Won't take but just a few minutes if we use that. I'll bring 'er over first thing and help y'all get the gravel smoothed out. I can't get down and do trowel work like I used to, but pushing a mess of gravel around's no trouble."

While the men made their plans, Isabel leaned in close to me and said, "Now don't you let Haywood sit down at your table tomorrow morning, Deb'rah. He don't need to eat two breakfasts again. The doctor wants him to lose another ten pounds."

"We'll be finished long before nine," I promised.

"Just put away all the biscuits. You know how he can't pass even a cold one up if he sees them."

I had to laugh at that. "Bel, do you know how long it's been since I made biscuits for breakfast?"

Jingling the car keys in his hand as he turned to open the car door for me and looking almost as hopeful as Haywood, Dwight said, "You making biscuits for breakfast?"

On the way back to Dobbs, I drove while Dwight read through Haywood's list. I was still hung up on that missing pillow case and now remembered how the bed was positioned when we got there with Lois. Patients can't be restrained anymore, so hospice beds can be lowered almost to the floor so that it's less likely someone will get hurt if they roll off the edge.

"I only noticed because Lois raised the bed," I said.

"Noticed what, shug?" he asked without looking up from his notes.

"The pillow. I guess y'all didn't think to really look for the pillow case?"

"We looked. Checked the laundry bins on that floor and all the wastebaskets. No lace-edged linen pillow slip. It's probably on somebody's bonfire by now."

As I turned onto 401 and headed south, he read from the list the old woman had given him.

"*Teenage girl, yellow dress,*" he read. "Ring a bell?"

"Sounds like Jessica," I said. The description fit what my brother Seth's daughter had worn Wednesday.

"*Blue hair.* Sally's was purple so would that be May or June?"

I nodded. "They dye it with Kool-Aid."

Aunt Sister's twin granddaughters now go to great lengths not to look like the identical twins they are. I still couldn't tell them apart unless I was close enough to see the tiny scar near May's right ear.

"What about *bald man*, *big red nose*?"

"That would be James Collins. I don't know what he does, but he contributed to my last campaign. He was telling Minnie how he used to stop by Aunt Rachel's vegetable stand as much for her talk as for her corn and tomatoes."

"Pretty blonde teenager, blue shirt."

"I think that's Emma." Zach's daughter has turned into the family's videographer, so her cell phone has extra memory and she probably got some good footage. "How's Mayleen doing with all the pictures and videos?"

Red-haired, freckle-faced Mayleen Richards is one of Dwight's top detectives. She had tried sitting at a desk after finishing a two-year computer course out at Colleton Community College, but she was farm bred, knew how to handle a gun, and liked physical work, preferably outdoors. After three years of trying to fit her awkward square nature into a comfortable round hole, she quit her job in the Research Triangle, took some law-enforcement classes, then badgered Sheriff Poole to hire her. What further enraged her family was that she finally stopped waiting for them to accept Mike Diaz, a naturalized citizen who owns a landscaping business, and married him this past Easter at a joyous wedding festival. Bo Poole walked her down the aisle and gave her away when all of her own people refused to come. Dwight was one of the ushers.

"She's patching them together to make one continuous sequence," he said. "Good thing Minnie thought to ask for them before they got deleted. The biggest help is that they're time-stamped." He pointed to a barbecue shack that was coming up on our right. "Want to grab lunch?"

I looked at my watch and shook my head. "I promised I'd get to court before one and it's almost that now."

"What time you think you'll take a break? Three? I could send you up a sandwich."

"That's okay," I said. "It won't hurt me to skip a meal, but if you've got a can of tomato juice in your refrigerator, that might taste good."

"You got it, honey."

He put his hand on the back of my neck to give a soft squeeze and I decided that maybe I *would* make him biscuits for breakfast.

God, I love being married!

CHAPTER
7

For as wise old men are charmed with well-disposed youth, so do young men delight in the counsels of the old.

— Cicero

True to my promise to Bel, breakfast was finished and done with next morning, and the leftover biscuits I'd made to go with the scrambled eggs, country ham, and redeye gravy were all stowed away before Haywood showed up in his truck, followed by Robert on the Farmall Cub. I learned how to drive on that small red tractor long before I was old enough for driver's ed, and even back then it was held together with baling wire, sweat, and WD-40. It'll probably still be running when I'm eighty.

By nine o'clock, the lower slope to the pond was crowded with pickups that carried rakes and shovels in the back and a few dogs, too. Cal's dog Bandit knows all the farm dogs and soon they were frisking alongside the pond.

Daddy, Seth, Andrew, and Andrew's son A.K. were there to help and offer advice, and so were Zach and his son Lee. Zach's the next brother up from me, one of the "little twins," which is what we say to distinguish them from Haywood and Herman, the "big twins." Ostensibly, he had come to bring us a dozen brown eggs from his hens, but he and Lee didn't seem in much of a hurry to leave either.

The twenty-by-twenty footing for the floor of the pond house had been dug and the perimeter poured the weekend before. With so many men here today, they could have dispensed with the tractor altogether, but Robert signaled to Cal, who eagerly climbed up onto his lap and followed his instructions as to how to lift and lower the pusher blade. After a few minutes' practice, Robert began teaching him how to change gears and steer and I saw Cal's earnest concentration. He's tall for his age so his feet reached the pedals, but he had to come up off the seat to push down on the clutch hard enough. His face was a mixture of pride and trepidation when Robert got up and stood behind him on the tow bar to put him through the paces. By the time the gravel truck arrived and emptied its contents inside the footing, Cal seemed to have the hang of it and was soon maneuvering the blade to level the gravel.

I glanced at Dwight, who stood off to one side with the same mixture of pride and trepidation on his own face. Heavy equipment, even when it's a little red Cub, is nothing to fool around with but Robert's a careful teacher and he never let Cal take it out of low gear.

Daddy sat down on a stack of cinderblocks in the shade of a nearby tree with his hound dog Ladybelle, who was now too old and dignified to frisk with the other dogs, and I walked over to join them. There was laundry to wash and fold, beds that needed changing, bills I should be paying, not to mention some legal documents I needed to read, but hey—it's not every day you get to watch your son drive a tractor for the first time.

Eventually, Robert had Cal steer the Cub off the gravel and park it alongside one of the trucks.

Cal jumped down from the tractor and ran over to us. "Hey, Mom! Granddaddy! Did y'all see me drive the tractor? Uncle Robert says I can maybe help him on the bean picker this fall. And he's gonna show me how to hitch up the cultivators so we can plow our garden."

No bigger than our garden is, an hour or two with hoes would be quicker and more efficient than using a tractor, but a hoe doesn't have an engine or make a lot of noise, so I just smiled and said, "We'll see."

"Gonna make a farmer outen him yet," Daddy said as Cal darted past dogs and men to reach Dwight, who tousled his hair with a big grin.

The cement truck arrived, cutting more deep ruts in the grass, and then the hard work began. Dwight pulled on heavy rubber boots, as did some of the others who had remembered to bring them, and they waded in with hoes and rakes. In less than twenty minutes, the concrete was spread level over the gravel and ready for the trowels. Again, those many hands made it go fast. They deliberately left the surface slightly rough and even sprinkled a little sand over it so that the finish wouldn't dry so smooth that we'd be slipping and sliding every time it got wet.

A.K. and Lee brought buckets of water they'd dipped out of the pond and we rinsed our hands and the men washed off their boots and the hoes and rakes they'd used in the concrete.

Before the slab could set, Dwight used a stick to inscribe the date and we each pressed our hands into the gloppy mixture and signed our initials underneath.

"Bandit, too," Cal said. "He's part of the family."

Daddy nodded approvingly. Dogs have always been a part of his life. Bandit's only three but I knew the day would come when he would lie with Blue and my own beloved Tricksy in the pet section of our family graveyard alongside all the other dogs that have been fiercely loved and sadly mourned over the years.

I'd brought down a cooler full of soft drinks and everyone stopped to open a can and admire the morning's work.

"Hey, Deb'rah," Seth called to me, holding up his phone. "Sally's been trying to get you all morning and she says you're not answering your phone."

"My phone's up at the house," I called back, which got me a roll of the eyes from Dwight. He questions why I even bother to own one when I leave it off or forget to carry it most of the time.

I rinsed my hands and dried them on the seat of my

jeans, then went over to take Seth's phone. "Hey, Sally. What's up?"

"I need to talk to you," my cousin said. "About whether or not somebody's broke the law."

"Sorry, honey," I told her. "Judges aren't allowed to give legal advice."

"This isn't advice. We just need your opinion about something."

"We? We who? You and Jay-Jay?"

"No. Me and the Daughters."

My mind blanked for a moment until I remembered that this was the name of her support group for caregivers. The Designated Daughters.

"Please?" Sally begged. "Mama was always so proud of you going to law school and getting to be a judge."

Even though I knew this was a calculated use of her recent bereavement, I couldn't say no.

"I'll listen," I said, "but I mean it, Sally. I can't give any legal advice."

"It's not legal advice. I promise."

Dwight had heard when Seth called to me and now he strode toward me. "Is that Sally?"

I nodded and he took the phone. "Sally? You reckon you or Jay-Jay could meet me over at the courthouse in about an hour? My deputy's finished putting together a tape and we could use your help...What?...Well, I'll ask her, but—"

He pushed the mute button and said, "She wants to know if you'll come, too?"

I nodded. "But remember that we have to get back for Cal's ball game."

"Okay, Sally. See you in about an hour."

We handed Seth's phone back to him and, as the others were turning to start packing up and leave, Dwight said to Daddy, "We've got a tape of Wednesday. Could you and Miss Sister come back here tomorrow and watch it? Maybe tell us the names of some of the people we missed if it won't be too hard on you?"

He nodded grimly. "Iffen it'll help catch whoever did that to Rachel, then it won't be too hard on me or Sister either. Just tell me what time."

"*You're* going to call her?" I asked, astonished. He almost never dials a number of his own volition.

"I'll call her," he said, and the look on his face warned me off making any smart-aleck comments.

CHAPTER
8

*I never heard of an old man's forgetting where
he had buried his money.*

— Cicero

We left Cal and two of his cousins shagging flies hit
by my nephew Reese, who's assisting one of the Little League coaches this summer. This is Cal's second
summer playing in his age group and young Jake's first
year with T-ball. Mary Pat's not sure how much she
likes softball, but she won't let the boys leave her behind and she does okay with her glove if Reese hits her
easy flies.

Reese can be a feckless screw-up at times. With
twenty-five in his rearview mirror and fast heading for
thirty, he's an electrician in my brother Herman's electrical contracting business along with Annie Sue, his
younger sister. Actually, Herman and Annie Sue are
the licensed electricians. Reese can pull wire and put it

where it needs to go, but he won't buckle down and get his own license. He'd rather hunt and fish than crack a book. He lives in a singlewide at the backside of Seth's place where various women come and go. Come, because he can be charming as hell. Go, because he won't commit. He's surprisingly good with kids, though, and always seems to find time for his younger cousins.

Rather than take two vehicles, Dwight and I drove to the courthouse in his truck. I figured that if we went together, he couldn't decide he needed to stay in Dobbs and work, because I certainly didn't intend to miss Cal's game. Aunt Rachel's death might be of personal concern to both of us, but it wasn't the only item on his plate.

In addition to the usual petty crimes, there had been a rash of break-ins over near Black Creek, the SBI was keeping an eye on a potential meth lab, and allegations of brutality had been lodged against one of the jailors.

An unidentified male body had been found in a drainage ditch out by the interstate. His tats indicated that he'd been a member of a gang active in Baltimore, so Dwight had hopes that the Maryland State Police might take that body off his hands.

The kid who got shot in a Cotton Grove barroom brawl last night was his problem, though, and at that point, none of the customers in the bar would admit to seeing anything.

Unless time is a factor, Dwight always chooses to drive the back roads to Dobbs. Despite all the development our county's seen these last few years, there are still plenty of open fields away from the main highway. Cat's-ears and coreopsis were patches of bright yellow along the edges of the cultivated fields. Corn and cotton were several inches tall and someone was setting out a few last acres of tobacco plants near Pleasants Crossroads.

"You ever miss working in tobacco?" I asked Dwight.

He shook his head. "Not for one single minute. You?"

"I know I ought to say yes, but I can't. I'm glad it's not being raised on the farm anymore, but in a way I'm sorry Cal will grow up not knowing what it was like."

"Because it taught us about hard work?"

"And the value of an education if you don't plan to earn your living sweating in a hot gummy tobacco field."

"Yeah, it did do that," he agreed.

Where the fields hadn't yet been planted, drifts of blue toadflax and dark red sourweed swayed in the warm breezes. Purple wisteria blossoms still twined through the pines on north-facing roadsides and as we drove into Dobbs, every yard sported masses of azaleas in reds that shaded from pale pink to deep scarlet.

"I love this time of year," I said, drinking in all the beauty of a Carolina spring.

He smiled. "Tell me a time of year you don't love."

"Good news, Major," Raeford McLamb called out to Dwight as we walked down the hallway to his office in the basement of the courthouse. "Tub found us a witness from last night's shooting and we're about to go arrest the guy."

"Great," said Dwight. "That was quick."

Tub Greene was the newest member of the detective squad and he was shaping into a competent investigator "real fast for a fat little white boy," according to Ray, who was mentoring him.

"Mayleen left you these," he said, handing Dwight a packet of DVDs. Richards no longer worked weekends as a regular thing, but Ray said she'd spent the morning sequencing the various pictures and videos my family had provided and she had made several copies before leaving thirty minutes ago. "I'm not sure how much longer we're gonna have her."

"What do you mean?" Dwight asked.

"Well, you know how she likes to be outside and now that she and Mike are married? I get the feeling she might want to work with him. Landscaping." He shrugged. "We maybe ought to take a look at the kids graduating in criminal justice out at Colleton Community this spring."

"Hope to hell you're wrong," Dwight said glumly.

"Yeah, me too." Ray slipped on a brown poplin jacket and holstered his gun.

As he headed out to meet Deputy Tub Greene, he held the door open for Sally. Before he could ask who she was there to see, Sally spotted us and waved extravagantly.

"Hey, Dwight! Deb'rah! Y'all been waiting long?"

She pushed past Ray McLamb, who stood with his mouth agape.

Whereas her last two wigs had been short, today's was a mass of long blonde ringlets that fell below her thin shoulders to spring out in every direction and bob up and down across her forehead like wire coils. She wore skintight black jeans and a fringed black leather vest over a flesh-colored top that fit so snugly she might as well have been nude under the vest. Nails and lipstick were also black.

Sally's idea of mourning?

"Jay-Jay stayed with us last night," she said when we were seated inside Dwight's office, "but he had to go home to Raleigh to get his dog. He'll be back tonight, though."

"Us" would be her and her husband, Buzz Crenshaw, who owns Crenshaw's Lake, an RV campground that does a thriving business thanks to the interstate highway that skirts the lake. We're about halfway between New York and Florida and a lot of vacationers seem to find Crenshaw's a convenient and picturesque stopping point. In his way, Buzz is as colorful as Sally—his nickname comes from his reckless handling of speedboats out on the lake—and both seem popular with their customers.

Dwight handed her a couple of the DVDs Mayleen had made. "Mr. Kezzie and Miss Sister are coming over to our house tomorrow to watch with us. Why don't y'all come, too? Around two o'clock?"

"That'll work for Jay-Jay and me, but Buzz can't come. He's giving a waterskiing class then."

"Still a little chilly for that, isn't it?" Dwight asked.

"Oh, you know Buzz. He's well insulated and we've got wet suits if someone wants them."

Like Haywood, Buzz must weigh close to two-seventy, so yes, he's very well insulated. I spent a moment trying to imagine him on water skis in a Speedo and then I spent another few minutes trying to get that image out of my head.

"Now about the Daughters," Sally began, but I stopped her because Dwight had suddenly become absorbed by something on his computer screen.

"We'll be up in my office if you finish first," I said and warned him that I'd be ready to go in a half hour.

He gave me a distracted nod. "It's Baltimore," he murmured.

"Thirty minutes," I said again.

"Let's go to the old courtroom," Sally said when we reached the elevator. "More room."

More room?

When the doors slid open on the second floor, I saw why. It was the same group who had been in my courtroom earlier. The elderly woman who had looked around in bright-eyed interest was now asleep in a wheelchair, her small white head drooped onto her chest. The old man who had occupied it yesterday was seated on a nearby bench.

"Well, it's about time you got here," he said testily.

He tried to rise to his feet, grabbing a startled Marillyn Mulholland's arm for leverage. The pretty young woman who had been pushing his chair yesterday hurried to help. "Now, Grampa, we've only been waiting about ten minutes."

"At my age, I don't have all that many ten minutes left to waste, Katie. Why are we hanging around here anyhow? I say we take my gun and just—"

"We're not doing guns," Sally told him firmly. "Not yet, anyhow."

"Not *yet*?" I said. "Sally?"

Before she could answer, the hefty middle-aged man who hovered near the old woman asked the octogenarian gunslinger if he wanted his wheelchair back.

"Naw, I can walk just fine if these two don't let me fall." Half pulling them along, shoulders humped with what looked like osteoporosis, he hobbled toward the double doors that opened into our old superior courtroom.

As the others followed, I heard the same faint squeaking sound I had noticed when I first saw them earlier in the week but I couldn't tell if it came from the wheelchair or from someone's shoes.

All the courtrooms in the new wing are stripped-down modern, but here in the original part of the building, it was dark oak benches, oak paneling, and large gilt-framed portraits of earlier superior court judges. All males. All white. The floor had a gentle slope and with the support of Marillyn and his granddaughter, the old man made it to the nearest bench and eased himself down stiffly. The rest found seats and the young woman showed the other man how to set the brake on the wheelchair.

Sally pushed aside some of the exuberant blonde coils that had fallen over her eyes and said briskly, "Y'all, this is my cousin, Judge Deb'rah Knott. She's gonna help us."

"She's going to listen," I corrected sternly.

"Yeah, yeah," said Sally, waving off my stipulation. "Judges can't give legal advice, but she'll listen to us and then we'll listen to her."

She quickly introduced her friends.

The woman in the wheelchair was Charlotte Ashton. Her caregiver was her sixty-something son Charles, who wore white socks and black leather orthopedic sandals that squeaked with every step he took. "Charlotte's got Alzheimer's, but she can still walk and she has good days when she can talk and understand."

The crusty old man was Spencer Lancaster. His granddaughter was Kaitlyn Lancaster.

"You already know Marillyn. She helps look after her mother-in-law, who's in the last stage of breast cancer."

"I'm Frances Jones," said the remaining older woman. I put her at about seventy-five. She had a finely wrinkled face but she held herself erectly and her words were clear even if her voice was thin and trembly. "And this is my niece, JoAnn Bonner."

The niece looked to be three or four years younger than me. Like her aunt, she wore a cotton shirtwaist dress in a light flowery print. Both had sweet if somewhat plain narrow faces, both wore their straight hair in bangs. The niece's hair was a light brown and tucked behind her ears; her aunt's was white and curved into her chin line on either side. Neither woman struck me as someone who needed care.

"Frances was one of the first Daughters," said Sally. She had perched on the back of a heavy oak bench with her black leather boots planted on the seat. "Back then, she was taking care of her father and JoAnn's little girl, too, while JoAnn worked."

"That little girl's in college now," JoAnn said in a soft voice. "Aunt Frances took us in after my family turned their backs on me when I got pregnant."

"And now JoAnn's taken me in," said Frances Jones. Her narrow face lit up when she smiled at her niece, and from the answering smile JoAnn gave her, I sensed a true fondness between the two women.

"That's why we're here," said Sally. "Frances finally told us why she's losing her house, and we need to figure out how to get it back. Tell her, Frances."

Clearly embarrassed, Miss Jones said, "Oh, Sally, what's the use? I signed the papers, it's all legal, and even if it wasn't, Judge Knott has already said she can't advise us."

"Shit in a henhouse, Frances! Would you just *tell* her?" Sally exclaimed, stamping one of her boots.

The sound echoed through the empty courtroom and old Mrs. Ashton's head popped up. She blinked twice as if to clear her head, then gave me a polite smile.

"Hello," she said, holding out a thin bird claw of a hand. "So nice of you to come. You're Chuckie's teacher, aren't you?"

"Please tell her yes," said the middle-aged Charles Ashton, gently rocking the wheelchair as if it were a cradle. He swayed back and forth and his squeaky sandals kept time with the rocking chair.

"Chuckie's teacher? Yes," I said, taking her hand. "Yes, I am."

"I hope he's not giving you any trouble?"

"Not a bit, Mrs. Ashton. He's doing real good in school."

"He's a good boy…" Her eyelids slid to half-mast and her hand went limp in mine as the motion of the chair lulled her. "…good boy…"

With that she was asleep again.

"Thank you," said her son, and mirrored in his sad smile was the good little boy he must have been.

"Okay, Frances," Sally said. "No more false modesty here. Deb'rah's heard it all, right, Deb'rah?"

"Probably," I said.

Frances Jones straightened the collar of her flowery shirtwaist and spoke in a tremulous voice. "What you have to understand, Your Honor, is that my father and mother used to have money. Papa had the Ford dealership here and he made a handsome living, then sold it for a handsome amount when Mama got sick. Before that, though, they traveled all over Europe and they brought home many nice things. Mama belonged to the Daughters of the Confederacy and she had a sterling silver Georgian tea service that she used whenever it was her turn to host the meeting."

Tears flooded her eyes. "She was so proud of it. I can't believe I let him talk me into putting that in the sale. I should have kept it for Amy."

JoAnn squeezed her aunt's hand in consolation and I gathered that Amy was her daughter in college.

The story that eventually emerged differed only in details from so many I'd heard over the years. The cash money Miss Jones's parents had accrued dwindled through the years. Bad investments, taxes, and huge medical bills—the sheer cost of living drove her father to take out a reverse mortgage.

"He could have sold Mama's diamond engagement ring, her pearl-and-emerald pendant, and her diamond earrings, but he couldn't bear to part with them. They were Tiffany and he had them insured for two hundred thousand up until there wasn't enough money to pay the insurance. But he said I could sell them after he was gone and pay off the mortgage if I needed to."

At that point, he had hidden them somewhere in the old two-story house situated in what used to be the richest side of Dobbs but which had now gone downhill.

"Somewhere on the first floor, though, because he couldn't climb the stairs the last few years of his life," JoAnn said. "When Amy was a little girl, he used to keep them in a secret compartment in the fireplace surround and bring them out and let her try on the necklace, but after he died, the compartment was empty."

"I'd almost forgotten about them," her aunt said.

(*"She forgot about a set of Tiffany jewels?"* asked my disbelieving internal pragmatist.)

(*"Not everyone's as materialistic as you,"* said the preacher who never misses the moral of any story.)

The old man had died eighteen months ago and they had searched the house from top to bottom. No Tiffany jewelry. That's when Frances decided to sell her parents' best antiques, under the impression that they would bring enough for her to keep the house and keep looking. She had inquired among her friends and quite soon, Rusty Alexander, the owner of an auction house over in Widdington, had approached her about consigning the best pieces to him. She had spoken to two others, but they wanted fifteen percent of the sale, whereas Alexander Auctions agreed to take only ten plus advertising costs.

Papers were signed. The furniture, the silver tea set, the Limoges china—all were trucked over to Widdington. Frances and JoAnn had gone to the auction and were shocked at how little those things brought. That was last fall. Shortly before Christmas, Frances passed by an antique store in Raleigh and saw her tea set in the window. She went in and inquired about it and got another shock when she was told the price—almost exactly what the whole sale had brought in.

"You didn't have a reserve on any of the items?" I asked.

"I didn't know I needed to," Frances said tearfully.

"The bank's going to foreclose next week," Sally

said. "We've helped her look and we can't find the jewelry without ripping up every floorboard, which I still say we should do since it's only the ground floor, but—"

"Stop!" I said. "I don't want to hear about any crimes you're planning, okay?"

"God, Deb'rah," Sally said. "This judge thing's really gone to your head, hasn't it? You used to be willing to take it off the road and straight through the underbrush. When did you get to be such a tight-ass?"

"When I took my oath of office," I snapped, knowing I sounded like a sanctimonious prig.

Sally tried to give me a sneer but her face is so tight after that second face-lift that I didn't feel the full force of it. "I've gone online," she said, "and I've read about how dishonest auctioneers have a bunch of crooked dealers in their pocket. The dealers won't bid against each other, the prices stay low, and then later they get together, divvy everything up, and pay the auctioneer a percentage of the real value. So what we want to know is, can Frances sue that auctioneer?"

"Depends on what kind of contract she signed," I said. "But I'm willing to bet that everything he did is absolutely legal as far as the paperwork is concerned. If you could prove that it wasn't an honest sale, then you might have a chance of recovering part of it, but can you do that?"

From the look of despair on Frances's narrow face, I knew she couldn't.

"My brother Will's an auctioneer here in Dobbs," I said. "Too bad you didn't consult him."

"Knott? Will Knott? But I did. He was one of the ones that wanted fifteen percent of the sales."

"Fifteen percent of a lot would've been a hell of a lot more than ten percent of nothing," my cousin said sourly. "But Will! I forgot all about Will."

A big grin spread from her Botoxed lips to her eyes and my heart sank.

"He's totally legit now," I told her, hoping it was true.

"I still say we need to get my gun," croaked Spencer Lancaster.

CHAPTER
9

*There are two kinds of injustice: the positive
injustice of the aggressor, and the negative injustice of neglecting to defend those who are
wronged.*

— Cicero

So what did Sally want?" Dwight asked as we drove
out of Dobbs barely an hour after we'd arrived.

He was thoughtful as he listened to what I had to say
about the crooked auctioneer who had conned Frances
Jones out of her antiques.

"Alexander Auctions? I keep hearing about them," he
said. "I don't suppose there's any recourse, is there?"

"Nothing legal that I'm aware of. She said the guy
got her to sign the contract in front of a notary, supposedly to protect her, but of course, it was to protect
himself."

"Too bad."

"If you've heard about him, Dwight, why haven't
you shut him down?"

"Same reason, shug. No proof. I keep thinking we ought to run a sting operation, but you know what our budget cuts were. Violent crime's up all over the county and there's still a hiring freeze on."

"It may not be a violent crime, but Miss Jones is losing her house and will probably need welfare for the rest of her life because of him. And you won't go after him because he used fast talk instead of a gun to rob her?"

"Not true, Deb'rah, and you know it. We can't go after him because no one's filed a complaint."

"But he gamed her with legal-looking contracts."

"Preaching to the choir, shug. Let her swear out a warrant and we'll haul him in. Enough people complain, even our lazy DA might step up to the plate."

I sighed, knowing there was little likelihood of that happening.

Instead, we discussed the unidentified body that Baltimore was going to take possession of, then he told me how the alleged shooter in last night's barroom incident planned to plead self-defense. "He's already hired Zack Young to represent him."

"Don't tell me another word," I said. "Or I'll have to recuse myself if he shows up in front of me for a probable cause hearing."

We had worked out a mutual agreement clause as soon as he proposed: I wouldn't ask about any case with district court potential and he wouldn't second-guess any of my rulings if I dismissed the charges or lowered the penalties on people his department had arrested.

Because a lot of his work is with major crimes that would go directly to superior court, it hasn't been much of a problem.

We got home in plenty of time for Cal's game, and even though his team lost, he scored one run on a grounder past the shortstop and caught a pop-up foul, so he and Dwight high-fived each other and we parents treated the team (and Reese) to pizzas afterwards. Dwight's brother Rob and his kids came, too. Jake's T-ball league doesn't keep score. They're focused on just teaching the kids which way to run to first base, but Mary Pat's softball league does and they had won, so she was ragging on Cal in the car.

Her mom Kate wasn't with us. R.W. still takes naps, and Kate had elected to stay home today.

"To be perfectly honest," she confided to me as Dwight and Rob loaded the car with bats and gloves, "baseball bores me to tears. If I'm forced to watch grown men chase around after small round objects, I much prefer hockey."

"You New Yorker," I teased.

She laughed. "Go, Rangers!"

The sun had dipped below the tall pines when we got back to the house. We walked down to the pond to see how the concrete was drying and discovered that Bandit had run across the smooth surface while we were gone.

"Sorry," Cal said, abashed. "I tried to call him back but he wouldn't listen."

"It's okay," I told him. "Look there. Aren't those squirrel tracks? That's probably why he didn't listen to you."

"And those look like crow feet," Dwight said, pointing to a set of large avian prints in the middle of the slab.

"Maybe a possum or a coon or a fox will go across it tonight," said Cal. "Then we'd have a whole zoo."

"Not as fast as it's drying." Dwight pressed down lightly with his fingers and they left no mark. "In fact, with all this sunshine today, it's drying too fast. C'mon, buddy, grab one of those buckets and let's get some water on it before it cracks."

I left them to it and headed back to the house to see what I had in the way of drinks and munchies for tomorrow.

Above the pines, wispy clouds blazed orange and red. Sailors would be happy with tomorrow's weather if red skies really did mean anything.

CHAPTER
10

Spring typifies youth, and shows the fruit that
will be.

— Cicero

Even though there were no sailors in our vicinity,
Sunday morning did indeed dawn bright and clear.
Dwight wanted to adjust the carburetor on our riding
mower and then start looking at the DVD Mayleen had
put together, so Cal and I drove back into Dobbs to go
to church with Aunt Zell, something I try to do at least
once a month, in addition to dropping by the house for
lunch every week or so.

Aunt Zell is my mother with some of the
strong-minded edges smoothed down, not that she's
anybody's pushover. But she never challenged the
status quo the way Mother did, and when she married, it was to a respectable and educated buyer for
one of the large tobacco companies, not a fiddle-

playing bootlegger with a houseful of half-wild little boys.

She was the dutiful one who joined all the expected small-town social groups: Junior League, the DAR, the United Daughters of the Confederacy, and the Democratic Women. She helped organize the town's first Friends of the Library and she continues to raise money for the community college, the hospital, and the shelter for victims of domestic violence.

Aunt Zell and Uncle Ash had no children, so she sublimated with Mother's brood. When I ran off to dance with the devil after Mother died, she never gave up on me, and when I was ready to come back to Colleton County, she let me use the apartment on the second floor of their house, where Uncle Ash's mother had lived until her death.

Cal and I got there in time to sit down in the kitchen and share a cup of coffee while Uncle Ash went up to put on a tie. She poured chocolate milk for Cal, and their little dog Hambone jumped up in his lap as soon as he patted his knee.

"Well, young fellow," Uncle Ash said when he came back down. "I hear you drove a tractor yesterday."

Cal beamed and was soon describing how he'd had to stand up on the pedals to change gears and how balky the blade had been when he tried to raise it, but he'd managed to do okay.

I put our cups and Cal's glass in the dishwasher, Aunt Zell picked up her Bible and her purse, and we went out the back door. It was only three blocks to the church and too pretty a day not to walk. Cal held still long enough to let me get rid of his milky mustache and slip him a dollar for the collection plate, then hurried to catch up with Uncle Ash's long strides. Aunt Zell and I followed at a more leisurely pace because she wanted to hear my take on Aunt Rachel's death and funeral.

She hadn't known Aunt Rachel all that well, but she had visited a time or two after Sally brought her to live at nearby Crenshaw's Lake.

I described the low-cut red dress Sally had worn to the funeral and how scandalized Bel and Doris were by her collection of wigs. "Why didn't you ever mention them?"

She smiled. "Didn't realize I hadn't. They're just so Sally, I guess I assumed you'd seen her."

"Not since her hair came back in funny," I admitted, feeling vaguely guilty that I hadn't visited more often.

As if reading my mind, Aunt Zell linked her arm in mine and gave it a gentle squeeze. "You've had a busy spring, honey, and Bel and Doris don't have enough to do if they've got time to keep finding new ways to fault Sally. Maybe she never got over being a teenager, but she's been through a lot and she was good to Rachel."

"Do you know her support group?"

"The Designated Daughters? Oh yes. I was one myself once."

"You?"

"When Ash's mother was dying. She was a dear woman and a wonderful mother-in-law, but those last few months were bad. Congestive heart failure. Uncomfortable for her and so hard to watch. The Daughters were such a comfort. Ash was still having to travel in his work. South America. Mexico. I couldn't talk about it with my regular friends—it would have sounded self-pitying and very disloyal to her. But the group understood and didn't judge. And they had such practical suggestions for coping."

"You must have missed Mother terribly then," I said, remembering how close they had been. "And I wasn't here for you either."

She squeezed my arm again. "You'd already had your bad time, honey, nursing her. And you didn't have much of a support group yourself, did you?"

I was eighteen that summer, newly graduated from high school, the only child still at home, and yes, my mother's only daughter. My last summer at home. I should have been looking forward to college. Parties. New clothes. Instead, it was sickness and grief. Aunt Zell came as often as she could get away from her caretaking duties with her mother-in-law, but it was Maidie Holt, our longtime housekeeper who was dealing with her own grief, who helped me through it on a day-to-day basis. She was my rock. I was her broken reed.

Looking back, I don't fault my brothers anymore. The boys were building their own lives, getting married, starting families, preoccupied with earning a living and totally unnerved by her dying. Even Daddy. He was so heavy into denial that he couldn't—*wouldn't*—talk about it to her, to me, to anyone, so he hid behind farm work. Tobacco. Corn. Beans. He was out on a tractor twelve and fourteen hours a day.

I forced back the lump in my throat that always rises if I let myself remember too clearly and cast about for another subject. "Do you know a Frances Jones? Lives over on West Elm?"

"Jones? Would that be Olive Jones's daughter?"

I shrugged. "All I know is that she lived on West Elm and her mother used to belong to the UDC."

"Must be Olive Jones, then. She was president of our UDC before me. Why?"

"Sally's trying to help her and her niece save the house," I said, and told her what I knew about the situation.

Aunt Zell was surprised that they were in such financial straits and dismayed to hear they had been cheated by a dishonest auctioneer. "Her Georgian tea set? Oh dear. Olive was so proud of it. Not proud in a 'Look what I can afford' way, but more like 'I'm so lucky to have such a thing of beauty.' It would break her heart to know her daughter couldn't keep it."

Before I could ask if she ever saw the woman's Tiffany jewelry, we reached the side entrance to the church, where Cal held the door for us.

"Such nice manners," Aunt Zell said, and I felt a wave of maternal pride that still catches me by surprise even though Cal's lived with us for over a year now.

With so many nieces and nephews to cuddle, babysit, yell at, or ignore, I've never felt any yearning for a child of my own body, especially now that I've adopted Cal. When Doris or Bel or Nadine started asking pointed questions about when were Dwight and I going to have a baby together—"You ain't getting no younger," they told me—I quickly let them know that Cal was all the child we needed or wanted.

"If you want another one, sure," Dwight said amiably when the subject came up last summer, "but don't do it on my account. I'm fine with Cal."

"Good," I'd told him, "because I'm fine with my ready-made son, too."

That didn't stop my sisters-in-law from sniping or warning me that I might feel differently when it was too late.

Not a chance, I thought, as Cal and I shared a hymnal and he stumbled along earnestly with the words of "Safely Through Another Week."

Amen.

CHAPTER
11

*Nor, while lust bears sway, can self-restraint
find place.*

— Cicero

As soon as we stepped out of the car after church,
Cal and I smelled the succulent aroma of roasting
meat. We followed our noses around to the screened
back porch, where Dwight had fired up the gas grill. He
finished swabbing some ribs with barbecue sauce and
lowered the lid before Cal or I could snitch a sliver of
crisp pork.

"Another twenty minutes, and no lifting this lid," he
said sternly. "Peas are in the kitchen and I'm gonna go
scratch a few potatoes."

"Wait for me!" Cal cried and hurried off to change
out of his Sunday pants and hard shoes.

Digging for new potatoes in our soft sandy soil
means gently feeling around under the roots to find

those gumball-size spuds without hurting the sturdy green plants. It's like an Easter egg hunt for farm kids and Cal never seems to tire of it. A trail of hastily discarded garments led down the hall to his room and he was out the back door before Dwight reached the garden.

I hung up his pants, tossed his shirt in the laundry, and left his shoes where they were for him to stumble over and maybe think to put them away.

I changed, too, shucking my two-piece blue linen dress and open-toed heels for cutoffs and sandals. Out in the kitchen, a pan of tender young sugar snaps waited for someone to string them.

When Dwight and Cal returned with a double handful of baby potatoes, I washed the dirt off and steamed them in their thin red jackets.

Ribs are like fried chicken, best eaten with the fingers, and we didn't stand on ceremony when they came off the grill, smoky and tender. These were from one of Robert's pigs, so most of our meal had been grown right here on the farm.

"Can't get more locavore than this," Dwight said, spearing a potato no bigger than a marble.

I couldn't help smiling.

"What?" he said, smiling back.

"Nothing," I lied, but I'd suddenly remembered the reasons he'd given me for wanting to get married. "I'm tired of living in a bachelor apartment," he'd said plaintively. "I want to plant trees, cut the grass, buy family-size packs of meat at the grocery store."

And here we sat, less than two years later, surrounded by trees he'd planted and grass that he'd be cutting this week if he could get the mower's carburetor adjusted, and a family-size platter of meat on the table.

While we ate, Dwight told me that he had fast-forwarded through Mayleen's DVD and taken a few notes. "When Mr. Kezzie's brother drowned, was there ever any talk that it might not have been an accident?"

Cal's eyes grew wide. "Granddaddy had a brother that drowned?"

This was the first time the subject had come up in front of him and I kept my voice matter-of-fact in telling him about Daddy's younger twin brothers and how Jacob had drowned in Possum Creek, while Jed died at Fort Bragg.

Cal listened, then turned back to Dwight. "Why'd you say it might not've been an accident, Dad? You think somebody killed him? The same guy that killed Aunt Rachel?"

He knows what Dwight's job entails, but we try not to talk about it too much in front of him, and Dwight seemed a little taken aback that Cal had leaped from one possibility to another so quickly.

"I don't know, son, but if someone did do both, he'd have to be pushing eighty now, wouldn't he, Deb'rah?"

I nodded. "At least. Their friends would've been teenagers back then, too."

"Weird," said Cal. In his video games, all the bad

guys were brawny and muscular and young, not octo-
genarians.

"On the other hand," I said, when Cal had gone outside to give Bandit some rib bones and to check for
new animal tracks on the concrete slab, "there were a
lot of elderly people in and out of Aunt Rachel's room.
People who knew her and know our family from years
back. It wouldn't take much strength to smother an unconscious old woman."

"Was she talking coherently the whole time? Making sense?"

"Coherent, yes, and probably making sense, too.
You'd have to ask the others about that, though. I didn't
know half the names she mentioned, but that's why she
was killed, isn't it? To keep her from going on and on
about Jacob's death? That it wasn't an accident and
someone was afraid she was going to name who she
suspected?"

"Looks that way to me," he said. "Why else kill a
woman likely to die in the next few hours?"

The family started coming in around two. Daddy and
Aunt Sister arrived first, followed in short order by
Seth and Minnie, Sally and Jay-Jay, Aunt Sister and
her daughter, several of the nieces and nephews who
had contributed pictures, and lastly by Haywood and
Isabel, Herman and Nadine, and even Robert and his
wife Doris. Except for Herman, none of those last six
had been there on Wednesday, but they didn't want
to be left out—or at least their wives didn't—because

they were sure they could help identify any that the others couldn't.

"Robert'll probably know everybody Miss Rachel talked about," said Doris. "If y'all remember, he used to take some of his extra vegetables and watermelons down to her vegetable stand and sit and talk with her for hours, didn't you, hon?"

Robert allowed that this was true. "She liked my mother and told me a lot of good things about her I didn't remember."

Aunt Sister sniffed at that, but held her tongue.

I was surprised by Robert's words. He and my older brothers almost never mention Annie Ruth, Daddy's first wife. My impression of her is that she was short-tempered, grim, and worked in her house and garden from first light to full dark. Ironing, mending, canning, and preserving, even though she must have been pregnant most of the time. Eight babies, two of them twins, in eleven years. Nine babies, if you count the stillborn first son. Poor as Daddy was, she came from even more abysmal rural poverty and, according to Aunt Sister, never had a new dress or pair of new shoes till after they were married. She encouraged Daddy's illegal activities because it put food on the table, clothes on her expanding brood, and a stash of paper money under the kitchen floorboards.

"But he could've made a million dollars and it won't never going to be enough," said Aunt Sister. "I reckon when you've been that poor you don't never feel easy in your mind. She sure was proud of pumping out them boys, though. Thought she was raising up a real work crew."

Daddy seldom spoke of Annie Ruth and only once was it halfway negative. "We had it rough, too," he had said, "but there was always time for fiddling or story-telling. 'What's the good of it?' she used to ask me. She never stopped to smell the roses and she won't one to walk out in the fields with me of a moonlight night or catch lightning bugs with the little 'uns."

To be fair, though, my mother had it easier. She was town bred, the daughter of a prosperous attorney with a bit of money of her own, and she used that money to hire help instead of trying to do it all by herself. She always had time for a ramble with Daddy and any of the boys who wanted to tag along, and she loved hav-ing friends and family come visit for days at a time. Between her piano and his fiddle, our old farmhouse rang with music and laughter.

But there must have been some tenderness in Annie Ruth to make her firstborn find comfort in Aunt Rachel's memories and want to hear whatever stories she could tell him.

Dwight and Cal and I pulled extra chairs into our living room/den and we rounded up a bunch of cushions so that the younger ones could sit on the floor.

I could see the television screen from my seat at the dining table where I had my laptop ready to go when Dwight cued up the DVD. Mayleen had sent him an alphabetized list compiled from the notes that people had turned in, so it would be easy to insert any new names. Most of the still photos were focused on Aunt Rachel and those immediately around her bed. These had no sound to them, of course, and some were out of focus. Dwight paused the pictures whenever they showed other parts of the hospice room, and everyone called out the names of those they recognized. After five minutes, I'd only added one name to my master list—a Furman Snaveley. He was stooped with enormous age and turned out to be the former minister of Aunt Rachel's church.

"Well, I'll be blessed," said Jay-Jay. "I didn't see him there Wednesday. He's the one baptized you and me, Sally."

"Really? Oh wow! Look how he's shrunk. When he laid me backwards under the water, I thought he was six feet tall. Of course, I was only eleven, but still—!"

"Probably eat up with arthritis," said Doris, who had a touch of it in her thumbs.

Using his laser pointer, Dwight put a red dot on the profile of another white-haired man who stood between Seth and Dr. Howell near Aunt Rachel's bed. His head was turned away, so we couldn't see his face. "Who's that, Seth?"

"Never saw him before. Daddy?"

Daddy leaned forward. "I'm not rightly sure. You know him, Sister?"

She shook her head and Dwight moved on to the next picture. At that point, a three-minute burst of video flashed on the screen, and each time the camera strayed from Aunt Rachel's face, he would pause it so that everyone had a chance to comment.

"Oh, I know who that must've been before," said Jay-Jay. "That's his wife over there talking to you, Sally."

"Kitty Byrd? He's Sam Byrd?"

"We met her Friday after the funeral," I reminded Dwight, adding an asterisk to both names to denote someone over seventy-five. "She gave you a list of names, remember?"

"They live just up the road from Mama's and she used to let us come pick blackberries in their back pasture. Lord, the chigger bites we used to endure for Mama's blackberry cobblers. Remember, Jay-Jay?"

"Did you know them when y'all were young?" I asked Daddy.

"Naw, never met them till atter Rachel and Brack set up housekeeping," he said, giving me a speculative look.

It's always hard to slide anything past him. If he knew we were concentrating on the over seventy-fives today, he'd realize where Dwight was going with this.

"Who's that?" someone asked as Mrs. Byrd's "bald man, big red nose, blue shirt" passed in front of the camera.

Dwight immediately reversed the film and paused it there.

"I know him," Robert said unexpectedly.

"Jim Collins," said Sally before I could chime in. "He owns a big company down in Fayetteville. Something to do with medical equipment for the military, I think. He used to love to stop by Mama's vegetable stand on his way home and listen to her talk. Said she reminded him of his own mother."

"That's right," said Robert, "and there's his daughter right behind him. Real pretty, ain't she? I forget her name."

"Amanda," Sally said. "Mr. Collins says she goes to Meredith College now. Majoring in business so she can go to work with him."

I recognized that this was the girl whose pearls had broken when we both used the bathroom across the hall from Aunt Rachel's room. Slender and blonde, she was short like her father, with a narrow nose set in a very pretty face.

"She must take after her mother," I said.

Sally took a peppermint from the bowl on the coffee table. "No, Mrs. Collins was just as dumpy."

Jay-Jay leaned forward with a smile. "She's—"

Dwight immediately paused the picture again. "Something, Jay-Jay?"

"Naw," my cousin said. "Just thinking how lucky she was not to get his nose."

Dwight had moved on and we all focused again on the screen. Some of the videos were fuzzy and shot at an odd angle and none of them were very long.

I get it that videos taken with a cell phone can eat up a lot of valuable battery power that could better be used for texting and talking, but I also get it that teenagers have a short attention span and a hard time not talking while they're filming. Emma was the only one who managed to keep her mouth shut and her camera focused on Aunt Rachel for a full ten minutes.

We listened as she rambled on from Jacob to Jed to the house fire that had killed Richard Howell's sister and her two young daughters to bathing suits and recurring references to Letha, whoever she was. With so much background noise, it was difficult to hear everything.

"Mayleen's sent a copy of this DVD over to the SBI lab," Dwight said. "They say they can maybe clean up the sound and get more of what Miss Rachel was saying." He paused the action as Aunt Sister registered that mention of soup being ruined.

"Lordy, lordy!" she said. "I plumb forgot about that! It was hot as the dickens that day Jacob died, but the vegetables were ready and Mammy and Rachel were canning soup mixture. You young'uns don't know what hot is till you try to can vegetables in a water bath on top of a wood-burning range in the middle of summer. No air conditioning. No 'lectric stove. We'd shelled and shucked the night before and Mammy got started first light peeling tomatoes and slicing corn, but it was atter dinner and her and Rachel was still working on 'em when I went to the field. Hot as it was out there in the midday sun, me and Jed at least got a breeze. Not like the kitchen. When they hollered that Jacob was dead, Mammy just ran out of the house and—"

Her voice broke as the vivid memories of that day flooded over her.

"By the time we walked back in the kitchen, all the water had boiled out of the pot, the soup was burned, and three of them half-gallon jars had busted," she finished quietly. "That's what Rachel meant."

We all sat silent for a minute, and Dwight looked over at me.

"Let's take a break," I said. "Cal, would you get Aunt Sister a Pepsi, please? Anybody else want one? How about a glass of tea?"

"I could use a glass of that last beer you made," Seth told Dwight, and some of the others joined them at the tap Daddy had given him as a wedding present. Doris allowed as how she wouldn't mind a little glass if Robert was having one, but the rest of us opted for tea or soft drinks.

Emma helped me set out bowls of chips and nuts while some took turns in the bathrooms. As we waited for everyone to settle again, I said, "Who was that Letha she kept mentioning? Was she Jacob's girlfriend or something?"

"She's why Jacob died," Aunt Sister said tightly.

Daddy was as surprised as the rest of us. "What're you saying, Sister?"

"Well, she was. Jacob wouldn't've been down there at the creek if not for her. I never said before and then she ran off to Widdington to live with her sister right after that and I thought I wouldn't never have to think about her again, but Rachel going on and on about her's brought it all back. The way she led all the boys on. You, too, Kezzie. She tried it with you. Tried to turn you from Annie Ruth."

"She might've tried, but it didn't work." Daddy shook his head as if clearing away cobwebs of memory. "I knowed what she was and I never looked at her twice after me and Annie Ruth got together."

"That's 'cause you had more sense than the boys did. She played them off against each other and that last day, Jed came storming up from the woods and went right to the field and started on them suckers. Wouldn't even come to the house for dinner. I asked him if he'd seen Letha and he said he never wanted to hear her name again. All the same, she'd been by that morning on her way to the creek, swishing her tail in a skimpy bathing suit and looking for somebody to go swimming with her. Me and Rachel had to work. Not that we'd've gone. Mammy never let us go swimming when other boys were around lessen you was there, but Letha's mammy just let her run wild."

Daddy frowned. "She's what the boys were fighting about that morning?"

Now it was Aunt Sister's turn to look bewildered. "They fought?"

"I had 'em splitting logs for the cooker and they got into it so bad, I sent Jed back to the house to start suckering. Jacob wouldn't say what they was fighting about, so I told him to finish splitting the wood and stay away from Jed till they could act civil. Last words I ever spoke to him. Always felt like it was my fault he went to the creek alone."

"What actually happened?" asked Sally, who had opted for a Diet Mountain Dew that matched the pale yellow green of today's wig. She had dressed more conservatively for today's meeting. White cotton capris and a high-necked black tee that was so loose even Doris and Bel couldn't fault it. "Y'all keep saying he drowned, but why? How?"

"We had us a rope tied to the limb of a big ol' water oak," Daddy said. "We'd swing out and drop down in the middle of the creek where the water was real deep. They said the rope broke and Jacob, he hit his head on some rocks near the edge. They got him outen the water 'fore I got there, but I seen his head." He laid his hand on the side of his own head above his right ear. "It was all caved in."

"Who was 'they,' Mr. Kezzie?" Dwight asked.

"Ransom Barley and Billy Thornton."

"Not this Letha?"

"Letha McAllister." His voice came harshly. "If she was there, she must've run home soon as it happened, 'cause she won't there when I got to the creek and today's the first I knowed she was even anywhere around."

"Well, maybe if you'd've told us they fought that morning—"

"I *couldn't* say nothing, Sister. Jed was hurting so bad. Last time he seen Jacob, they was cussing each other. I won't gonna rub more salt in his wounds."

"Did you know he'd enlisted in the army?" Jay-Jay asked.

Daddy shook his head. "He took off the same day we buried Jacob. Didn't know where he went. I put out the word but nobody'd seen him. Was almost a month 'fore Mammy got a postcard from him. I drove down to Fort Bragg to get him. Even took his birth certificate to prove he won't old enough to join up, but I got there four hours and twenty-eight minutes too late. I fetched him home anyhow, though. They wanted me to wait and let 'em send him home proper, but I told 'em the hell with that. I'd take him home my own damn self and they could go f—"

He broke off abruptly and there was a grim silence as images of what that ghastly trip home must have entailed flashed in our minds.

"Granddaddy?"

I realized that Cal was about to blurt out a question, but Dwight said, "Not now, buddy," and he subsided.

The other grandchildren were looking subdued and anxious. They had never heard him use language before. Even my brothers and their wives were silent.

To get us back on track, I said, "On Wednesday, Daddy, you said Ransom Barley and his family moved back to Georgia a few years after that. What about this Billy Thornton?"

"What about him?"

"Where's he now?"

"Ain't heard nothing about him in years."

"Won't he Davis Thornton's daddy?" Haywood asked. "Sharecropped with Leo Pleasant?"

"I reckon."

"I think they moved to Johnston County when me and Herman was in the eighth grade. Ain't that about right?" he asked his twin.

Herman nodded. "Last I heard, Davis was working in a welding shop in Benson. Don't know about his daddy."

I made notes of what they'd said. If this Billy Thornton was still around, Dwight would find him. In the meantime, we moved on with the pictures. Church friends and family made up the bulk, of course. There was one more old-timer in the crowd, but he was one of Aunt Rachel's longtime customers and not someone who'd lived in our neighborhood as a boy.

At the very end, a pudgy male figure dressed in blue scrubs walked past the camera and Dwight paused. "Who's that?"

Sally squinted at the screen. "Just one of the orderlies. They sent up a supper tray every evening for whoever's there and he always brought it up. Real pleasant. Asked a lot of questions about you, Uncle Kezzie, and what it was like growing up on a farm. He said his name, but I forget it. You remember, Jay-Jay?"

Her brother shook his head.

"Doesn't matter," Dwight said easily as the last pictures flashed across the screen, but I knew he'd have the guy's name by midday tomorrow.

CHAPTER
12

Youth has many more chances of death than those of my age.

— Cicero

Shortly after he came back to Colleton County and was sworn in as Sheriff Bo Poole's second-in-command, Dwight had gone fishing on one of the farm ponds with the man who was now his father-in-law. Kezzie Knott had been almost like a father to him after the early death of his own dad. All through his adolescence, he had hung out with the Knott boys—fishing, hunting, swimming, and playing whatever ball was in season. Their house had drawn him like a magnet. Miss Sue always seemed to know when he needed to talk during those tough years when his own mother was stretched to the breaking point to earn a living for her four children and get the academic degrees that eventually made a better life for all of them. And half the time he wasn't sure Mr. Kezzie realized he wasn't another son to be cuffed or praised, depending on the circumstances.

The rowboat was drifting in the middle of one of the farm ponds and their hooks were in the water when the older man said, "So you're gonna be a deputy sheriff now, boy? Lot different from working in Washington, I reckon."

"I dunno. Crime's crime."

"And it's always black and white to you?"

"'Fraid so, sir."

"Well, as long as you stay straight and play fair, you'll do good."

Up until he was in his early teens, when Miss Sue finally got Mr. Kezzie to quit making whiskey himself, Dwight had actually helped the boys chop firewood for cooking the mash in one of those large copper stills, so it felt weird to say, "I hope you won't take this wrong, Mr. Kezzie, but I've got to say it—"

"No, you ain't," he interrupted. "You catch me doing what's against the law, you gotta do what the law says."

Like the sly old fox he was, he gave Dwight a sardonic grin. "'Course now, you gotta catch me doing it first."

And Dwight had laughed as a sun perch took his hook and dived for the bottom of the pond.

He had not yet had to arrest Deborah's father, but they both knew he would if the proof was there. Not that the old man was still actively making it. Dwight was pretty sure of that, but there was a suspicion that he might be bankrolling the smaller productions of men who were, just to keep his hand in. So far, though, it was all rumor and speculation. No one had offered evidence or even made a direct accusation. But nature and moonshiners both abhor a vacuum and Colleton County still had stretches of isolated woodlands and plenty of men who knew the trade. Word was out that a fairly large still must be in operation somewhere close to the line between Colleton and Johnston Counties, and he'd been asked to a strategy lunch with some of Johnston's officers and a couple of Alcohol Law Enforcement agents.

With Sheriff Bo Poole sitting in on the morning briefing, Dwight said, "Long as I'm down that way, I'll go on over to Benson and see if I can locate this Billy Thornton or his son."

Poole looked skeptical. "You really think Rachel Morton's death goes all the way back to that drowning?"

Dwight shrugged. "Seems to me that the only reason to kill her was to stop her from talking about something bad that happened years ago and her brother's drowning is what she kept going back to. Don't know if it's relevant but we've gotta start somewhere and it's the only thing I know to go with right now." He turned to the red-haired deputy he had come to rely on for all things related to computer searches and data bases. "Mayleen, see if you can locate a Ransom Barley down in Georgia. He'd be around eighty now. His father worked for CP&L fifty years ago, and his younger brother's name was Donald. I'm afraid that's all the information I have."

Richards smiled. "Should be enough, Major."

"And there was a Letha McAllister. She moved to Widdington back when she was a teenager, so she'd be around eighty as well, if she's still alive."

"That might take a little longer," Richards said. "Especially if she got married."

"Five or six times probably," Dwight said and repeated some of Miss Sister's assessment of the girl.

Both of the other two detectives on duty had court appearances that morning, but he asked them to take a look at the end of Mayleen's video, then go over to the hospital when they were finished in court and see if they could ID that orderly. "And question the staff again. Maybe we'll get lucky and they'll remember seeing someone enter or leave that room after the family left."

Sheriff Poole gave them a quick update on the jailor accused of brutality. Three former prisoners had filed a formal complaint and he had been arrested last night. "Hate to say it, but it looks like they have a case. I've suspended him, but he's waived his PC hearing and now we wait for the DA's office to indict. I've called a meeting for the other jailors and the bailiffs, too. Sometimes the uniforms go straight to their heads and they forget they're not in charge of the universe."

The youth Tub Greene had arrested for Friday night's barroom brawl was sitting in a cell two corridors over. His probable cause hearing was that morning and he would no doubt be bound over for trial in superior court.

"Good work," said Poole, and the rookie detective turned bright red under the praise.

A little before ten, Mayleen Richards tapped on the open door. "Major? I've located a Donald Barley down in Waycross, Georgia. He says his brother Ransom died six years ago. You want to talk to him?"

Dwight nodded.

"Line two," she said.

Dwight pressed the lit button and was soon introducing himself to one of the last living friends of the Knott twins.

"Yes, I remember them," Donald Barley told Dwight. "What's all this about?"

"We're trying to reconstruct the day Jacob Knott supposedly drowned," Dwight said. "Were you there?"

"*Supposedly?* What do you mean, 'supposedly'? He drowned in the creek, didn't he?" Before Dwight could answer, he said, "What was it called? Possum Creek? Save me, Jesus! I haven't thought about that creek in years."

"Were you there when it happened?"

"No, but my brother Ransom was."

"Did he tell you what happened?"

"Oh. That's what you meant by 'supposedly.' It was that fall on the rocks that probably killed him, not drowning, right?"

"What did your brother actually tell you, Mr. Barley?"

"Do you know how long ago that was, Major… Bryant, was it?"

"Yes, sir. More than sixty years."

"And I was just a kid brother who didn't get to tag along that day."

"Why not?"

"My brother was a horny teenager, if you really want to know, and he didn't want me around, cramping his style while he showed off for this girl he liked."

"Do you remember her name?"

"Sorry."

"Could it have been Letha? Letha McAllister?"

There was a long silence.

"I'm sorry, Major. That could have been her name. But there were a couple of girls after that—a Lisa and a Valeta—and I used to get the names mixed up."

"What about a Rachel?" asked Dwight. "Rachel Knott?"

"The Knott boys' sister? I know she liked Ransom because she was always asking me about him when she'd see me at church, but I don't think she was the one he was after right then. I'm pretty sure it was a Lisa or Leta or something like that. But yeah, Rachel's brother didn't drown. At least not outright. Ransom said a rope he was swinging on broke and he landed on his head. Scared the hell out of them. One minute the kid's playing Tarzan and the next minute he's lying there, facedown in the creek. Ransom said all the water around his head was bright red. They pulled him out and tried to give him artificial respiration, but it was too late. So did he drown or was it the rocks? Whichever, Ransom never went swimming there again and I know he was glad when Dad said we were moving back to Georgia."

"You said 'them.' Were any other kids around that day?" Dwight asked.

"There must've been, but don't ask me who. Like I say, I wasn't there. And after that first day, after he talked to the sheriff, Ransom never wanted to speak about it. This is the first time I've even thought of it in years."

After another few minutes in which Barley could add nothing new, Dwight gave him his phone number and said, "If you think of anything else, I'd sure appreciate a call."

But after he cradled the receiver, Dwight leaned back in his chair with even more questions running through his head. *Did that rope really break or did someone bash young Jacob Knott with a rock? He and Jed had fought over that girl. Was there another fight down on the bank of Possum Creek?*

CHAPTER
13

*So near is falsehood to truth that a wise man
would do well not to trust himself on the narrow edge.*

— Cicero

Monday morning and my calendar was filled with
the ordinary messes humans keep getting themselves
into: assaults, drunk and disorderly, shoplifting, check
kiting, drug cases, and one case of elder abuse. There
was also a probable cause hearing for the shooting
death in a Cotton Grove bar Friday night.

Deputy Tub Greene, one of Dwight's younger officers, testified against the accused, as did a witness to
the shooting who said the fight was over some young
woman. The public defender did his best to squelch his
client, but the tearful young black man was clearly and
vocally remorseful.

And just as clearly guilty.

Although his attorney argued that the evidence was

insufficient, I found probable cause to bind him over to superior court and set his bail at fifty thousand.

"Please, Your Honor," he said, tears streaking down his cheeks. "The funeral's today at two o'clock and I really need to be there. Please? He was my best friend."

"I'm sorry, sir," I said, and I really was. They probably *were* best friends until a girl set their testosterone levels soaring. "If you hadn't had that gun in your pocket, you'd've likely blacked his eye and he'd've bloodied your nose and you two would probably be having a beer together tonight. As it is ... ?" I shook my head. "If you can't make bail, I'm afraid you're going to have to miss his funeral."

As the bailiff led him away, I couldn't help thinking about Jacob and Jedidiah. Twins. Best friends. Until a girl named Letha came between them. "Swishing her tail in that skimpy bathing suit," Aunt Sister said. If Daddy hadn't pulled them off each other, would their fistfight have ended with one of them using a knife or picking up a rock?

"Call your next case," I told the ADA.

"The State versus Melva Rouse Pennington, Your Honor," said Julie Walsh, who was prosecuting today's calendar.

Reduced to its basics, Mrs. Pennington was a thirty-year-old white woman who had several previous misdemeanor convictions for drug possession and one for driving with a revoked license. She had been living with the seventy-four-year-old grandmother who raised her. After the grandmother refused to sign over her last pension check, Mrs. Pennington had slapped her, then kicked the chair out from under her and broke her arm. When the grandmother went to the emergency room for treatment, the hospital was required by law to report it to DSS, who made it their business to investigate, which led to Mrs. Pennington's arrest for misdemeanor Assault Inflicting Serious Injury.

Rather than delay the inevitable, she had waived her right to a jury trial and was ready to plead guilty, but before I sentenced her, her court-appointed attorney asked if I would hear the grandmother.

Despite her drug addiction, Melva Pennington was an attractive brunette and she bore a distinct resemblance to the neatly dressed white-haired woman who came forward to speak on her behalf, her arm still in a sling. She seemed frail and unsteady on her feet and her voice trembled as she asked me to send her granddaughter for drug treatment rather than to prison. "It's the drugs that made her do this, Your Honor. She needs help. If she could just get clean, she could keep a job, make a better life for herself."

This was not the first time a victim had stood before me to argue that the abuser was not a bad person/hadn't meant to do it/wouldn't do it again. Pick one. Hell, pick them all. It was a common refrain in cases of domestic violence.

But I had read the DSS report. "This isn't the first time she's hurt you, is it, ma'am?"

The old woman's shoulders slumped in an acknowledgment she didn't want to voice. "She's all I've got,

Your Honor, and it's not really her fault. Her mother—
my daughter—she did heroin. She ran off when Melva
was only ten. We haven't heard from her in years. If
you send Melva away, I won't have anyone."

"I'm sorry," I said for the second time that morning,
"but if we don't put her where she can't hurt you,
it's only going to get worse. Next time, you could
be killed, and I'm sure she wouldn't mean to do it,
but you'd be just as dead. What's the State asking,
Ms. Walsh?"

With five priors, I could and did sentence Mrs. Pennington to 150 days and added a recommendation that
she be admitted to the prison's drug treatment program.
I hoped that this longer sentence might give a treatment
program time to work even though it usually takes a
full six months and a true desire to quit.

I adjourned for lunch a little before twelve and called
my brother Will at his auction house to see if he wanted
to meet me somewhere. I really had no intention of
getting involved with Sally and her Designated Daughters group, but it wouldn't hurt to get his take on Rusty
Alexander, that auctioneer over in Widdington.

"Why don't you come here?" he said. "I've got stuff
in the microwave and drinks in the fridge. Always
room for one more."

There was a hint of laughter in his voice, and hearing him say that made me smile, because Daddy used
to swear that this was Mother's motto. "We could be
sleeping four in a bed and pallets on every floor and

you'd still tell the preacher and his family, 'Y'all stay the night, we got plenty of room.' You been a-keeping that inn, Jesus would've been born inside right next to the fireplace." But he would be grinning even while he grumbled, because he loved company as much as she did. Any excuse for a little pickin' and singin'.

Mother and Aunt Zell's parents used to open their spacious home for a large formal Christmas party every December. The rest of the year, they entertained at the country club or in restaurants. My grandmother Stephenson died before I was born, but they say she disliked the social side of my grandfather's practice.

"He could have been governor if he'd run," his former law partners have told me, "but she hated to mix with strangers and she certainly wasn't going to shake hands with riffraff or potential voters that we'd managed to keep out of jail."

"She was a snob?" That had surprised me because neither Mother nor Aunt Zell had ever seen a stranger.

"Not a snob exactly," said my very proper cousin John Claude Lee, son of the firm's original founder.

"Sounds like a snob to me," I'd said.

"Well, maybe," he conceded. "But in the kindest possible way. I think she felt it wasn't their fault if people didn't meet her standards."

"She must have hated having Daddy join her family." This was something I'd really never given much thought to. Despite their differences in social standing and education, Mother and Daddy seemed so perfectly matched that I couldn't imagine them *not* being married to each other. "It's a wonder Daddy ever had the nerve to propose."

"We-l-l-l..." John Claude had looked faintly embarrassed. He, too, had standards that weren't always met.

"You mean Mother proposed to *him*?"

"Really, Deborah, this is something you should be asking your father, not me," John Claude had said firmly, and for him, the subject was closed.

At the time of that conversation, I had been in my first race for the bench and too caught up in campaigning to pursue it. The summer she was dying, Mother had told me most of her secrets, but I realized now that she hadn't told me everything. One of these days, maybe I *would* get up the nerve to ask Daddy.

The older boys remembered her coming but not how or why. "It was like *The Wizard of Oz*," Frank once told me. "Everything was black-and-white till she come, and then it was color."

Aunt Sister got defensive when she heard that. "Pa couldn't afford paint just to make a place look pretty while he and Mammy was alive. And Annie Ruth wouldn't spend a nickel on fripperies. Them boys was lucky if they got a piece of bubblegum on their birthdays."

"Not true," said Robert. "Daddy always used to come home from one of his whiskey runs with a sackful of candy."

"And every time he did, Annie Ruth would fuss about wasting money," Aunt Sister told me later.

*   *   *

Will was the oldest of my own mother's four children and a perpetual exasperation to her. He was always poking through junkyards and the neighbors' barns, learning the history of rusty machines or dilapidated furniture, looking for deals. Give him a bicycle with two missing wheels in the morning and he'd have traded it up to a television by dark, then sold the TV the next morning to buy something else. And when I say "give him," it would probably be more accurate to say "don't turn your back or he'll take." He didn't consider it stealing to rescue an item he was sure no one really wanted, no matter how many times Daddy took him to the woodshed for not asking first.

By the time he got his driver's license, he'd figured out that people would pay him to clean out their garages or basements and let him keep whatever trash he hauled away. I'm not real sure his customers always remembered what was in those barrels and boxes that went off in the back of his pickup. Mother reluctantly got over the idea of turning him into a lawyer—she barely kept him in high school long enough to get a diploma—but with his easy charm and glib tongue, she thought she had a good chance of making him an insurance broker or a real estate dealer if he would just buckle down and pass the state's minimum requirements for a license.

She didn't live long enough to see either of those happen. When she died, he was married to his second wife and barely scraping a living, hauling junk and selling it at flea markets. By the time I came back to

Colleton County, though, he'd gone to auctioneering school and was a fully licensed auctioneer, working on his third marriage. He somehow acquired an old tobacco warehouse on the west side of Dobbs and began holding auctions every Saturday night as well as doing appraisals for a flat fee.

He collected books on silver, crystal, and china, and taught himself how to tell whether a piece of furniture was handmade and old or machine-made and new.

These days, he runs estate sales from the mountains to the coast and has a pretty good reputation for knowing the market values that let him get top dollar for his consignors. So far as I know, everything is totally legitimate.

When I got to Will's, four other vehicles were parked near the back entrance of the new auction house that replaced the old original warehouse after it burned. (And nearly took me with it.) In addition to a brand-new van with his business logo on the sides, there were two SUVs with handicap tags dangling from their rearview mirrors and the fourth set of wheels was a dismayingly familiar blue VW convertible with a bumper sticker that read: MY OTHER CAR IS A TARDIS.

I should have known. No wonder my brother had sounded so amused when he invited me over.

As soon as I stepped inside the air-conditioned coolness, I saw Sally behind the high counter that separates the kitchen area from Will's conference room. The air was redolent with the mingled smells of hot bread, onions, and Texas Pete chili sauce. She held up two squirt bottles, one yellow, the other red. "I forget. You like mustard on your hot dogs or ketchup?"

Today's outfit was almost as conservative as yesterday's: a blue-and-white checked newsboy cap with black bangs and a fringe of black curls peeping out all around, electric blue shirt, and blue gladiator sandals that laced up several inches above her ankles. And yes, blue eye shadow and blue nails and lipstick.

With a gotcha grin on his face, Will said, "Coleslaw and onions?" and handed me a can of soda.

"Mustard, slaw, and chili, yes. No onions," I said and took a seat at the round conference table beside Frances Jones, who was folding paper towels into individual napkins. Once again, she and her niece wore shirtwaist dresses in similar summery prints.

Cheap red microwaved wieners floated in a bowl of steaming hot water on the counter, and JoAnn Bonner was gingerly pulling hot buns from a plastic bag that had almost melted from the microwave's heat. Marillyn Mulholland and Kaitlyn Lancaster had an assembly line going with pickles and chips on a row of paper plates, and old Mr. Lancaster sat in his wheelchair with a bag of potato chips in his lap, happily munching away and strewing greasy crumbs down the front of his shirt.

Charles Ashton sat across from me at the table and fed bits of hot dog to his mother, who had her own wheelchair today. He saw my raised eyebrow and said, "I know, I know. Not good for her. But right now she's aware of enjoying this hot dog. A month from now, she may not. So what difference does it make?"

"Yeah, and when Katie takes my blood pressure tonight, it'll be up from all this salt," said Mr. Lancaster, popping another potato chip in his mouth, "but who gives a damn?"

"What the hell, what the hell, what the hell?" Sally chanted, cheerfully misquoting Mehitabel the Cat. "There's life in the old dog yet."

"You better believe it," he cackled.

Will handed me a paper plate with the hot dog he'd fixed for me. I carefully wrapped it in a paper towel because I'm bad for dripping things and I know from past experience how hard it is to get chili sauce and mustard stains off of a white silk blouse.

"I suppose they're here to tell you about Alexander Auctions?" I asked him.

Pushing fifty, with the first touches of gray at his temples, Will's still my best-looking brother. Tall and flat-bellied, he was trim in a dark blue golf shirt unbuttoned at the neck and khaki slacks. Laugh lines crinkled around his blue eyes. He was smiling now, sharing the joke with Sally. "See? I told you she wouldn't be able to resist."

"Resist what?" I said indignantly. "I'm not getting involved. I just want to know if Rusty Alexander is as crooked as they think."

He shrugged. "Probably. Business has been slow these past few years. Mediocre antiques and the more common collectibles aren't bringing what they used to now that eBay lets us know that some things aren't as rare as we thought they were, so it's tempting to cut a few corners, try to fatten up the profits."

"You don't do that, do you?"

His smile broadened. "You think I'd tell you? And you a judge? Married to a sheriff's deputy? Not hardly likely, little sister." He shook his head. "Besides, that last come-to-Jesus session with Daddy put me on the straight and narrow. Well, on the straight anyhow. Funny that a man who spent the first half of his life breaking the law would take it so seriously when we did it. You ever think about that?"

Of course I had. "I think that cheating the government out of its whiskey tax never struck him the same as stealing from a neighbor or somebody he'd looked in the eye. So far as I know, though, he never dealt dishonestly with a buyer or ever went back on his word."

"Well, neither have I. Not with any of my consignors anyway. And not since I got my auctioneer's license."

I took his carefully worded disclaimer with a grain of salt. Just because he was honest with them doesn't mean he's honest with everyone else, but I wasn't here to pick a fight or monitor his morals. I just wanted to know about Rusty Alexander.

"Yeah, I've heard things. Nothing blatant. The licensing board is pretty vigilant," he said, "but there have been a few times when he gets to auction off a nice estate and somehow the prices just don't meet expectations."

"Like Frances's mother's tea set?" asked Sally.

She and the others had brought their paper plates to the table and there was a companionable sound of munching as pickles and chips were consumed. Marillyn had placed another open bag of chips in the middle of the table and I was virtuously trying to ignore it.

"Like the tea set," Will agreed. "Georgian? Sterling? With its own sterling tray and hallmarks from one of the best silversmiths working in London at that time? It should have fetched at least seven or eight thousand, even in this market. Forget about the historical value. The melt value of silver's around thirty dollars an ounce now and a set that large would weigh several pounds. I don't know what all was in your house, Miss Jones. Sally says a lot of nice antiques and maybe they were. But maybe they were only high-quality factory-made pieces. Just because something's old, doesn't mean it's valuable, but a sterling tea set from the early eighteen hundreds has a recognized worth and no way should it have gone for the twelve hundred you say it brought."

"See, Deb'rah?" said Sally. "I told you so!"

Will finished his first dog in two bites and reached for the second one on his plate. "Another thing, Miss Jones. You say he charged you for advertising the sale but that there weren't many people in the audience?"

Frances Jones nodded. "He said it was such a nice day, people were probably out doing other things."

"And if it'd been raining, he'd've blamed the weather for that, too," Will said. "I keep my eyes open for quality auctions and if he put notices in the paper or sent out flyers, I never saw one."

JoAnn Bonner fumbled for the straw purse beneath her chair, opened it, and pulled out a sheet of pale green paper. It was folded in thirds and had been secured with a bit of tape. On one side was a mailing label and canceled stamp with the auction house's return address. On the other side was a long list of household items.

Marillyn looked at it with a printer's professional interest and held it disdainfully by one corner. "Cheap twenty-pound bond, Helvetica font, probably run off on his office printer, and he didn't even use the printer's highest-quality resolution."

She passed it to Will, and JoAnn said, "He told us he mailed out about two hundred of these and sent emails to another thousand of his usual customers."

I took the sheet from Will and ran my finger down the list till I came to *English Silver Tea Set*. Nothing about its age, its hallmarks and provenance, nor how many pieces the set contained.

Vintage costume jewelry.
Nice old walnut dining table with eight chairs.
China service for 10.

Everything listed was equally generic. "This is supposed to draw people in?"

"Only if he really did send this to someone other than these two," Will said grimly. "I'm willing to bet that he certainly didn't send it to any of his high rollers, only his low- to mid-range buyers. A detailed list would have gone to a ring of dealers who had agreed beforehand to keep the bidding low. Later, they would have the real auction among themselves and split the proceeds with Alexander."

"So how do we nail the bastard and get some of Frances's money back?" asked Sally.

Will shook his head. "I'm afraid there's no legal way."

"What about an illegal way?" asked Marillyn.

At that point, I decided it was time for me to get back to court.

CHAPTER
14

*O admirable service of old age, if it takes from
us what in youth is more harmful than all things
else.*

— Cicero

DWIGHT BRYANT—MONDAY AFTERNOON

Enforcing the state's local alcohol laws was no
longer the province of Alcohol, Tobacco and Firearms,
so Dwight was surprised when ATF Agent Ed Garrison
joined them at the lunch meeting set up by ALE's Virgil Dawson.

"An operation this active, this close to the interstate,
they're probably sending it on down to Florida or up to
Virginia," Garrison explained, which was why the feds
were involved.

Dawson laid a map of the highway on the table to
look at while they ate. He pointed to exits along the

section that crossed from Johnston County into Colleton. "Here, here, and here, we've had reports of sales being conducted out of the back of a white panel van. They must use magnetic signs to change the look, because one informant said it was a window cleaning service, but this time, it was a florist."

He showed them a fairly crisp picture that someone had given him. Although taken at night, it showed two men, both with their backs turned. A stocky man in coveralls appeared to be transferring gallon plastic milk jugs from the back of a van to the bed of a pickup truck parked beside it. A second picture showed several dozen jugs being covered by a tie-down tarp.

"He couldn't have gotten a picture of the license plate?" asked Garrison.

"She," said Virgil Dawson. "She manages the snack bar at that service station here." He pointed to an intersection on the map. "They were at the far side of the parking lot and she'd have been noticed. They caught her attention because it was around nine thirty at night, a real odd time for a florist to be making a delivery. As it was, she was plenty nervous but pretended she'd gone outside to make a call on her cell phone, not taking pictures."

Aerial flights along the route had given them nothing. It was maddening, because patrol cars up and down that stretch of highway had reported fleeting but distinct smells of the mash being cooked, yet thorough searches each time uncovered nothing in the woods or underbrush or any nearby barns and no lingering tell-tale aromas.

Garrison and Dawson were both old school, nearing retirement, and they spoke nostalgically of the days when a simple flyover might show smoke from a still during the day or red coals at night.

"Not that I miss it," said Garrison. "You'd lie out in the brush and briars for two or three days at a time, fighting mosquitoes and chiggers and snakes, eating cold beans and Vienna sausages, waiting for the still hands to come work the mash. Nowadays, it's barns and basements, under hogpens or inside chicken houses. They cook it with propane or electricity and pipe in cold water rather than set up by a creek."

Dwight grinned. "Next thing you know, they'll add wheels and— Hey, wait a minute! We've got mobile meth labs now, right? Idiots cooking it up in the back of their SUVs?"

His Johnston County counterpart immediately saw where he was headed. "Well, damn! You know a semi would hold at least two of those five-hundred-gallon pots. They could just trundle it up and down from one rest stop to another."

"We only have one rest stop for trucks," Dwight said, touching the map where the interstate entered and exited the bulging western edge of Colleton County, "but I'll have my patrols start running the plates on every rig they see parked there or anywhere else along this route."

The others were thumbing their phones as lunch

broke up and they scattered from the restaurant to their cars. Ed Garrison was parked next to Dwight. "Tell Deborah I said hey, okay?"

"You're really going to retire this fall?" Dwight asked as he unlocked the door to the prowl car he'd driven over in. "How's Linda gonna like having you hang around the house twenty-four hours a day?"

Garrison grinned. "I'm gonna ease her into it. Catch up on my reading. She'll barely notice I'm there." He got into his own government-issued car and, with a wave of his hand, headed back to Raleigh.

Benson was still so small that Dwight soon found the metal works two blocks off Main Street near the railroad tracks. The sidewalk in front of the place was lined with decorative iron gates embellished with flowers and trailing vines. The double shed doors that fronted on the street had been rolled up for ventilation and the interior was noisy with the clang of hammers against iron and the hiss of blowtorches.

"Help you?" said one of the workers, lifting his mask and dialing back the flame on his torch.

"I'm looking for a Davis Thornton," Dwight said.

The man gestured to a co-worker at the rear of the shop and went back to welding a break in a wrought-iron lawn chair.

"Davis Thornton?" Dwight asked as he approached.

A stocky gray-haired man with muscular arms that bulged from a sleeveless denim shirt, the blacksmith was in the process of turning an iron rod into a ram's-head fireplace poker. "With you in a minute," he said as he put the touches to the small head with a curved neck that would form the hanger. He had already twisted one horn into place around the ram's face. Now, with the inch-long head clamped in a vise, he used a blowtorch and heavy-duty needle-nose pliers to twist the second red-hot horn into a curlicue shape. He gave it a brisk scrub with a wire brush, then held it up for Dwight to see. In just those few seconds, the metal had gone from fiery red to a gleaming black.

A row of finished pokers hung nearby, no two heads precisely alike, each with a twist in the rod and a pointed tip and spur at the end for moving hefty logs around a hearth.

"How can I help you?" the man said.

Dwight introduced himself. "Actually, I'm looking for Billy Thornton. Would that be your dad?"

Davis Thornton nodded. "It would. What's this about, Major Bryant?"

"We're trying to locate someone who might have witnessed a death about sixty or so years ago," he said, "and we're told that your father might have been there."

"Death? Whose death?" Thornton hung the unfinished poker on the wall with the others and lifted one side of his leather apron to reach into the pocket of his jeans. He pulled out a lollipop and tossed the paper wrapper onto the hot coals of his fire. Seeing Dwight's amusement, he shrugged.

"You ever smoke? Hell on wheels trying to quit and stay quit. So who'd my dad see die?"

"A Jacob Knott."

"Knott? One of Kezzie Knott's crowd?"

"You remember hearing about it?"

"Don't remember a Jacob, but there were so many of them boys. Used to go to school with Haywood and Herman. They were smack-dab in the middle as I recall. Was Jacob older or younger?"

"He would've been their uncle."

"Uncle? Oh yeah. I do sorta remember some talk about how Mr. Kezzie had twin brothers and one of 'em drowned and the other got shot or something?"

"Jacob was the one that drowned. In Possum Creek. Your dad ever talk about that?"

Thornton shook his head, his jaw distended by the lollipop. "Don't think so."

"Where can I find him?"

"He lives with my sister over in Cotton Grove, but I'm afraid it may not do much good to try to ask him anything. He's eighty-three and his memory's going fast. Half the time he won't even know who I am."

Thornton gave Dwight his sister's name and address, then said, "Don't suppose you want to buy a fireplace set, do you? Poker, shovel, and hanger? I can let you have one cheap."

"How cheap?" Dwight asked.

By the time Raeford McLamb and Tub Greene finished testifying in their separate cases and then met to watch Mayleen's DVD, it was past noon. They stopped for takeout at one of the fast-food places and drove on over to the hospital, where they ate in their unmarked cruiser with the windows rolled down to let the warm May air flow over them.

Up in the hospice wing, they showed a picture of the orderly to the receptionist at the desk.

"Chad Rouse," she said promptly. "But he's not on duty till two."

They filled the time questioning the staff who had been around the previous Wednesday and checking the layout of that floor.

The hospice wing was part of the original hospital built in the fifties and extensively remodeled. The current main entrance was several yards farther down a curving sidewalk, but the public could still enter through the original doors. A wide wooden staircase rose from that lobby to the family waiting room and more stairs from there up to the third floor. An elevator was tucked behind the stairs. The hospice wing was completely open on every floor to the newer parts of the building, where larger elevators could accommodate gurneys, rolling trays, laundry carts, and cleaning equipment, which meant that staff and visitors could move back and forth freely.

There was a fire exit on each floor at the end of the halls, but the doors opened only from the inside and were supposed to be kept locked at all times. An orderly on duty sheepishly admitted that sometimes he sneaked out onto the third-floor fire escape for a quick cigarette, leaving a mop bucket or broom in the door-jamb to keep from locking himself out.

"Worse than Swiss cheese," said McLamb. "Holes everywhere and the nurses' stations don't seem to be manned full time."

"That's right," a passing aide said cheerfully. "We don't keep any drugs here either. They're dispensed elsewhere and brought over on an as-needed basis."

Like that aide, several staff members were ready to stop and gossip and voice the surprise they'd felt when they heard how Rachel Morton had died, but none of them had noticed anything out of the ordinary.

"Although that sure was the biggest family gathering I ever saw here," said one. "So many people in and out, how would you know who was supposed to be there and who wasn't?"

"Was that really Kezzie Knott's sister?" asked a young nurse who had grown up on stories of moonshining and epic car chases.

All agreed that the privately hired aide who had attended Rachel Morton was a dedicated and conscientious woman.

"Lois Boone has a true calling for hospice work. Not everybody does," said one of the registered nurses who worked in that wing as needed. "Some people find it morbid and depressing and I admit it can be sad, especially when it's a child or young person who's dying. By the time someone's admitted here, all hope of recovery has been exhausted. Our job is to help terminal patients get through this last stage of life as painlessly as possible. It's palliative care only, you know, not curative, and Lois is wonderfully calm and reassuring about that. She helps the family understand that when they authorize the doctors to turn off all the life-support systems and move the patient to this unit, they aren't giving up on their loved ones, just accepting the fact that death is a natural end that can be as beautiful in its way as birth."

The nurse was indignant when asked if Lois had ever hastened someone's end, perhaps with an over-dose of painkillers? An injection? Or, yes, a pillow?

"Absolutely not! In the first place, she's an aide, not an RN nor even an LPN. She has no access to drugs and wouldn't know how to give a proper injection if she did. And she certainly wouldn't do what you're suggesting."

Chad Rouse arrived at the hospital a few minutes before two. A native of Widdington who hadn't rolled far from the tree, he appeared to be in his early twenties, a slightly chubby young man with fair skin, a pleasant face, and an open friendliness. There was no apprehension in his manner when the two deputies approached him in the staff locker room. As Rouse changed into green scrubs, McLamb was amused to see that he wore boxer shorts imprinted with little red hearts. He volunteered the information that he had just come from morning classes out at the community college.

"This time next year, I'll be an LPN," he told them. "Pays about twice what I'm making now."

He spoke willingly about Rachel Morton's last day. "Yeah, I knew who she was. I mean, I knew she was Kezzie Knott's sister. I been hearing stories about him forever. Thought he must've died years ago, yet there he was, big as life. I almost asked him for his autograph first time I saw him here last week. Lois didn't know too much about him, but Mrs. Morton's daughter—Mrs. Crenshaw? Or her son, Mr. Morton? If nobody else was here when I brought up a supper tray, they'd talk to me about him some. Things she'd told them about what it was like growing up with moonshiners. Their granddaddy did it, too, you know."

Tub Greene listened with a fascinated interest that made Ray McLamb smile. No one in the department except maybe Sheriff Bo Poole would ever come straight out and mention Major Bryant's father-in-law to his face, but it was a source of head-shaking amusement around the courthouse that a judge and a chief deputy would be so closely related to someone who was a cross between Jesse James and Junior Johnson if half the stories told could be believed.

Eventually, McLamb led Rouse back to the day in question. They learned that the wing held twelve rooms, six here on the third floor, six on the second, but it was unusual to have more than two or three occupied during the week.

"Now on weekends, we might have a full house because we give respite care to folks who're still at home so that their caregivers can have a day or two off. Like if they have to go somewhere and don't have anybody else to step in."

Rachel Morton was the only patient on this floor last

Wednesday, though. "I came on at two o'clock and first thing I did was collect the lunch trays from her room. When I saw all the people, I thought maybe she'd died, but no, they were there because she suddenly started talking. It was so crowded that I just took the trays and left, but I did come back with some soft drinks later. I knew they wouldn't want a supper tray because their church people were setting up in the family room, but I was hoping to meet Kezzie Knott. Didn't happen, though. After that, I was busy on the other halls."

"Did you come back after her visitors went downstairs to eat?"

"I wish! You could've knocked me over with a feather when I heard what happened."

Back in Dobbs, Dwight transferred his new set of fireplace tools from the trunk of the cruiser to the cab of his pickup. He met Richards on the sidewalk, her phone in her hand.

"I was just going to call you, Major," she said. "There was a home invasion at that trailer park out past Crenshaw's Lake. An old man and his wife are both on their way to the hospital. Tub's going to wait there till the EMS truck arrives, and Ray's headed to the scene."

As she hurried past, Dwight called after her, "Any luck locating that McAllister woman?"

"Sorry," she said. "No McAllisters in Widdington."

One of the department's clerks had left some files on his desk that needed attention and he saw that another break-in in the Black Creek community had been reported.

The phone on his desk rang and he was tempted to let the answering machine take it, but yielded to duty on the third ring.

"Bryant here."

"Major Bryant? This is Donald Barley. We talked this morning?"

Barley. Brother of the boy who dragged Jacob out of the creek.

"Yes, Mr. Barley?"

"I'm over here at Ransom's house. I was telling his wife—or rather, his widow—about your call and she remembers Ransom talking about how Jacob died. You want me to put her on?"

"Please."

"Hello?" The woman's voice was thin and quavered with age, but she sounded quite clear in her thoughts and memories. "You were asking Donald about that boy who fell off a rope swing and died in a creek up there?"

"Yes, ma'am."

"Donald said Ransom never said much about it to him."

"Did he talk about it with you?"

"Not a lot, but he did tell me about that girl Donald said you were asking after.

"One night after we got engaged, we were talking about puppy love and the people we'd liked before we met. Sort of clearing the deck, before the wedding, you know?"

"Yes, ma'am?" he said encouragingly.

"I told him about a boy that flipped his car right when he was coming to propose to me with the ring in his pocket, and he told me about a girl up there that all the boys were silly over."

"Did he tell you her name?"

"Letha McAllister."

"You're sure?"

"Oh yes," she said dryly. "He had an old history notebook that he used to keep baseball scores in and one whole page at the back was covered in her name where he'd written it over and over. Liked to've embarrassed him to death when I found it. Said she was like a sickness in his blood that summer. From what he told me, she was one of those girls who flirted with all the boys, kept 'em stirred up. He said he fought with his best friend over her and then she went off with somebody else. He said that she was the reason another friend got himself killed. I reckon that would be this Jacob Knott you were asking Donald about?"

"He told you that?"

"Said the boy was showing off for her. Tried to do a somersault off a rope swing and the rope broke so he landed wrong."

"Did your husband say anything that would lead you to believe it might not have been an accident?"

"No, but then he didn't actually see it happen. Said he was on the path to the creek when he heard her yelling and crying. By the time he got down there, the boy was lying on some rocks with his face in the water. There was another boy—Ransom never said his name, or if he did, I forget it—and the two of them got Jacob up on the bank. He said Letha just ran. Didn't call for help or anything, just ran away like a yellow hound. That soured him on her right then and there. He couldn't even say her name without looking like it tasted like vinegar on his tongue."

And then there was one, thought Dwight.

Billy Thornton.

Whose memory was going fast, according to his son.

He glanced at his watch. Plenty of time to get over to Cotton Grove before he needed to pick up Cal.

CHAPTER
15

But memory is impaired by age.

— Cicero

As he pulled up in front of 402 Magnolia Street, Dwight realized that he had driven by this house several times over the years. The street was typical of small southern mill towns, which Cotton Grove once was. The houses here were 1930s working class— well-tended single-story clapboard bungalows, painted white or soft earth tones, wide front porches shaded by old oaks and the occasional magnolia or pecan tree. Most of the porches had hanging baskets of bright flowers or ferns, swings, and rockers, as did 402. Indeed, as he approached the house he saw an old man seated in the swing, gently rocking to and fro.

A middle-aged woman dressed in a pink scooped-neck T-shirt and black slacks rose from one of the rockers. Her wiry gray hair was at least two weeks overdue for a trim and she tried to smooth it down as he came up the short walkway. "Major Bryant?"

Dwight nodded. "Mrs. Sterling?"

"Yes. My brother called and said you were coming. That you wanted to talk to Dad about a drowning or something that happened when he was a boy? Sixty-five or seventy years ago?"

"That's right. We heard he was present when a friend of his hit his head and drowned in Possum Creek."

"One of the Knott boys, Davis said."

"That's right. Your dad and two other kids were there—a Ransom Barley and a Letha McAllister. Are those names familiar to you?"

"Never heard them," she said, shaking her head and then pushing her hair away when it fell into her face. "A lot of people, when they start getting old, will go on and on with stuff about their childhood, but Dad never did much of that. He might say how hard the work was, and I can remember a little bit of that myself, but we lost touch with everybody out there in the country after we moved to Benson. Davis says we were in school with some of Kezzie Knott's sons, but I don't remember. Is this about his sister getting killed when she was dying?"

"Yes, ma'am," he admitted.

Even though they had tried to keep it low-key, too many people knew about the murder because anything connected with Kezzie Knott would always make the local news. Fortunately, the public seemed to have a short attention span and there wasn't enough sex or titillation about the death of an eighty-year-old woman to keep it on the front pages or on television after the first news cycle ended.

"We're trying to locate people who were in her hospital room that day."

"But what does that have to do with us? We weren't there. I don't think Dad knew her, and even if he did, he hasn't been out of the house alone in three years."

"We're just hoping he could tell us what happened back then. It might help our investigation."

"Well, you're welcome to try. He's a little hard of hearing, though."

She invited Dwight to a white wicker rocker near the swing, where Billy Thornton gave him a welcoming smile. A sturdy white bentwood table between the two rockers held a newspaper with a half-worked crossword puzzle and a radio tuned to a country music station.

"Good to see you again," said Mr. Thornton.

So far as Dwight knew, he and the old man had never met. His white hair was thin across the top of his head and the pale green shirt he wore was at least a size too big, as if he had shrunk considerably since it was first bought. In shape, though, he was a slightly smaller version of his chunky son. Probably built like a nail keg when he was younger.

"Nice of you to stop by. We're just setting out here watching them wrens."

He gestured toward a hanging basket of ferns at the other end of the porch. Sure enough, a Carolina wren with a white eye streak came winging in, an insect in its mouth. Immediately, Dwight heard the nestlings' loud competitive peeps as each vied for food.

"Every year I swear I'm not gonna let them nest in my flower baskets," said Mrs. Sterling with a rueful smile. "If I catch 'em at it before they lay their eggs, I'll pull the straw out, but I just can't bring myself to smash wren eggs. I pulled this one's nest out that fern around seven o'clock one morning and bless me if she didn't have a new one built and one little speckled egg in it by seven o'clock the next morning. So now I have to spend the next two weeks being careful how I water so that I don't drown the babies."

Springy curls fell forward over her eyes and she brushed them away again. "I was fixing to get him a glass of tea. Can I bring you one?"

"No, ma'am, thank you," Dwight said and turned to Mr. Thornton, who looked at him expectantly.

Mrs. Sterling turned off the radio, then speaking distinctly, she said, "Daddy, this is Major Bryant. He wants to ask you about when Kezzie Knott's brother Jacob drowned. Can you remember?"

"Well, of course I can, honey," he drawled. "I ain't lost my mind, no matter what you and Mamie think."

He leaned toward Dwight, his blue eyes shining with amused male solidarity in that wrinkled, liver-splotched face. "You married, son? Your womenfolks

treat you like you ain't got sense enough to come in out
of the rain?"

On the other side of him, Mrs. Sterling paused before opening the screen door and murmured, "Mamie
was my mother, Major. She died three years ago."

She proceeded on into the house and Dwight said,
"Would you tell me about it, sir?"

"Tell you what?"

"About how Jacob Knott died?"

"Jacob Knott...? One of the Knott twins?"

"Yes, sir."

"Well now, let me think..." He leaned back in the
gently moving swing and stared up at the ceiling. Like
many porches of that style and age, it was painted light
blue, like a cloudless spring sky. An occasional car
passed on the quiet tree-lined street. "Darn birds make
a heckuva lotta noise, don't they?"

"It would have been back when you were a boy,"
Dwight said. "You lived out in the country then."

"Yeah. Tobacco and wiregrass. Some of them wiregrass roots go halfway to China. You can chop up a
hill of grass and leave it in the sun a week and it'll still
sprout soon as it rains." He paused and gave Dwight a
puzzled look. "What was it you were asking me?"

"When you were a boy?"

"That's right. When I was a boy. My pap farmed
cotton till the weevils got too bad, and I sharecropped
tobacco till I walked out of the field one day and went
to work in Benson, driving a heating oil truck. Dirty
work, too, but better'n a tobacco field."

Mrs. Sterling returned with two glasses of tea and a handful of paper napkins, which she laid on the wicker table that stood between the two chairs. She wrapped a napkin around the base of each glass and handed her father one. As he gulped it thirstily, she took a sip from her own glass and said, "His short-term memory's pretty bad but sometimes he's real clear about things that happened years ago. I still don't see why you want to ask him about that drowning."

Her father frowned. "Somebody drowned?"

"We're just trying to get a fix on who was there that day," Dwight said.

"After all this time?" she said. "Why?"

"I can't really discuss that right now, ma'am. Like I said before, it might be pertinent to our investigation. Did he ever talk about it?"

She shook her head and then had to brush back the hair that fell down over her forehead. "Davis says he remembers some of the Knott boys talking about it, but if Dad ever did, I never heard it."

Mr. Thornton rattled the ice cubes in his glass. "I could sure drink some more tea."

Without complaint, Mrs. Sterling took his glass and went back inside for a refill, and Dwight found himself thinking about Sally and her support group. Designated Daughters. That's what they called themselves. All over the country, middle-aged children were taking care of their elderly parents, and yeah, the majority were indeed women, just like Mrs. Sterling. They didn't all wait to be designated either. They just stepped up to the plate and did what needed doing. If and when his pepper pot of a mother ever needed care, he knew his sisters would be elbowing each other aside to take it on. They already tried to make her slow down, worried over her blood pressure, and sneaked in when she was at work to wash her windows or scour her bathrooms, "because Bessie Stewart's not getting any younger either," they said, speaking of their mother's longtime household help.

Mr. Thornton stopped the swing with his foot and gave Dwight a long puzzled stare. "Jack?"

"No, sir. Dwight Bryant."

"You here about the termites?"

"No, I'm here to talk about Jacob Knott, Mr. Thornton."

Mrs. Sterling had returned in time to hear the last exchange. In a soft voice, she said, "Call him Billy. Sometimes that works."

"What works? You talking about me again like I'm a baby?"

"No, Dad. Major Bryant wants you to tell him about Jacob Knott."

"Jacob's dead."

Encouraged, Dwight leaned forward. "That's right, Billy. He's dead. And you were there, right?"

That got him a hesitant nod.

"You and Jacob Knott and Ransom Barley and Letha McAllister. What happened?"

"Letha?"

"Letha McAllister."

"Letha?…Yeah, Letha." Suddenly his eyes seemed to focus and his voice went hard as iron. "*Her* fault. God *damn* that little bitch to holy hell!"

He shook his glass at Dwight and half of his tea splashed onto the floor. He tried to stand and the swing went out from under him. Dwight barely managed to catch him before he fell.

By the time they got him seated again and Mrs. Sterling had mopped up the tea with paper napkins, Dwight could almost see the anger leaving the old man's eyes, as if a door was closing. An instant later, Billy Thornton looked down into his nearly empty glass. "Good tea, Mamie. Don't you want some, Davis?"

With a wad of wet napkins in her hand, Mrs. Sterling shook her head in bewilderment. "I'm sorry, but that's the first time I ever heard him cuss."

She touched her father's knee. "Dad, who was Letha?"

"Who?"

"Letha McAllister."

"She the new preacher's wife?"

"No, Dad. She was an old friend of yours. Letha."

He gave her a troubled look and didn't answer.

Further questions seemed to confuse and upset him.

Resigned to failure for the moment, Dwight stood and handed Mrs. Sterling one of his cards. "I'd appreciate it if you'd give me a call if *you* remember anything. Anything at all."

Still holding the wet napkins, she took the card and

put it in the pocket of her slacks. "I'll ask Davis, but I doubt he knows anything either."

Frustrated, Dwight walked back to his truck. To come so close and then to lose it. Maybe Jacob's death had nothing to do with his sister's death sixty-odd years later, but now it was a matter of principle to find out exactly how he had died.

According to Ransom Barley's widow, only Billy Thornton and Letha McAllister had actually been there. "*Her* fault," Thornton had snarled, and then he'd cursed her.

Why?

CHAPTER
16

I am not ashamed to confess I am ignorant of what I do not know.

— Cicero

Harkers Island—Monday afternoon

And *those* are some of our oldest," said the docent, who seemed to speak in italics. She gestured toward a glass case ahead of them. "I'm *sure* your editor would be interested in them."

Monday afternoons were usually slow here at the Core Sound Waterfowl Museum and Heritage Center. With a half hour to go before closing time and no other visitors, she had time to give her full attention to this reporter from *Our State Magazine*, who had arrived out of breath but happy to see that the museum was still open.

"I was afraid I was going to be too late," the woman said, after identifying herself.

"I just *love* your magazine. Have you written for them very long?"

"Oh, I'm not a writer," the brown-haired woman said, although she was dressed like one in a beige photographer's vest that matched her slacks. "My job's to roam around the state looking for offbeat subjects that might make a good article for us. I don't think we've done an article devoted solely to decoys. Is it true that the old carvers just did it with no instruction?"

"No *formal* instructions, if that's what you mean," said the docent, who was a descendant of Harkers Island fishermen. "Boys learned by watching their fathers. Some were better than others, of course. My granddad never *did* get the hang of it, but his brother? You'd *swear* it was a real duck. They didn't need models because they hunted the birds for food every winter and they knew *exactly* how the heads were colored or how the feathers lay along their backs. It was just something they *did* when the weather was too rough to take the boats out—like mending the nets or making crab pots."

"Did they use any special wood?" The woman focused her iPhone on a handmade buoy.

"Not *really*. Just whatever was laying around, mostly scrap juniper from one of the boat builders here on the island. They'd rough-carve the shape with knives, then scrape 'em smooth with a piece of broken glass."

"Any special paint?"

"Boat paint, house paint, whatever was *cheap*."

The self-identified *Our State* scout drifted over to the locked glass case. The decoys here were weathered and faded and one of them was pitted with small holes. "Why do some of these have cracks in their necks?"

"Usually the heads were made separately and then pegged on. Over the years, as they got wet and then dried out, the wood would swell and shrink and *that's* when the heads would try to separate."

"Do you think you could take some of them out and let me get a close-up?"

Normally, this would not be allowed, but everyone else had left for the day and this *was* an *Our State* representative, the docent told herself. Every time the museum was mentioned in the magazine, attendance picked up.

"Sure thing." She went back to the counter in the outer room and returned with a key ring.

"Why are these under lock and key and some of those prettier decoys are just sitting out on shelves?"

"*These* are pretty special." The docent carefully lifted a duck from the case and set it on top. It had a red head and a white body with black breast and tail. The paint was chipped and worn, but the feathering was exquisite. "This one's a 1902 Hanley Willis. He *loved* redheads. Just *look* at the details. And you can barely see where the head is joined. If you wanted to buy one like *this*, it would cost you six or eight thousand dollars."

"Really?" She zoomed in with her camera and clicked off several shots. "Back then, though, how much would one like this sell for?"

"Oh, fifty or seventy-five cents. Certainly no *more* than a dollar."

"What's that metal thing on the bottom?"

"Just an iron weight to help it ride level in the water."

The docent turned it over so that the other could take more close-ups. "Are those his initials?"

"HW," said the docent. "He was one of the *few* who signed their work back then."

The H was slanted like the W and the right upright of the H formed the left downstroke of the W, with a crossbar to indicate the H.

"But *we'd* know his work even without the initials because he always put a tiny little dot of white in the center of each eye."

Click, click, click and close-ups of the eye joined those of the initials.

"Did he ever do other kinds of ducks?"

"There's a pintail in the North Carolina Wildlife Museum in Raleigh and a ruddy duck in a museum up in Virginia and he was known to have carved at least *one* green-winged teal that's owned by a private collector in Maryland, but those are *very* rare." The docent put the redhead back in the case and brought out a rather plain, dark brown decoy. "Now we don't know *who* carved this canvasback, but it's all one piece of wood. A cypress knee. Dates back to the Civil War. It's even more valuable than the redhead."

"Wow! Never have to worry about him losing *his* head."

The docent laughed. "Except that he *almost* did. See those pit marks? *Some*body hunted over this one and wound up putting a few buckshot in his side."

CHAPTER
17

Nor am I afraid to read sepulchral inscriptions...my recollection of the dead is thus made more vivid.

— Cicero

The last item on my calendar that afternoon was a final DWI, and with what had gone before, I was not surprised when it was called and the ADA shrugged her shoulders. "Another one of Mr. Young's clients, Your Honor."

"And he still hasn't surfaced?" I asked.

"No, ma'am."

I can't decide whether to be amused or exasperated by Zack Young. But thanks to him, I'd get to leave a little earlier than usual. The defendant, a neatly dressed young woman of Asian heritage, had come forward when her name was called and stood there looking at me in a mixture of fear and bewilderment. This was probably her first time in court and certainly her first time to be represented by Young or she might have looked a bit more confident.

I dismissed the trooper who'd ticketed her and scheduled her to come back on his next court date.

"You may want to join the rest of Mr. Young's flock," I told her and pointed toward some five or six others who clustered together on benches at the back of the courtroom. Some of them had brought along friends or a family member for support, so there were at least a dozen altogether. Black, white, Latino, and Asian, they ranged in age from late teens to a gray-haired woman who sat shoulder to shoulder with a youth who was probably her grandson.

"Anything else?" I asked the prosecutor.

She thumbed through the shucks and shook her head.

For the most part, those people at the back of the room looked tired and somewhat puzzled, unsure of what was going to happen now. Except for meals and bathroom breaks, some of them had been here all day, waiting for their cases to be called. At times like this, I'm never totally sure if they were told beforehand what was going on or if they understood why, but I always feel compelled to apologize.

"I'm sorry that you've had to sit here all this time," I told them, "but none of you waived your right to representation so I can't hear your cases without your attorney. That means you'll have to come back to court another day. This is not the court's fault. It's not the district attorney's fault. It's Mr. Young's fault. He seems to have disappeared, but don't worry. I'm sure he'll show up before you leave the courthouse."

Judge-shopping is as old as the court system and the first time it happened to me, the first time I realized that an attorney had deliberately disappeared when I was due to hear his client's case, I admit it—I was rather pleased. It meant that the case for the defense was weak and the attorney preferred to have it continued in the hope of drawing a different judge, one who might be more sympathetic or more easily persuaded by flimsy arguments. It meant I was being taken seriously.

So I could sit here on the bench, gossip with my clerk and the prosecutor, read a book, and wait till five thirty to adjourn, or I could make it easy on all of us and adjourn now. Whichever way I decided, I knew that within five minutes after adjournment, Zack would somehow hear about it. I'm not sure who his informant is, but he'd be ambling in to talk to his clients about rescheduling their appearances.

I lifted my gavel and rapped it lightly. "Court's adjourned."

"All rise," said the bailiff.

Out in the courthouse parking lot, I put my briefcase and laptop in the trunk of my car and thought to check my phone for messages. There were three.

From Minnie: "Coat hangers!!!"

From Dwight: "C U at Mr. K's."

From Cal: "dont 4get marshmellas."

Coat hangers? Marshmallows? See me at Daddy's?

Memory flooded in. So that's what Will meant when he said he'd see me later as I was leaving his place.

To my relief, the dry cleaning shop around the corner was still open and yes, the clerk was willing to sell me a bunch of wire hangers. Marshmallows would be cheaper at a grocery but quicker at a convenience store. I bought three of their largest bags. I couldn't remember if I'd promised to bring anything else but whenever we have one of these family projects, there's always more than enough food to go around.

There was just time to swing past the house, change clothes, and pick up a pair of pliers to straighten out the hangers. Some families use fancy skewers to roast their hot dogs. We've always threaded ours on coat hangers.

(*"Hot dogs twice in the same day?"* my internal preacher said disapprovingly.)

(*"So tomorrow we'll eat grapefruit and salads,"* said the pragmatist.)

Over at the homeplace, Dwight and Cal were already at work in our family graveyard, along with Robert, Andrew, and Seth. Bandit and the pampered beagle Andrew keeps as a house pet lay panting nearby, which made me think they'd had a good run together.

Up the slope from them, Haywood was adding to Daddy's brush pile with trimmings from the live oak trees that shade the graves. Will had picked up Herman and brought him out from Dobbs, but meetings had kept their wives in town this evening. No sign of Isabel, Minnie, or April. They were probably still putting together the fixings in Minnie's kitchen or April's: the coleslaw, pickle relish, chili sauce, chopped onions, mustard, and mayo that make hot dogs so sinfully delicious. A washtub full of ice and soft-drink cans sat on the tailgate of Andrew's truck.

I myself was perched cross-legged on the tailgate of Dwight's to start straightening out the wire coat hangers when Zach and Barbara drove in, followed a few minutes later by their kids, Lee and Emma, on a four-wheeler.

Seth and Minnie's Jess and Andrew's Ruth had ridden their horses over and I was sure we'd see more of the nieces and nephews as they finished with work or after-school activities.

Mother had started this May tradition of cleaning the graveyard on the first Mother's Day weekend after she married Daddy. She wanted the boys to talk freely about Annie Ruth and remember what they could of her, and she figured that working with their hands would loosen their tongues and make them less self-conscious about speaking. Robert, Frank, and Andrew actually have what they say are clear memories of their mother; and as the younger ones got old enough to realize they would never have true memories of their own, she encouraged each of the three older boys to give a special memory to a little brother. Robert gave Ben such a vivid memory of Annie Ruth kissing his little pink toes that he's now convinced he really does remember those kisses and how they tickled.

I have a feeling that Andrew made up the memories

he gave Seth and Jack. Annie Ruth had died within a year of Jack's birth and Seth was still a toddler. Herman and Haywood say they can remember her tucking them into opposite ends of a dresser drawer to make room in the cradle for Ben, but I have my doubts.

Not that I would ever say it to them.

Due to Aunt Rachel's dire condition last Sunday, we were late getting to it this year, but none of my brothers—none of them who live around here anyhow—ever want to skip. We always cut the grass, wash bird droppings off the gravestones, and weed around the flowers. We prune the rosebushes Mother had helped the boys pick out for Annie Ruth and the rosebush the boys planted for Mother the first year after she died. We repaint the names and dates on the large rocks outside the low stone wall that mark where our pets are buried. And as we work, we talk about those who lie here, remembering funny stories that we share with the grandchildren.

Aunt Sister's ugly pet goat is always good for a laugh, which for some reason always prompts Andrew to tell about the first (and last) time my Stephenson grandmother came to dinner and scared the bejeebers out of Frank.

As a child, I always took it upon myself to clean around the little white marble stone topped with a small white lamb. It was hard for me to wrap my head around that baby, a brother dead before he actually lived.

Daddy and Annie Ruth's first son.

Stillborn.

The oldest grave belongs to Daddy's great-grandfather, who bought the original ninety acres back before the Civil War. The newest was Uncle Rufus, Aunt Sister's husband.

There's the black marble obelisk that Daddy raised to the memory of his father as soon as he could borrow the money for it, an act of defiance by a teenage boy who burned with rage against the ATF agents who caused the car crash that killed him. His mother is buried under a more modest stone, but then she died peacefully in her own bed.

There's a pair of twin stones for Jacob and Jedidiah—same birth date, the death dates only weeks apart—and a flat bronze tablet for Andrew's carney grandson, another boy we never got a chance to know.

The graveyard is bounded by a waist-high stone wall and Daddy sat there to watch as Cal wandered from one marker to another, reading the names, adding and subtracting dates, and asking dozens of questions.

"Is that where you're going to be someday, Granddaddy?" he asked, pointing to the space between Mother's marker and Annie Ruth's.

"I reckon," he said.

"But not before I'm an old, old woman," I called, reminding him of his promise to me when I was a child and went to him in tears because I had just realized parents could die, too, not just pets.

"What about us, Dad?" Cal asked.

I rested on my hoe to hear Dwight's answer, because this was one topic we'd never thought to discuss yet. My people are here, of course, but his are scattered around at various churches.

"I imagine they could tuck us in somewhere," he said lightly.

"Let's go over there," Cal said, pointing to an empty corner shaded by the live oaks on the other side of the wall. "Near the pets so Bandit can be near us."

"Your wife might have something to say about that," Will teased, as he gave the Marshal Niel rosebush a final snip to keep it in manageable shape.

"How come Aunt Rachel's not buried here?" Cal hadn't gone with us to her funeral, and only now was he realizing that she might have had a place here.

"We talked about it," said Daddy, "but her husband wanted to be with his family and she wanted to be with him."

"*Thy people shall be my people*," said Robert, who goes to church with Doris almost every Sunday.

Daddy, who only goes to church for weddings and funerals, gave him a half smile and finished the passage: "*Where thou diest, will I die, and there will I be buried.*"

Will's head came up in astonishment to hear him quoting scripture, not something he does very often, but not all that odd considering that his mother read aloud from the King James Bible every night before bedtime.

With so many of us working, the graveyard was pristine and all the animal names repainted an hour after

I arrived, with another hour of fading daylight still to go. The moon, a few nights from full, had cleared the eastern trees and shone with dull luster in a cloudless blue sky.

Haywood had the bonfire blazing and Isabel, Minnie, and April had ridden over on Bel's golf cart with a basket of warm buns and the side dishes. Everyone grabbed a straightened coat hanger. Everyone except Will and Daddy, that is. Those two had walked off to one side and put their heads together for what looked like a serious talk on Will's part. I heard him say, "...if you could let me borrow your shotgun to shoot the duck?"

Daddy had an amused look on his weathered face. "Well, for ducks, don't you need to use lead shot? I might have one or two of them old shells still laying around."

Then the two of them had gone up the slope to the house together.

Lead shot? For ducks? Federal law prohibited the use of lead shot for waterfowl years ago. Too many wild ducks and swans ingested them and then died of lead poisoning. Worse, when eagles and buzzards ate the sick birds, they, too, died. Besides, Will's no Deadeye Dick, so even if he planned to use illegal ammunition, how was he going to kill a duck with only one or two shells?

I was almost nosy enough to follow them and ask, but Dwight had roasted two dogs on the same hanger and one of them had my name on it.

* * *

They were gone only a few minutes, then the back door slammed up at the house and I saw Will put a shotgun in the trunk of his car before he and Daddy walked back down the slope to rejoin us.

Before I could ask about the gun, Andrew's wife April called to him. "I saw your ad in the paper, Will. You're selling Mrs. Lattimore's things next Saturday?"

He nodded. "You ought to come bid, April. Check out my website. I just finished updating it. There's a stained glass panel that would look good over y'all's front door."

"Really?" April's a sixth-grade teacher, but she relaxes by moving walls, relocating doors and windows, or adding built-in bookshelves, cupboards, or other architectural embellishments to their 1930s house. Andrew swears he's afraid to go to the bathroom at night for fear that the bedroom will be on the other side of the house before he can get back.

Will pulled out his cell phone and brought up some pictures to show her while Cal handed me a coat hanger with two nicely browned marshmallows on it so that we could share. I showed him how to pull the outer crispy shells off so that the cores could be toasted again, the only way to eat them as far as I'm concerned.

There wasn't much wind this mild evening, but the breeze shifted and we did, too, to keep the smoke out of our eyes, as I waited my turn for pictures of the Lattimore auction.

Dwight and I were probably the only two there who had spent a social evening in that big house before Mrs. Lattimore died, and that was only in the public rooms on the first floor, so I was as curious as my sisters-in-law about the furnishings that would go under Will's hammer on Saturday.

By the time Will's phone and pictures had gone around our group, Doris and Isabel had decided they might drop by even if they couldn't afford anything. Barbara and Emma looked interested, too.

"They're selling that bronze deer?" asked Minnie. "That's been a Cotton Grove fixture forever."

Will shrugged. "There's a hefty reserve on it, so it may not go. If it doesn't, they'll donate it to a park or something and take a charitable donation against estate taxes."

"Will Anne or Sigrid be there?" I asked, referring to Mrs. Lattimore's New York daughter and grand-daughter.

"None of the family," Will said, retrieving his phone. "They went ahead and took the things they wanted right after the funeral and told me they didn't want to watch strangers pawing over the rest."

I thought about my court case last week where the brother sued his sister over their mother's things. "No squabbles?"

"Not really. Mrs. Lattimore set it up so that the ap-praised value was on everything. I added up what each of them took and it'll be deducted from her third. The only time it got heated was when the two older gals both wanted an enameled clock that came from Gilead. It went for three times its appraised value."

As he explained it, Saturday's sale would be of the less valuable antiques and collectibles. The following week, he would auction off the major items.

I described an end table from the living room that had caught my eye.

"Nice but not terribly valuable," Will said. "If you're coming Saturday, though, you'll see it."

"I couldn't just go ahead and buy it now at the appraised price?"

"Sorry. That's not how it works," he told me virtuously. "There's no reserve on it, though, so maybe you'll get lucky and nobody else will want it."

"What about Alexander Auctions?" Dwight asked. "You ever do business with him?"

Will shook his head. "We've bought from each other, but I'd never partner with him on an estate sale. Deborah tell you how he snookered Sally's friend?"

Dwight nodded. "Any chance she'll file a complaint?"

"Doubt it, but you know something? Birds do have a way of coming home to roost, don't they?"

"Be nice if they'd settle on a branch right over his head," I said.

Will laughed. "Maybe we should dab a little peanut butter on that branch."

Throughout the past hour, one after another had asked Dwight how close he was to finding out who killed Aunt

Rachel and each time he had said, "Not very." Now, with everyone gathered together around the bonfire to roast marshmallows and finish eating, he told us about the phone calls with Ransom Barley's brother and widow and his interviews with Davis Thornton and his father.

"I made a note of the date Jacob died," he told Daddy. "But we've only gotten back to the seventies in digitizing our department's records. Was there any sort of investigation at the time? Who signed the death certificate?"

Daddy frowned. "Don't know about the death certificate. Maybe Duck's daddy?"

Aldcrofts had been burying Knotts for two or three generations and Duck Aldcroft is the current owner of the funeral home.

"No, wait a minute," Daddy said. "The sheriff did come out and the coroner, too, now that I think about it. Asked a lot of foolish questions. Thought we should've left Jacob a-laying in the water instead of bringing him up to the house. They went down to the creek and looked, but the sheriff was more interested in me and what I might be doing than in what happened to Jacob. They saw the broke rope, heared what Ransom and Billy had to say, and then left. If there was any death certificate, it would've come to Mammy, but I don't remember ever seeing one."

"I'll see what I can find tomorrow," said Dwight. "If the sheriff came out, there should be a record."

He took a final bite of his third hot dog and tossed the bun end to the dogs. "I'm not ready to say Jacob was murdered, Mr. Kezzie, but see, the thing is, Ransom Barley may have talked to the sheriff, but he wasn't actually there when Jacob fell. *If* he fell. According to Barley's widow, Jacob was facedown in the water with his head bleeding. Only Billy Thornton and this Letha McAllister were there and I'm afraid Thornton's dementia's too bad to say what happened. He got real agitated when I kept asking him about Letha. Then he cussed her and said it was all her fault."

"All her fault?" asked Daddy.

"I know," said Dwight. "It could mean that it was her fault that Jacob fell because he was showing off for her, or it could mean that Jacob and Billy fought over her like you say he and Jed had fought a little earlier."

"Or it could mean that Billy picked up a rock," said Andrew.

Dwight nodded. "Yeah, it could mean any of those."

"And Rachel kept worrying about it," Daddy said slowly. "Talking about it."

The sun had set completely now, but between the fire and the nearly full moon, he could see all of us quite clearly. He gave the glowing coals a strong poke and a fountain of orange and red sparks spurted straight up into the night sky.

"Y'all think somebody kin to the Thorntons or the McAllisters was in Rachel's room last Wednesday?"

"I don't know," I told Dwight when we were getting ready for bed later that evening. "What if it's not about Jacob's death but something else? Letha McAllister's probably dead and you say Billy Thornton's senile. Even if he actually did kill Jacob, it's not like anybody could prove it after all these years. So why kill Aunt Rachel? She wasn't even there."

"It must have been an impulse thing," Dwight said through the open door of the bathroom as he stripped off his work clothes and tossed them in the laundry hamper. "Whoever picked up that pillow couldn't've been thinking clearly. Probably just wanted to stop her from talking again, keep her from blurting out something bad about a parent or grandparent."

"But what if it's something else? Would you try to stop somebody from saying your grandfather was a killer? I sure wouldn't."

"Yeah, right," he said, and from the tone of his voice, I knew he was remembering some of the impulsive things I've done in the past without fully thinking them through.

"You know what I mean. What if it was about domestic violence or something to do with money?"

Toothbrush in hand, he smiled while watching me shed my own clothes for the oversize Carolina T-shirt I wear at night.

I took the other sink to brush my teeth, then we put out the lights and got into bed. Both of us take morning showers so the minty smell of toothpaste mingled with the woodsy smell of smoke as we turned to each other.

"You sleepy?" Dwight asked.

"Not really," I murmured. "You?"

(Ping!)

CHAPTER
18

The life of the dead is in the memory of the living.

— Cicero

DWIGHT BRYANT—TUESDAY

Shortly before noon, with most of the paperwork cleared from his desk, Dwight joined his detectives in the squad room to bat around their current investigations.

There had been another of those annoying break-ins in the Black Creek area and Sheriff Bo Poole was starting to get an earful about it from county commissioners and nervous residents alike.

The elderly victims of yesterday's home invasion had been treated and released from the hospital. The eighty-three-year-old husband, a Mr. Jenson, had four stitches in his head, and his eighty-year-old wife had been mentally traumatized but not physically harmed. Not surprisingly, they could name one of the men who had kicked in the door of their doublewide. Too often, criminals prey on people they know, and this man had done landscape maintenance for the owner of the trailer park, so it was only a matter of time before he and his partner were picked up.

"Most of the residents are retired," Mayleen Richards reported, "and neighbors say this isn't the first time that guy's roughed up someone. Usually he tries to bully them into paying for jobs like cutting the grass, pruning bushes—stuff that the owner's already paid for—but Mr. Jenson wouldn't pay and said he was going to report it to the owner. That's when it got violent."

"One good thing, though," Tub Greene said. "The owner has liability insurance so whatever Medicaid doesn't cover, his insurance will. That was really worrying the Jensons. This could've wiped them out."

"Ray gave the owner one of Mike's cards in case he wanted a different lawn service," Mayleen said. Her new husband had begun with a single broken-down lawn mower and now owned a thriving landscaping business.

"Not coercing the public, are you?" Dwight asked.

"Just being helpful, boss."

Dwight leaned back in his chair and tried to look stern. "To the owner of that trailer park or to Mayleen and Mike?"

"Whichever." Ray McLamb's flashing smile was unrepentant beneath his pencil mustache. "He doesn't have to use the card."

"Except that he already did," said Mayleen, who was smiling, too. "He told Mike our rates were less than the other guy's, so it's win-win all around."

She was letting her cinnamon-colored hair grow out and it softened the angles of her freckled face, freckles she no longer tried to cover up. But it wasn't just the hair, thought Dwight. There was a new softness to her face. Marriage must agree with her, too.

"We talked to that orderly in the video," McLamb said. "Chad Rouse. No help, I'm afraid."

"And still no luck locating Letha McAllister?"

"Sorry," said Mayleen. "But I'm checking one more possibility."

While her sturdy fingers moved over her keyboard, Dwight turned to McLamb and Greene and told them to go back to the Black Creek area. "Take another hard look at these break-ins, talk to the victims again, hit the local pawnshops. By now, someone over there should be hearing something useful."

On the way back to his own office, Dina Willner, a wheelchair-bound departmental clerk, called to him down the hallway. "Major Bryant? You asked me to look for a record on that drowning?"

Dwight walked down to meet her. "Find anything, Dina?"

"Just these." She handed him a couple of papers. The first was a photocopy of a page from a long-gone sheriff's logbook. It was dated the day of Jacob's drowning: "*Called out to Pleasants X-rds. Jacob Knott, age 15¾. Son of Robert A. Knott, deceased, & Martha Knott, widow. Drowned in Possum Ck. Coroner certified death.*" The second sheet was a copy of Jacob Knott's death certificate and it was signed by the man who'd held the coroner's office all those years ago.

"That's it? No inquest? No pathology report?"

"I'm afraid not, Major. Accidental deaths didn't get much attention back then."

Dwight thanked her and carried the papers back to his office, where he added them to the folder he was compiling.

He turned to the list of hospice visitors the day Rachel Morton died and was making notes for follow-up when Mayleen came through his door with a big smile on her face. "Got her!"

"Yeah?"

"I ran the name McAllister back through the archives of the Widdington *Post* and came up with an obituary for a Clarence McAllister, who died twenty-four years ago up in Rockville, Virginia. Among the survivors was a sister, Letha Wallace of Widdington, North Carolina. I tried variations of *that* name and bingo!"

She handed Dwight the printout of an obituary dated eight years earlier for a Letha McAllister King Wallace Cornwall. "Three husbands."

"I'm surprised it's not four or five given all we've

heard about her when she was a girl." After a moment, Dwight looked up from the printout. "Did you read this carefully?"

"You mean, did I notice that one of her survivors was a grandson named Chadwick Rouse? Yes, sir!"

"Invite him in for a talk," he said, and as Richards headed back to the squad room, he added, "Good work, Mayleen."

Less than an hour later, Richards met Chad Rouse at the front desk and escorted him to an interview room around the corner from Dwight's office.

"I don't understand," he said when Dwight introduced himself. His round chubby face looked puzzled. "Like I told that other officer yesterday, I didn't go back to the hospice wing that evening, so I don't know anything about what happened except what I heard. Is this going to take long? I'm supposed to go on duty at two and I still haven't had lunch."

"You never met Rachel Morton before she became a patient?"

"No, sir."

"Or knew who she was?"

"They said she was Kezzie Knott's sister."

"You know him?"

"Well...not to say *know* him. Know who he is, though. Heck, everybody around here's heard of him."

"Did you know about his brothers?"

"Brothers?" The young orderly shook his head. "I thought he just had sisters."

"Your grandmother never mentioned them?"

"My grandmother? She lives in Pennsylvania. How could she—?"

"Your grandmother Letha. Letha McAllister"—he glanced at the printout in his hand—"King Wallace Cornwall."

"Letha? She passed years ago."

"Did she ever talk about when she was a girl?"

Chad Rouse shrugged. "Not really." Enlightenment spread across his wide face. "Hey, that's right! She came from out near Cotton Grove. Did she know the Knotts? Is that what you mean? She'd've been about Mrs. Morton's age, wouldn't she? Were they friends?"

"That's what we're asking you," Dwight said patiently.

"My mom might know." He gave them her name and address and seemed surprised to hear that there might have been a connection between his grandmother and the Knotts when she was younger. "Mom might know" was his dubious answer to every question.

"Tell you the truth, Major Bryant, I don't think she liked kids. My mom's got a half sister by Letha's first husband, but that's it. She gave both girls to their daddies and didn't bother with them again till after they were grown and she needed to borrow some money once in a while. I've got two sisters and a couple of cousins, and she made us all call her Letha. She wasn't the kind of grandmother who babysat or made cookies. She liked to roadhouse, if you know what I mean. Big hair. Tight leather pants. Long red fingernails. I forget how old she was when she crashed her car coming home from a dance, but my mom says she started hitting on one of the troopers that pulled her out of the wreck."

"Sounds like the Letha we've come to know and love," Dwight said wryly when they let Chad Rouse leave for work after wringing as much family information from him as they could.

"She left her children for someone else to raise?" Strong disapproval was written all over Mayleen's freckled face. "Doesn't seem like somebody whose reputation needed protecting, does it?"

Dwight was too experienced to say that he could never be conned, but Chad Rouse certainly didn't feel like a killer. "All the same, it's a pretty big coincidence that Letha McAllister's grandson was in that hospice room Wednesday, so get me some confirmation, Mayleen. Talk to the mother and some of Rouse's cousins. See if they're as disconnected as he says. In the meantime, I'm going to ride out to Miss Rachel's house and talk to her old neighbors."

"Another fishing expedition?" she asked.

Dwight nodded. "Just wish I had some fresh bait."

Driving over to the Morton home felt more like running in place than fishing, though. Mr. Kezzie had already stated that he'd never met any of his sister's neighbors until well after her marriage, so it seemed highly unlikely that any of them could add anything about that long-ago drowning, but you never knew what Miss Rachel might have told them over the years.

Maybe Deborah was right, Dwight thought. Maybe her aunt's death had nothing to do with Jacob's. Even though he'd never been out to the Morton homeplace, he knew that the road he wanted was the last left turn before the county line, but he'd forgotten to look up the address. Luckily, he'd only driven a quarter mile down that sparsely settled track before spotting Sally Crenshaw's bright blue VW convertible parked among other cars in the driveway of a rambling one-story wooden farmhouse. There were no railings on the wraparound porch and three pickups with their tailgates down were backed up side by side to the front edge. A couple of muscular young men were loading the trucks with furniture and they paused to stare as Dwight got out of the cruiser.

He was wearing his usual lightweight summer sports jacket and khaki slacks instead of a uniform, and he pushed back the flap of the jacket so that they could see his badge.

"Sally Crenshaw here?" he asked.

"Hey, Ma!" the taller man called. "Somebody here to see you."

He reached out to shake the hand Dwight offered. "Kevin Crenshaw, and this is my brother Andy."

"Dwight?" Sally Crenshaw came down the central hall of the house and dodged around a third young man, who was bringing out a couple of dining room chairs. Today's purple wig was slightly askew and her white capris had smudges on her thighs where she must have wiped dusty fingers. The faceted glass "jewels" on her sandals flashed in the afternoon sun. "What are you doing out this way? You remember my boys, don't you?"

Dwight nodded even though he didn't think he'd ever seen them before their grandmother's funeral last week.

Sally's brother Jay-Jay followed her out and they were joined by a couple of young women, Jay-Jay's daughters.

"We thought we'd get a start on cleaning out Mama's house," Sally said.

She rattled off names and relationships too rapidly for Dwight to keep track. In all, there seemed to be two nieces, a nephew, and their spouses as well as a wife and girlfriend of her own two sons.

"I don't reckon you're here to tell us who killed Mama, are you?"

"'Fraid not, Sally. Just more questions."

"Well, come on and let's get out of their way."

"Aunt Sally?" One of the young women stepped onto the porch with a shallow concave wooden tray. "Who gets Grandma's bread tray? Abby or me?"

"Neither one of you," Sally replied. "Mama made biscuits in that thing every morning of my life. Y'all can fight over it after I'm gone, but it's coming home with me for now, so just put it in my box."

"You still making biscuits?" Dwight asked as they moved out of the line of traffic to the west side of the wraparound porch.

"No, but it's the memory that counts. Don't reckon Deborah makes them either, does she?"

"As a matter of fact, we had biscuits Saturday morning."

She sat down in one of the wooden rocking chairs and looked up at him skeptically from beneath those purple bangs. "Real ones? Made from scratch or frozen from a can?"

"Made from scratch," he assured her.

Sally laughed. "You've got the smuggest damn look on your face. Good biscuits to go along with the good sex, huh?"

At the far end of this section of the porch, Jay-Jay emerged from the open kitchen doorway with cans of soft drinks, which he set on a nearby wrought-iron table, then held up a pocketknife. "You mind if I have this, Sal?"

"Dad's whittling knife?" She reached for his empty hand and pulled him down into the chair next to her. "Honey, you can have anything in this house you want. You know that."

He snapped the top on his drink can and winked at Dwight. "Even Mama's bread tray?"

"Well, maybe not that. I know he whittled out birds for our kids, but if you come across a bluebird, that one's mine, too. I forget what he carved you."

"A chuck-will's-widow," Jay-Jay said promptly,

rocking back in his chair. "It's setting on the mantel in my living room."

"Did he make Deborah's hummingbird, too?" Dwight asked, suddenly reminded of the little green bird with scarlet throat and long black bill that hung in their kitchen window. It was crudely carved and naively painted, but she'd had it back when she was living in her Aunt Zell's upstairs apartment.

As if echoing his thoughts, Sally said, "He wasn't all that good at it, but he loved messing with 'em."

The Morton house lay on a slight rise. Across a five-acre field from where they sat, above the distant treetops, a tall brick chimney stood starkly against the blue sky, its bricks burned black from that long-ago fire.

"That the Howell house?" he asked.

Jay-Jay nodded.

"I'm surprised the chimney's still standing."

"Mama wanted it knocked down," Sally said, "but Richard left it as a memorial to his sister and her little girls. He didn't want them forgotten. Like any of us ever would. After Jannie's marriage went bust and she moved out here, I used to go over and play with the babies."

Jay-Jay gave a sad smile. "Before Sally and me left home, we'd sneak out here to smoke pot because Mama always sat on the other side of the house where she wouldn't have to look at that chimney and remember what it felt like to watch that house burn and know who was inside."

"It did seem to be one of the things weighing heavy on her mind," said Dwight. "Was there ever any talk that it might be arson?"

"Arson?" Jay-Jay's gentle face looked bewildered. "Who'd burn down an old house with people inside?"

Dwight shrugged. "Kids who didn't realize the house wasn't still empty? Or a man who didn't want to pay child support?"

Sally snorted. "What child support? When it turned out that Mrs. Howell wasn't as rich as everybody thought, Jannie's husband left her. Left the state, too, and no forwarding address."

"Mrs. Howell?" said Dwight. "Their mother?"

"Grandmother. She was the one finished raising Jannie and Richard. Their grandfather owned a little piddly-ass feed store in town and he sold out when the new highway went through. We heard it was thousands, though that might have been wishful thinking. After he died, she let the house run down because she was too tight to let go of a dime. Richard was in school and Jannie was married, so she just lived in one or two of the rooms. Jannie's husband was sure she was going to leave them a fortune, but when they went to the bank after she died, there was only a checking account with a few hundred dollars and nothing in her lockbox but a garnet ring, the deed to the farm, and three thousand dollars in cash. Jannie got the land, Richard got the house and a couple of acres it was sitting on. Back then, land wasn't worth much but Jannie sold her part of the farm right then and there. Soon as the money was gone, though, her husband ran. Hadn't been for Richard letting her use that tumbledown old house, she'd have been out on the street."

Dwight frowned. "But surely Dr. Howell—"

"He wasn't making much money yet," she reminded him. "He was just finishing up his residency. That's what nearly killed him. That he was so close to being able to help her and her daughters move into a decent house."

Life's ironies, thought Dwight. All the money Howell had made since then, yet just scraping by when his sister needed it. "Tell me about Chad Rouse."

They gave him blank looks. "Who?"

"The orderly who worked the third floor last week."

"What about him?"

Both looked surprised to hear that he was the grandson of the Letha McAllister their mother kept talking about.

"Nice kid," Sally said.

"He wanted to hear stories about Uncle Kezzie," said Jay-Jay.

"You'd've thought we were kin to Robin Hood," said Sally. "Oh, and that reminds me, Dwight. Her pillow case has showed up."

"Huh? Where?" He looked around as if expecting it to appear in her hands.

"Lois called me this morning."

"Your mother's aide?"

Sally nodded. "She's helping another patient now. A young man with leukemia. How she can keep taking on new ones time after time, I don't know." She gave a deep sigh. "But anyhow, she said that it'd come back from the laundry with the other hospice linens and as soon as she saw it, she knew it was Mama's. Irish linen? With a lace edging? I don't want it back, but I told her I'd tell you. Not that it's going to be much use. She said it's been bleached so there's no stain on it, but I still couldn't bear to touch it."

"I'll run by and talk to her again," Dwight said. "See if we can figure out how it got from Miss Rachel's room to the laundry." He drained the last of his soda and set the can back on the table. "Tell me about some of those things she kept saying. It sounded like Mr. Kezzie's first wife, Annie Ruth, told her that someone had signed a note for a debt that was never paid?"

Neither could hazard a guess.

"What about the man who beat his wife?"

More blank looks.

"The cowbird remark?"

Again, brother and sister both shook their heads as one of Sally's sons came around the corner with a hall mirror in a carved wooden frame. "You want this, Mom, or can Abby take it?"

"She can have it," Sally said, "and that little table from my old bedroom, too." She rose to follow her son and give instructions. "Back in a minute, y'all."

Left alone with Dwight, Jay-Jay said, "You reckon you'll ever find who did it?"

"Hard to say," Dwight admitted.

"Um, about that cowbird egg."

"You know who she was talking about?"

"Mama really didn't gossip, Dwight." His round face was troubled. "Not like some people who can't wait to spread bad things about people. Folks did tell her things, though, and she did like to fancy them up and make people laugh without 'em knowing who they were laughing at, you know? She never meant anything mean about it."

"I know," Dwight said encouragingly. "But this time?"

"Don't tell Sally, okay? It was about fifteen years ago. I was laying on the couch under the living room window after Sunday dinner, almost asleep. It was right after my first divorce. Mama and I'd been to church that morning and she and Dad were out on the porch, round on the other side, and she was telling him about who was in church. Dad had his whittling knife out and Mama told him he needed to whittle out a cowbird for one of their customers at the vegetable stand. The window was open and I heard her say, 'His wife should've picked a crow to mess around with, not a goldfinch.' Soon as she said that, I knew who she was talking about. I didn't know their names back then, but I knew who Mama meant. They were visiting at our church that day with their little girl. Both of them were short and stout and had curly brown hair, but the little girl's was straight and yellow as a goldfinch. The wife said that Jim's grandmother had been just that blonde at her age."

"Jim?" asked Dwight.

"Jim Collins." The name came reluctantly. "His wife Mavis had diabetes and died about six or seven years ago, but Jim used to stop by the vegetable stand every chance he got and he brought Amanda along from the time she was a baby till she left for college last year. Mama used to say, 'Jim Collins loves that daughter of his better than Peter loved the Lord,' but she never once mentioned anything to me or anybody else about cowbird eggs till the other day. And Jim was there, Dwight. Right there in Mama's room. Him and his daughter both. I was so afraid she was going to blurt out the whole story. She almost said his name. Remember?"

"Remember what?" asked Sally as she rejoined them.

"Jay-Jay was reminding me about your neighbors out here," Dwight said easily. "The Byrds?"

"Sam and Kitty?"

"Which is their house?"

"You passed it coming in," Sally told him. "That house with the red tin roof. First one on the left after you turn back toward the highway. Want me to come with you?"

"That's okay," he said. "You've got your hands full here."

At that moment, one of Jay-Jay's daughters appeared with some handmade bed quilts. "Do you know who made these, Aunt Sally?"

"Catch you later," Dwight said and headed for his cruiser.

CHAPTER
19

Let the punishment match the offense.

— Cicero

Like Deborah's Aunt Zell, indeed like most elderly Southern women of that generation when they go out to garden, Kitty Byrd was swathed from head to toe despite the warm May day. A man's faded cotton shirt was buttoned at neck and wrists, loose cotton slacks reached to the ground, gardening gloves protected her hands, and the floppy brim of a straw hat shaded her face from the sun. In times past, such a costume kept a lady's skin from tanning; today it was to prevent skin cancers.

Mrs. Byrd gingerly straightened up as Dwight parked in the gravel driveway and smiled in recognition when he got out of the cruiser and came closer. Her first few steps toward him were stiff, as if her joints had briefly frozen. "The older I get, the more I agree with Charles Dudley Warner," she said, stripping off her gloves and extending a thin white hand.

Dwight took her hand in his and was careful not to squeeze too hard. "Who?"

"Mark Twain's friend. He said that what every gardener needed was a cast-iron back with a hinge in it." She gave a rueful laugh. "My hinges are so rusty, it would take half the oil in Texas to keep them working. I just wish I could take my skin off and give my poor old bones a shot of WD-40."

She led him up two shallow steps onto a porch shaded by huge oaks and did not insist when Dwight declined her automatic offer of something to drink. She seemed grateful to sit down in a rocker with a high seat and took off her hat to use the broad brim as a fan. Her short white hair was damp with perspiration and the hat had pressed it flat against her skull. "If you were hoping to see my husband, I'm afraid he's gone to try to find some more cabbage plants. The cutworms got most of the first planting. I told him to put a paper cup around the stems till they got some size on 'em, but did he listen?"

Dwight sat down on the wide wooden railing and smiled. "I'm guessing the answer is no."

She ran her fingers through her thin hair to fluff it up until stray white tufts stood straight out from her pink scalp, giving her the look of an elderly punk rocker.

"And I'm guessing you didn't drive all the way from Dobbs to hear how two old people bicker. How can

I help you, Major Bryant?" She settled back in the rocker with her feet hooked over the bottom rung and continued to fan herself with her hat.

"You were Mrs. Morton's longtime neighbor. I was hoping you could help identify some of the things she talked about last Wednesday."

"Oh, Lord, son! She was all over the map with her ramblings, wasn't she? But I did recognize a lot of what she was saying. About her brother Jacob, for instance, even though we'd known each other for years before she told me about him. Rachel could keep her counsel when she wanted to. I never heard a peep about it till the Howell house burned. She said how her other brother felt guilty even though he wasn't there and she bet that Richard was going to feel guilty for Jannie's death, too."

"Did you ever get the impression that she thought he was murdered?"

"Murdered? Not really." Her voice dwindled off in uncertainty and her hand slowed until she dropped the hat on the floor beside her chair. "Not *murder*, but she did blame the ones that were swimming with him that day. Like the accident might've been their fault. That was the only time she opened up to me about it, right after Jannie's funeral, and I doubt she mentioned it more than once or twice in the last forty years. Rachel wasn't one to hang her private laundry out on the line unless it was to tell a funny story on herself."

"She mentioned unpaid debts several times. Any idea what that was about?"

"No. I'm sorry, but I don't."

"What about somebody who used to hit his wife?"

Mrs. Byrd sat up in the rocker and planted her feet squarely on the floor. "You sure I can't get you something to drink?"

"I'm sure, thank you."

She made a show of looking down the road. "Don't know what's taking Sam so long. I worry about him off driving without me even though his eyesight's better'n mine. Can you believe they just renewed his license for another five years and him ninety-two?"

"Who was it, Mrs. Byrd?" Dwight said quietly.

She started to deny knowing, then sighed and leaned back in the chair again. "Sam didn't notice when Rachel said that, and I was hoping maybe nobody else did either."

"Were you that wife?"

"Me?" She gave a soft snort of laughter. "Sam and I may fuss at each other and one of us might slam a door or two, but in sixty years, he's never once raised a hand to me." She smiled again. "Or me to him, for that matter."

"But you do know who she was talking about, don't you?"

Again she ran her fingers through her hair. It had dried enough to let the stiff tufts soften into smoothness. "I'm embarrassed to say that I'm the one who told her. She was such a good listener. Sally's usually too busy talking to listen, bless her heart, but Jay-Jay's more like Rachel. Hears more than he says. Back then, living out here on this empty road, I'd get hungry for woman talk and sometimes I'd say more than I should've. I'm probably the only one besides Furman Snaveley left to remember. And Sam, of course."

Dwight was surprised. "The preacher that baptized Sally and Jay-Jay?"

He'd seen enough domestic violence over the years to know that wife-beaters came from all walks of life and that preachers could erupt with as explosive a temper as any layman. Still...?

"It was back when he was first called to Bethany. Right before Rachel married Brack and moved down here. First time his wife came to church with a bruise on her cheek, the deacons called on him and prayed with him and he promised it wouldn't happen again. A few months later, it was a black eye and a swollen lip. She didn't come to church, but somehow they found out why she was staying home. That time, the deacons sent word for him to meet with them at the church. He came in all shamefaced and apologetic, said he was sorry, he didn't know why he'd flared up like that, wanted them to pray for him again."

She paused and looked at him earnestly. "What you have to understand, Major Bryant, is that back then, those old country deacons didn't know about counseling and psychology and such. They believed in deeds, not words. They said that they would indeed pray for him, but first they made him drop his trousers. He tried to fight but they bent him over the back of a pew and used a leather strap on his bare backside till he was squalling like a baby. Next day, he handed the deacons his resignation, but they wouldn't accept it. They told him that he was a fine preacher and as long as he didn't hurt his wife again, it would never be mentioned, but he needed to stay right where he was for at least five years and learn how to control his temper. If he tried to resign, they would see to it that he never got another church anywhere in this country. Not like those bishops who let all those pedophiles move from church to church instead of giving them a good strapping."

"Did he stay for five years?" Dwight asked.

"He stayed for twenty-five, till he was called to a church in Raleigh," she said. "He changed into a wonderful man—patient, kind, humble. And his wife bloomed like a rose after that. I doubt she ever knew because she always gave God the credit. She used to say that Bethany was his road to Damascus, where he really found Jesus and started walking in his footsteps. She's buried at Bethany and he wants to be buried there, too, when his time comes."

"So how'd you hear about it?"

"My dad was one of those deacons."

"He told you?"

"He didn't mean to. But Sam was made a deacon three years later and the others thought he needed to know. Dad swore him to secrecy and told him the whole story. Of course, Dad was half-deaf at the time and didn't realize how his voice carried. Sam doesn't know I know and I'd appreciate it if you didn't tell him."

"But you did tell Miss Rachel?"

"Lord forgive me, I did." She gestured toward the front windows. "Right inside my living room there. It was a rainy winter afternoon and Rachel came over to help me finish up a Star of Bethlehem quilt I was making to raffle off at church. In his sermon the day before, Mr. Snaveley had talked about how God had helped him control his bad temper and Rachel said he was such a gentle person, he was giving God a bushel of credit for a pint of work, and the next thing I knew, I was telling her he hadn't always been that gentle. I don't know if it was the rain or how warm and cozy the room was or how peaceful it was to be quilting with a friend on a cold day, but that was the first and only time till today I ever told another soul."

She shook her head with regret. "I was so ashamed of myself and she just reached over and patted my hand and said not to worry, she'd never repeat it. So far as I know, she never did. Not till last week. And Mr. Snaveley was there! His hearing's right bad these days, though, so I don't think he caught it."

"Was he still there when everyone cleared out of her room?"

"Oh yes, we left to come home then and he walked out with us."

So scratch the Reverend Furman Snaveley off the list, thought Dwight.

"But then he went back in to find a bathroom," said Mrs. Byrd. "He said it was a forty-minute drive back to his retirement center in Raleigh, and you know how old men and their bladders are."

With a mental sigh, Dwight put the Reverend Furman Snaveley back on the list of possibilities and asked for the name of his retirement home.

Distressed, Mrs. Byrd said, "Oh no! Please! Don't ask him about that."

"If there's someone who can alibi him for the first thirty minutes after you left, I won't need to," Dwight promised.

CHAPTER

20

The beginnings of all things are small.

— Cicero

Before Dwight could turn the key in the cruiser's ignition, his phone rang and Mayleen Richards's name popped up on the screen.

"I'm just leaving Widdington," she said. "Rouse's story about his grandmother checks out. I talked to his mother, his aunt, and a cousin and none of them ever heard her mention a drowning. According to them, they weren't close enough for that, and even if they had been interested enough to ask about her childhood, Letha never looked back. They barely remembered that she'd come from the Cotton Grove area."

"Any word from McLamb or Greene?"

"No, sir."

"See you tomorrow then."

As the call ended, Dwight saw that he had a text message from ALE Agent Virgil Dawson.

"Bingo!" it read. "2 300-gal pots n a semi nr Wilson."

He relayed the news of the traveling whiskey still to the department's dispatcher so that their patrols wouldn't have to keep checking every semi parked along their stretch of I-95, then headed back to Dobbs.

Even though his shift was technically over at four, it was four on the nose by the time Dwight got to the hospital and located the aide who had tended Rachel Morton that last day of her life.

He soon learned that all the towels and linens were stamped with the hospital's name. Used ones were deposited every morning in canvas-sided carts that were trundled down to the laundry where everything was washed with scalding hot water and bleach to disinfect and whiten.

"If patients want to use their own familiar bed-clothes, family members take them home and wash them. Every once in a while, though, a personal item will wind up in a laundry cart. If it's something colored, somebody down in the laundry will pull it out and bring it back, but if it's white, it might not get noticed till after it's been washed and is getting folded. That's what happened with this pillow slip."

"We searched the carts on this floor," Dwight said.

"Even the ones in the main wing?"

He nodded. "But not on all the floors."

Normally a cheerful extrovert, the aide had a troubled look on her small round face. "Someone would have had to carry it away on purpose."

"That time of day, would carts be out on the hall for anyone to use?"

She shook her head. "The empty carts come back before lunch and are stored in utility closets on each floor. The doors are marked STAFF ONLY, but they aren't locked. Anybody could open a door and toss something in."

"What about the old laundry chutes? We were told they aren't used, but could they be?"

"Most of the ones in this wing are sealed, but there is one on the floor that still works and sometimes people who don't know better will throw sheets and towels in it."

She had put the lace-edged linen case in a plastic zip bag and now she held it out to Dwight. "Sally says she doesn't want it back. Do you?"

After being washed and bleached, there was nothing they could learn from it, but Dwight knew a defense attorney could make a big deal out of its not being available if and when this case ever came to trial, so he had the aide mark it and gave her a receipt.

On the off chance that she might remember, Dwight described Furman Snaveley and asked if she had noticed him in the hall when she went back to the room that evening.

Earlier, the room had been so crowded that she didn't recall seeing him at all, "but like I said before, nobody was here when I came back up with my pie.

Miss Rachel was the only patient on that hallway, so I'd've noticed."

"We're not gilding the lily too much, are we?" Will Knott asked.

"I don't think so," said Marillyn Mulholland. Even though semiretired, she still kept her hand in here at the print shop her grandfather had founded back in 1901. "Where on earth did you find this old receipt pad?"

"You'd be surprised what turns up in old houses," Will Knott told her. "Paper doesn't take up much room and people don't seem to like throwing away unused sheets of it."

"Is that why you kept it?" she asked, gently rubbing the paper between her thumb and index. The cheap paper was foxed with age and had such a high wood-pulp content that it was flaking around the edges, but there was a blank margin at the top. Quite enough to work with.

"You never know when period paper might come in handy," he said innocently. "So what do you think?"

"I'll have to use my granddaddy's old hand press, but I think it's doable."

Two hours later, they examined what she had produced after several attempts. She had torn a page from the old receipt pad Will gave her. It was ruled in pale blue and had columns for prices. She had matched the ink to print the name and address of a now-defunct hardware store in Beaufort, using a font that shrieked pre–World War I.

"Looks good to me," Will said. "I like the way part

of the store name's missing. Like it was torn off carelessly."

"How many should I print?" she asked, wiping ink from her fingers.

"Another four or five in case I mess up."

When the ink had dried, he took a soft-leaded pencil with a blunt point and began to scribble, using an old Sears catalog as a price guide.

The latest victim of a break-in down in Black Creek Township had a bemused look on his face when McLamb and Greene caught up with him in a back field where his wife had sent them. He was tilling corn with a four-row cultivator in preparation for rain predicted by morning.

The tractor rolled to a stop beside the two deputies and the farmer cut the engine so they could talk. "I meant to call you guys. It's the damnedest thing. Yesterday, I decided to try to call my phone again and a guy answered. Said he had a feeling the phone must have been stolen since his buddy let him have it for so cheap, but he'd paid for it and he wasn't of a mind to give it back. I told him I'd give him what he paid for it and ten dollars on top of that, but he wouldn't do it. Then I told him it had pictures of my mom's eightieth birthday party and that seemed to get to him. He asked me my name and address and said he'd see what he could do. This morning, when my wife went out to mail a letter, she found a jump drive in the mailbox with all our pictures on it. Only there's one picture we didn't take. I was going to take it in tomorrow and show you."

He followed them back to his house and led them into the den where an old PC sat on the desk. "I've heard they're only stealing laptops. I guess this one's too old and clunky to mess with. My wife transferred all the pictures last night and then uploaded all the albums to a cloud, whatever that is."

A few clicks of his mouse and they were looking at pictures of a family celebration. At the end of a series of group pictures of people with lifted mugs and drink glasses was a picture of two young men in a barroom lifting mugs of their own.

"They must not've noticed they crashed the wrong party," the man said. "I don't recognize them, but I bet somebody will."

The flash drive that he handed them had a cheap red plastic casing and probably sold for less than two dollars in any discount store that carried office supplies. "My wife tells me that this little gizmo has more memory than our first computer had. Can you believe it?"

Kaitlyn Lancaster adjusted the white silk ascot at her grandfather's throat and smoothed the green velvet throw draped over his legs, then pushed his chair over to the full-length mirror in Mrs. Ashton's bedroom. "Oh, Grampa! Look at you! You look like a million dollars."

Mr. Lancaster inspected his image. This was the first time he had put on a suit in three years. His own suits were now too large but this one, a beautifully tailored summer-weight blend of pale gray linen and wool, had belonged to Charles Ashton's late father and except for being a little long in the legs was a near-perfect fit.

"Humph!" said Mr. Lancaster. He turned his head back and forth and frowned as he tried to smooth the strands of white hair across his pink scalp. "I need a haircut. A real haircut in a barber shop, not you with the clippers, Katie."

"We'll pay for a haircut," said Frances Jones, even though she still owned the barber set with which she used to cut her father's hair after money became so tight in that big house.

"My dad had a Panama that might work," Charles said. His black leather sandals creaked as he walked over to the closet and brought out an old hatbox.

"Do I really need a nurse's uniform?" Katie asked.

"Sally thinks so," JoAnn Bonner told her, tucking her hair behind her ears. Like her Aunt Frances, she wore a crisp white cotton shirt and a beige skirt. "One of my friends is a nurse. What size are you?"

From her own wheelchair near the bed, Mrs. Ashton lifted her small head and smiled at them benignly. "I'm so glad you all could come. Charles, dear, did you offer our guests some tea?"

Rusty Alexander set the screen of his laptop to its highest magnification. The picture in this online catalog was labeled "...*signed H N*." Was it possible that Will Knott was that ignorant? "One man's ignorance is another man's bliss," he told himself happily.

CHAPTER
21

*By our law, fathers of families who mismanage
their property have its administration taken
from them.*

— Cicero

Pork barbecue is the official entrée in eastern North
Carolina and it's served at almost every bar association
dinner, so I expected to find it on my plate tonight along
with the usual coleslaw, mushy string beans, and rubber
hushpuppies. Instead, we were surprised when the waiters
set before each of us a poached fillet of catfish on a bed of
buttery spinach with a side of tiny new potatoes steamed
in their red jackets and squares of tender cornbread.

I was amazed. "Are we at the right dinner, Por?"

Seated across from us at our table for six, Portland's
husband Avery gave us an exaggeratedly formal nod of
acknowledgment. "You may thank the hospitality com-
mittee, ladies, of which, in case you haven't noticed, I
just happen to be the new chair."

"The job is yours for life, as far as I'm concerned," said my cousin and former law partner, John Claude Lee, who sat between Portland and me. "For the first time in years, I may not have to take an antacid pill after one of these meals."

"You get my vote," said Luther Parker on my right.

Luther is the district's first black judge, the man who defeated me the first time I ran for the bench. We've been friends for years and he's the only one I could have been gracious about losing to, not that I didn't have a sour thought or two about it at the time. Happily, both of us had won reelection last time around.

"I'm just glad you didn't scrap the pecan pie for crème brûlée," said Reid Stephenson, who's also a cousin and junior partner of my old firm.

"Now you wait just one minute, young man," said Luther. "Crème brûlée's my favorite dessert."

"Then it will certainly be on the menu at the next dinner," Avery promised.

"Bribing a judge?" I asked.

Luther drew himself up in mock indignation. "Are you suggesting that a judge can be bribed with some caramelized sugar on a teeny little dish of custard?"

"If the shoe fits," I told him as I cut into my fish.

It was cooked to perfection: moist and flaky, the wine sauce was nice and lemony, and the spinach almost melted in my mouth.

The dinner was being held at a restaurant overlooking Crenshaw's Lake. Reid and John Claude had driven out with Luther, and I came with Por and Avery.

•

I had ordered a bottle of wine for the table but the
two drivers took only token sips when I lifted my glass
to toast the new partnership of Lee, Stephenson &
Brewer. Talks had been going on for several months
and the merger would become official on the first of
June.

Portland would handle criminal defense with Reid,
while Avery's experience with taxes and estate planning would enhance the civil side that currently took
up most of John Claude's time. I thought it was a perfect fit, since Portland wanted to cut back on her hours
until Carolyn was old enough for preschool, and I was
totally pleased for all of them.

"So who gets my old office?" I asked. "Por or
Avery?"

It was the one thing I really missed about leaving
the practice. My office at the courthouse was about the
size of a broom closet and I had to share the connect-
ing lavatory with Luther.

Half a block from the courthouse, the firm occupies
a white clapboard house built by John Claude's great-
grandfather shortly after the Civil War. Except for an
electric light over the door, the outside looks exactly as
it did in 1868. The interior's been extensively remodeled and modernized through the years but the offices
retain the original proportions. John Claude had the
double parlor on the left of the front door as you enter,
and I had used the lady's parlor across the wide hall,
with Reid's office behind mine in what was once the
dining room.

"I'll be moving into your old room," said John Claude. "I don't really need that much space and the pocket doors still work, so my office can go back to being two separate rooms."

"You really don't have to do that," Portland said. "There's room for two desks in Deborah's old office and I can take my laptop to the sunroom if Avery needs to confer privately with a client."

It sounded like an ongoing argument, and my cousin shook his head. "Julia's been itching to update those rooms for years."

His wife is a frustrated interior designer and she had redone my office right after I was appointed to the bench, in preparation for a replacement that had never been hired.

I offered my sympathies to Portland and Avery. "If I know Julia, you'll both be using the sunroom all summer."

As pie and coffee were served, our current president stood to introduce the evening's speaker, an earnest man from the attorney general's office who talked to us about some of the new scams that were being perpetrated on the elderly and how attorneys should use all their powers of persuasion to convince their older clients to sign a durable power of attorney for financial management before they fell prey to con artists. "In layman's terms, they need to appoint someone trustworthy to act for them in case they become sick or incapacitated," he said. "You should also encourage them to execute a living will *and* a health care power of attorney."

I know that these are standard procedures with John Claude and Reid, but several of the younger attorneys in the room were taking serious notes and the question-and-answer session afterwards lasted till nearly ten.

Portland listened politely but something about the set of her mouth made me think she was taking everything the man said with a grain of salt as big as a cow block.

"I'm not sure if Daddy's done that or not," I said on the drive back to Dobbs. John Claude was his personal attorney and neither had confided in me.

"Don't you reckon he's appointed Seth?" Portland said.

"Seth keeps the books for the farm, so he'd be the logical choice," I agreed.

"Not you?" asked Avery.

I laughed. "Daddy's come a long way in his eighty-odd years, but not to the point of trusting a woman to handle his affairs."

"Don't feel bad," Avery said. "Even women don't always trust women." He told us about a client whose mother had been robbed of several thousands by a so-called financial advisor she had trusted. "And my client couldn't do anything until her mother finally let her take a look at the bank records. Even then, it was hard to convince her that her own daughter, a woman who's run her own business for twenty years, had more smarts about investments than the man who had taken her for a ride."

"Maybe the mother's in the beginnings of dementia," I suggested.

"Oh please!" said Portland. "You know, everybody's so ready to think that because a person's old, they've lost the ability to act for themselves."

"Hey, when did I say that?" I protested. "Can you imagine anybody telling Daddy he's losing it? Or Aunt Zell?"

"Not you, but you'd be surprised how many do."

From my seat behind them, I saw Avery glance over at Portland, who had subsided into silence. "Case in point?" he asked mildly.

"Mrs. McElveen."

"Laurel McElveen?" I had a vague memory that Portland had just come from the funeral of Mrs. McElveen's niece when we had lunch together the day Aunt Rachel died. "Sharp as she is? She can't be much over sixty and she sits on half the boards in town. Who thinks she's getting senile?"

"Her niece did. If she hadn't dropped dead of a heart attack, Mrs. McElveen's convinced she would have had her committed by now."

"Huh?" Avery and I chorused together.

"You didn't tell me that," he said.

"Everybody talks about caregivers, how much they put up with, how hard it is to be at someone's beck and call. Like those Dedicated Daughters that your cousin Sally belongs to."

"*Designated* Daughters," I said, "not Dedicated."

"And who designated them?" she asked indignantly.

"Well, usually they step in when no one else will," I said and told them about the case I'd had last week,

when a son who had shirked all the day-to-day respon-
sibilities with his mother was right there for a full cut
of her estate.

"Oh, I'm not saying there's never a need." Portland
twisted around in her seat to face me. "But what about
the ones like Mrs. McElveen who have to fight off the
caregivers who think they know best when it comes to
making sure there's going to be an estate to cut up?
During that time after her accident when she was on so
many pain meds and having trouble thinking clearly,
that niece came close to getting her to sign an irrevocable power of attorney and to put everything in a trust
for her and three cousins. She says she was starting to
feel like buzzards were circling over her head."

"But don't you see?" said Avery. "That's exactly
why the AG's pushing this program. If she'd had a
proper plan in place, her niece wouldn't have had to
die in order to protect her interests. Do you want me to
talk to her?"

Portland didn't answer. Instead she turned back to
the front and stared silently through the windshield.

"Por?"

"Hmmm?" she murmured absently, as if deep in
thought.

"Do you want me to talk to Mrs. McElveen about
the safeguards she can take?"

"I'll ask her. She's got me drawing up a new will. At
this point she's ready to leave everything to charity and
nothing to any family members."

Avery started to say something more when suddenly

the sky ahead lit up with a jagged bolt of lightning. A moment later, fat heavy raindrops spattered the windshield. By the time we got to their house, a few blocks east of the courthouse, the rain was coming down like a hydrant had opened up over us. I had left my car parked on their drive but there was room for Avery to pull past it and into the garage.

"Why don't you spend the night?" Portland said.

"For a little rain? Don't be silly. Look. It's already starting to slack off."

Avery, ever the gentleman, took my keys and pulled my car far enough under the edge of the garage that I could get in without getting wet. Before they'd let me leave, though, they made me turn on my phone in case Dwight got worried and tried to call me.

"I'll be fine," I said and hugged them both for caring.

Heading for home, I turned on the radio to help me stay alert. I'd drunk only a single glass of wine and that was over two hours ago, but it had been a long day and I couldn't stop yawning. A local talk show was on and I started to switch to a music station when I realized that the topic was early-onset Alzheimer's. The expert du jour was describing early symptoms. (Forgetting where you put your car keys isn't one, in case you were worried, nor is forgetting to turn on your phone.) She also had suggestions for coping. An even-tempered cat or dog could help calm a patient, but contradicting him or insisting that he try to remember something could lead to agitation. Best was just to let him talk and go with the flow.

I thought of Mrs. Ashton mistaking me for her son's kindergarten teacher and how Dwight had described Billy Thornton's anger when he was pushed to remember Letha McAllister.

"Music can help, too," said the expert. "Especially the music that was popular in the patient's youth."

Really?

Hmmm. It certainly wouldn't hurt for Dwight to try.

CHAPTER
22

*There is, however, a calm and serene old age,
which belongs to a life passed peacefully,
purely, and gracefully.*

— Cicero

It was still raining the next morning when we sat down to breakfast and, according to the Weather Channel, rain was due to continue off and on throughout the day. Cal was disappointed. Rain meant no baseball practice, but Dwight was pleased for the garden. "As long as it stops by Friday."

"What happens on Friday?" I asked, passing Cal a bowl of freshly sliced strawberries and bananas. He scattered some over the top of his bran flakes and reached for the sugar bowl.

"The lumber yard's supposed to deliver the two-by-fours and the plywood for the pond shelter," Dwight said. "Hey, easy on the sugar there, buddy."

"The strawberries are sour," Cal argued even though

he hadn't yet tasted them, but he passed the sugar on to Dwight, who likes to sweeten his cereal and fruit, too.

"If the rain holds off this weekend and everybody shows up with hammers and saws, we could come close to getting it finished by Saturday night."

"Really?"

"Everything except for running a water line down for a shower and patching in the electricity."

"Annie Sue said that wouldn't take long." My niece had installed weatherproof outlets along the pier railing when she and her brother wired a multicolored geyser out in the pond as a Christmas present to us. Although they had buried the wire, she had marked its location so that they could splice into it when we built the shelter all the younger family members seemed to think we needed.

While Cal went to get ready for school, Dwight described his visit out to Aunt Rachel's old house yesterday, pledging me to secrecy about the cowbird story Jay-Jay had confided.

"The Collins girl really is a goldfinch, isn't she?" I said, remembering the pretty young blonde I'd run into in the empty hospice room and how her pearl necklace had broken. That reminded me that I still had one of her pearls, but my mind was drawing a blank on what I'd done with it.

"What about the neighbors?" I asked. "Did you talk to Mr. Byrd and his wife?"

"Don't know that they were much help," he said vaguely and told me what Mayleen had learned about

Letha McAllister over in Widdington and why none of her family seemed concerned about that thrice-married woman's reputation.

"Did you get a picture of her when she was young? Was she as hot as Jacob and Jed thought she was?"

"Mayleen said her daughter dug out an old snapshot, but I haven't seen it yet. I was thinking that a picture might jog Billy Thornton's memory."

That reminded me of the program I'd listened to on my way home. "I don't suppose you know what kind of music he likes?"

"I'd guess country. That's what the radio was playing when I got there."

I glanced at the clock.

"Yeah, I'd better get moving, too," he said, and took a final swallow of coffee before going off to brush his teeth.

Ten minutes later, he and Cal were out the door, but I had an extra hour, so I went to the computer and soon had a list of some thirty songs that had topped the charts sixty-five years ago. As I suspected, they were raw, nasal voices backed by unamplified guitars and fiddles. They sang of lost or unrequited love, hurting and cheating, and aching loneliness. Hillbilly and bluegrass flourished, together with gospel. Ernest Tubb, the Carter Family, and Roy Acuff. But the popular songs that would have been played on WPTF's late-night request programs were the lovesick ballads from Eddy Arnold, Bing Crosby, and Gene Autry. I didn't have time to download all the songs just then, but I stuck my iPod in my shoulder bag. There's always some downtime when ADAs separate out defendants who intend to plead guilty from those who want to argue the charges. By lunchtime, I had put together forty minutes of iconic songs that should certainly touch that old man's memory, and I carried my iPod down to Dwight's office.

He wasn't there, but Mayleen Richards was. Or rather Mayleen Diaz, as her name tag now reads. When I first knew her, there had been some awkward stiffness between us. For this past year, though, we were on a first-name basis, even if she did sometimes slip and throw in a "ma'am." I explained what I'd done so that she could show Dwight when he got back.

"He said you had a picture of that Letha McAllister when she was a girl?"

"Oh yeah. Want to see?"

She opened a folder and handed me a small shiny black-and-white photo of a young woman in a one-piece white bathing suit, one hand on her hip, the other holding a cigarette. Even though the suit was cut high at the top and low at the bottom in keeping with the style of the day, her pose left very little to the imagination. She had half turned away from the camera so as to show off her assets—full breasts, provocatively thrust forward, a tiny waist, and what looked like a nicely rounded bottom. Her dark shoulder-length hair was worn in a pageboy, her eyebrows had been plucked into arches, and her lips gleamed in what must have been a thick application of bright red lipstick.

The date written on the back was two years after Jacob's death.

"Wow!" I said. "If she looked anything like this two years earlier, no wonder those boys fought over her."

"Liked herself, too, didn't she?" Mayleen said.

I looked again and saw the complacent self-satisfied smile on her pretty face. "Well, in all fairness, she had a lot to like, didn't she?"

I handed the snapshot back. "Neither of us would stop a clock, Mayleen, but let's face it: most men wouldn't give us a second look if someone like this was in the room."

"Major Bryant would," she said loyally.

I laughed. "And I'm sure Mike would, too." Then I took that second look. "So when's the baby due?"

One hand immediately flew to her trim waistline and her freckles disappeared into the blush that flooded her face. "I didn't think I was showing yet."

"You're not," I assured her. "But there's something about your face. With so many sisters-in-law, I've had a lot of practice spotting early pregnancies."

"It's not due till Thanksgiving and we haven't told anyone yet."

"Don't worry," I said. "He won't hear it from me." I didn't feel one bit disloyal. After all, give her another month or two and everyone in the courthouse would have figured it out.

Even Dwight.

* * *

Back on the first floor, I ran into my cousin Sally,
who was furling a large wet golf umbrella outside
the clerk of court's office. Today's wig was a completely natural-looking brown that barely brushed the
collar of a man-styled white shirt. She was pushing a
wheelchair with a frail old woman who gave me what
would be a bright smile of recognition had she truly
recognized me.

"Hello, Mrs. Ashton," I said.

"Well, hey there, honey!" she said. "I'm so glad you
could come along with us."

"I'm giving Charles a little break," Sally explained.
"He hasn't had a day off in weeks and I needed to do
some paperwork here about Mama's house. She never
made a will, you know, so there's a ton of forms to fill
out and file, and Charlotte likes to get out, too, don't
you, sweetie?"

Mrs. Ashton held out her hands to me, palms down.
"We got our nails done."

Her nails shone with a soft rose polish.

"It matches your dress, too," I said.

"I know. Jean and I went shopping and I found
the exact same color. On sale, too!" She beamed and
smoothed down the front of a pink cotton dress that
had clearly been washed a time or two.

"Charlotte loves to shop and she has a good eye for
bargains," Sally said. "We always check by that dress
store next to the Cut 'n' Curl."

Dress store? Beside the beauty parlor?

"But that's—"

"—a wonderful place to shop," Sally interrupted me firmly and her eyes flashed a warning.

"Oh, it is," I hastily agreed.

Hey, if Mrs. Ashton thought that the Goodwill store was a ladies' dress shop, who was I to disillusion her? Aunt Zell is right, I thought. Sally might act like a flake at times, but she has a good heart.

Here at midday, the hallway was busy with people coming and going into Ellis Glover's office, hoping to take care of some paperwork on their lunch hour. Every other person seemed to know Sally or me, so we moved farther down the hall out of the flow and Sally positioned Mrs. Ashton's chair so as to partially block us from view, yet let Mrs. Ashton watch the passing parade.

"Who's Jean?" I whispered.

"Her older sister. She's in a rest home in Tennessee." She sighed. "Don't let's get old, Deb'rah."

"I won't if you won't," I said, looking at her firm chin line and trim body. Really, the only thing that gave away her true age were the faint brown spots on the back of her hands. She still moved with the ease of someone twenty years younger.

I realized she was examining my face, too. "You turn forty in August, right? Want the name of my plastic surgeon?"

"Not yet," I said and she grinned, hearing the "Not never" in my voice.

"Dwight told me he saw you and Jay-Jay down at the farm yesterday."

"Yeah, but we weren't able to tell him anything that

would help say who did that to Mama. I'm beginning to think we'll never know."

"Don't give up yet," I said. "It's only been a week and so many of the things your mother said could have touched on stuff someone didn't want known. Not just Jacob's death, but like that money someone lent that was never paid back or the wife-beater."

"Or who ate all the chocolates in both Easter baskets?" she said sarcastically. "Now *there's* a secret worth killing for. Unless it was somebody still lusting after whoever it was in that transparent bathing suit."

"I think Daddy and that neighbor of y'all's—Sam Byrd?—were the only men old enough to remember that," I said.

"Or Mr. Snaveley, who used to preach at our church."

Both of us stood quietly for a moment, remembering all the names that Aunt Rachel had called that last afternoon.

"Do you remember Annie Ruth?" I asked.

She shook her head. "Not really. I do remember going to her funeral and being told all those little boys were my cousins."

"Y'all weren't close?"

"Not really."

"But the way Aunt Rachel kept talking about her?"

Sally frowned. "Did she?"

The flow of people had slowed to a trickle and Mrs. Ashton turned in her chair. "Jean, dear, don't you think we ought to go in now? I'm sure the movie's about to start and I want some popcorn."

CHAPTER
23

The distinctive faculty of man is his eager desire to investigate the truth.

— Cicero

Dwight Bryant—Wednesday afternoon

Y our wife was here, Major," Mayleen said when Dwight stuck his head into the squad room after lunch. She handed him the iPod and showed him where Deborah had grouped the selections. "She said this was music that was popular around the time Jacob Knott drowned, thought it might help jar the Thornton man's memory."

"Thanks, Mayleen. Got anything pressing on your docket this afternoon?"

"Just the usual. Something you need?"

"One of the men in that hospice room was a

Jim Collins. See if you can arrange a meeting with him."

She was puzzled. "Isn't he too young to have had anything to do with that drowning?"

"Yeah, but remember that remark about a cowbird egg?"

Mayleen nodded and Dwight repeated what Jay-Jay had told him the day before. When he'd finished, she frowned.

"You want me to go ask the CEO of Mediway Technology if his daughter's not really his daughter?"

"Is that who he is?"

"Yessir. And he was one of Sheriff Poole's biggest supporters last fall, so shouldn't you be the one to talk to him?"

"I don't think so. Something like this? He'd take it easier coming from a woman."

Mayleen was shaking her head in dismay, but Dwight said, "Look, it's either you or Ray and how tactful you think he'd be? Where is he, anyhow?"

"You sent him and Tub to see if that preacher—Mr. Snaveley?—had an alibi for the time of Mrs. Morton's death."

"Oh, right." He started back to his office, then paused and said, "Look, if you can absolutely alibi Collins for the relevant time without saying why we think he might have a motive, fine. I saw Sally Crenshaw up in Ellis Glover's office a few minutes ago. Do you have her cell number? Maybe you can still catch her and see if she remembers when Collins and his daughter left. And do it without letting Sally know there's a question of paternity."

Back in his own office, Dwight called Billy Thornton's daughter and asked if it would be convenient for him to come out.

"Actually, this is a pretty good time," Mrs. Sterling said. "He's as clear-minded today as I've seen him all week."

"Have you and your brother had a chance to talk about that drowning?"

"Davis was over here yesterday, but really, Major, we lost track of the people we knew before we moved to Benson. Both of us were still in grade school. If Mom or Dad ever mentioned the Knotts, we don't remember it. Davis didn't remember ever hearing them talk about a Letha either. I guess I could try again since Dad seems lucid today."

"If you don't mind, I'd appreciate it if you'd wait and let me ask him," Dwight said. "I have a picture of her and I'd really like to see his reaction."

"You must be getting tired of all the questions," Mayleen told Sally Crenshaw after she'd been introduced to Mrs. Ashton. She moved a cardboard file box out of the way so that the wheelchair could be maneuvered through the squad room.

"That's okay," Sally said. "I just wish Mama hadn't been so careful about naming names."

"People might not have trusted her as much."

"Would've been fine with me," said Sally. She set

the brake on the wheelchair and then pulled her own chair close to Mrs. Ashton, who reached for her hand. "What is it this time?"

Mayleen held out a copy of all the names they had collated. "We're trying to eliminate everyone there who could have had an opportunity to slip back to the room."

Mrs. Ashton's eyes had closed. The chair had a reclining back, and before taking the paper, Sally positioned a small pillow under her chin so that she wouldn't wake with a stiff neck.

The first column beside the names was to indicate if a person was in the room before Mrs. Morton quit talking. The second was whether they could definitely be placed in the family waiting room when the aide came down to join them. "Check it if you remember them being there and put a question mark if you can't be absolutely sure one way or the other."

"Even family members?"

"Even family members."

When Sally handed the list back a few minutes later, Mayleen saw that Collins and his daughter had check marks for the room but Amanda's had a question mark for the waiting room. Hers was not the only name with a question mark. Three of the Knott grandchildren had question marks as well and so did Furman Snaveley, among others.

"I remember that Mr. Collins was there on the staircase talking to Richard Howell when we left Mama's room. Then a nurse came over from the other wing with a message for Richard. He went off with her and Mr. Collins went on down to speak to Deborah. I don't remember seeing Amanda or Emma or Jess, but they must have been there. If I saw Mr. Snaveley, I don't remember."

As the interview ended, Sally's face was bleak. "The worst of this is knowing it had to be somebody Mama knew and liked. Maybe even loved. Maybe even someone in our own family."

Mayleen showed them out, holding open the double doors out by the dispatcher's desk for the wheelchair and then ringing for the elevator. When the doors closed behind them, she took the stairs to the second floor where Judge Knott was holding court and slid into a seat next to an attorney waiting for his case to be called. At the next break in the proceedings, Deborah motioned for her to come up. "You wanted to ask me something?"

"I'm trying to verify some alibis," Mayleen said. "Your cousin Sally says that you spoke with a Jim Collins right before your aunt was killed?" She started to show a picture of him, but the judge was evidently more politically aware than Major Bryant, because she brushed the picture aside.

"Yes, we talked for a few minutes."

"Was his daughter there?"

Deborah thought a minute, then said, "Sorry, Mayleen. I can't remember. We used the same restroom, but I didn't see her after that. I think she probably left."

"Did you see anyone at all go back upstairs?"

"Not up the staircase, but the elevator wasn't visible from the waiting room. If it's any help, though, Collins was still talking to my sister-in-law Minnie a little while after Aunt Rachel's aide came down to eat, so I really doubt he's who you're looking for."

"What about these two nieces of yours?"

"Emma and Jess? They were there, but I think they left early before we knew about Aunt Rachel."

"And Furman Snaveley?"

"Who? Oh, the preacher. I don't remember seeing him downstairs."

Armed with a photograph of the Reverend Furman Snaveley that Mayleen had printed from the DVD, Raeford McLamb and Tub Greene parked the cruiser under the hospital's covered entryway out of the rain. Major Bryant had not told them why the old man might have a motive for murder, merely that he wanted to know if Snaveley had an alibi. They knew that Snaveley had left the hospice room with the Byrds and had walked out of the hospital through the main doors, then immediately returned, ostensibly to use the restroom.

A friendly middle-aged black woman sat behind the information counter opposite those doors. "Yes, I was here last Wednesday afternoon," she told them, and looked long and hard at the picture they showed her.

"Yes," she said at last. "I remember him now. That tie he's wearing. You can't really tell in this picture, but it was dark red, embroidered with little tiny gold crosses, and I was thinking a tie like that would make a good Father's Day present for my dad. He asked me where the men's room was and I told him down that hall, first door on the right."

She gestured toward her left, in the opposite direction from the hospice wing.

"Did you see him come back?"

She shook her head. "Sorry."

"But you saw him start down that hall?"

"That's right."

"Where's the nearest elevator from here?" they asked.

"Besides that one?" She gestured toward an elevator that was in her line of sight near the front entrance.

"Do you think you would've noticed if he got on it?" McLamb asked.

"Maybe. Especially if he had to wait, because that surely is the slowest elevator in the building."

"What about down that hall past the restroom? Where's the next elevator that way?"

"Not too far. See the second crossing down yonder? If you turn left, you'll walk right into it."

They thanked her and started timing the walk.

"You reckon he'd walk this fast?" asked Tub Greene, who still carried an extra thirty pounds of baby fat and sometimes had trouble keeping up with McLamb, who was lean and fit.

"He would if he was in a hurry to put a pillow over somebody's face," McLamb said. But he slowed his steps. The elevator arrived and they went up to the third floor, then walked down branching corridors toward the hospice wing. Four and a half minutes. Again, they were lucky. Two nurses sat at that last station in the newer hall making notations on their electronic charts, one a young blue-eyed white woman, the other an older brown-eyed man of Japanese descent. Both had been on duty the previous Wednesday. But there the luck ended. Neither of them recognized Snaveley's picture.

"We were right busy that afternoon," said the senior nurse. McLamb was disconcerted to hear the nurse's Southern drawl when he was expecting a foreign accent. "A lot of coming and going. We had a code about that time. One of our patients down on C Hall went into cardiac arrest and his wife freaked out. I thought we were going to have to sedate her before we could get him stabilized. A marching band could have gone past this station for all I know."

The young white nurse agreed.

McLamb thanked them and went on down the corridor and around the corner to the elevator that serviced the old wing. The desk there was unstaffed, as it had been last week.

"Okay," said Ray McLamb. "Snaveley and the Byrds left the room with the others. They then took the elevator down to the ground floor and walked through the halls to the main entrance, where their cars were parked."

"And don't forget that they would be talking as they went," said Tub. He looked at his watch. "Say ten minutes to get down and outside, then another five or six minutes for him to get in and back up, and that's not counting if he really did have to use the men's room. Yet nobody saw him."

"So I guess we drive over to Raleigh and ask him if *he* saw anybody after he left the Byrds," said Ray.

It was still raining when Dwight got to the Sterling home, but Billy Thornton was seated on the porch swing as before and seemed to be enjoying the sound of rain as it drummed on the roof and sluiced down onto the late azaleas that lined the foundation of the house with bright red blossoms.

"Daddy, this is Major Bryant from the Sheriff's Department," said Mrs. Sterling.

"Come to arrest me, young man?" he asked jovially.

Encouraged, Dwight said, "No, I brought you some music to listen to."

"Do you want me to stay?" his daughter asked. "I never know if I'm a help or a hindrance at times like this."

"Why don't I call you if I need you?" Dwight said, relieved that he wouldn't have to sugarcoat what he planned to ask.

"I'll leave the door open," she said and disappeared inside.

Dwight cued up the first song on Deborah's playlist, Ernest Tubb's "Walking the Floor Over You." A few bars into the song, Billy Thornton began to tap his foot in time with the music.

"Yeah, I like this one," he said with a happy smile on his face.

Next came a short Eddie Arnold cut, then a warm baritone voice began to sing about racing with the moon and Dwight realized that Deborah had chosen period love songs of adolescent loss and longing. He lowered the volume a little and softly asked, "You have a girlfriend?"

Thornton shrugged.

"C'mon, Billy. There must be someone special. Is it Letha?"

Dwight held up the snapshot of Letha McAllister that Mayleen had enlarged. "Remember, Billy?"

"Letha!" He reached for the picture and held it in both hands. Tears filled his rheumy eyes. "Letha," he whispered, then looked at Dwight angrily. "Where'd you get her picture?"

"Jacob Knott gave it to me," Dwight said. "She gave it to him."

"The hell you say!" His eyes went back to the photograph and resentment faded from his face, replaced by wonder. "Lord, but she was something else, won't she? You remember how she laughed?"

"Real pretty," Dwight said, realizing that the old man thought he was someone from out of a shared past. "But she liked Jacob best, didn't she?"

Thornton didn't answer.

"Down at Possum Creek, Billy. You and Jacob and Letha. Did you hit Jacob?"

"We all...me, Ransom, Jed. She let us all kiss her, but Jacob...She let Jacob—"

"How did Jacob die, Billy?" Dwight asked, his voice barely audible above the music.

"Always showing off, won't he? Swinging out on that rope, flipping off like he was Tarzan on a jungle vine. Laughing at me and Ransom 'cause we couldn't do it as good. And Letha looking at him like he was made out of sugar candy." His voice dropped to a whisper. "She saw me."

"Saw you doing what?"

"He fell. The rope broke."

"And you hit him with a rock because he wanted Letha, too."

"No! I didn't."

"What did she see you do, Billy?"

"She didn't know I was up there when she— She went right into the water and let him put his hand— She never let me touch her like that. She saw me out on that limb. Her and Jacob. They thought I was using my knife to pull the knot tighter."

Bing Crosby's mellow voice gently caressed a lovesick lyric.

"I didn't mean for him to get hurt so bad, but he wouldn't quit trying to take her away from me."

"So you cut the rope," Dwight said softly.

"She's *my* girl, dammit! *Mine!* It was all her fault!" His fingers clinched around the edges of the enlarged photograph and his eyes seemed to focus on the sexy image. "Letha," he whimpered.

"Tell me about Jacob," Dwight said, but Thornton sat mutely through two more songs that had been popular when he and Letha McAllister and Jacob Knott had been young and reckless.

If Thornton had all his marbles, thought Dwight, *I could arrest him. Now, though?*

He sighed, switched off the music, and reached for the photograph.

Thornton snatched it away and pulled back his fist. Dwight ducked, but not before a surprisingly hard blow landed on his shoulder.

"Get the hell off my porch!" the old man yelled in such a loud voice that Mrs. Sterling came rushing out.

"Dad? What's wrong?"

Flushed with rage, Thornton struggled to his feet, clearly intending to slug it out.

"*Dad!*" Mrs. Sterling cried, and as abruptly as the anger had come, it was already ebbing away and the old man looked at her in confusion. Without protest, he let her help him sit down on the swing. The chain creaked as he began to rock back and forth, soothed by the falling rain.

"Mamie?" he said. "Is it suppertime yet?"

"Not yet, Dad."

The picture had landed under the swing and Mrs. Sterling picked it up.

"Is this that Letha you were asking about?" She handed it to Dwight. "She looks like one of those old movie stars from back when I was a kid. What was her name? Betty Grable? Was she his girlfriend?"

"He thought so." Unbidden, came a line one of his Army Intelligence colleagues always quoted when he was in his cups: "*But that was in another country, and besides, the wench is dead.*"

He did not realize he'd spoken aloud until Mrs. Sterling looked at him curiously.

"Major Bryant?"

"Sorry," he said and slid the photograph back into his folder. Mr. Thornton did not seem to notice.

"Was he able to tell you anything useful?"

"Yes, ma'am. I got what I came for and I won't be bothering you again."

"No bother," she said brightly. "Dad and I are always happy to have company. Breaks up the day."

CHAPTER
24

*Old men who are moderate in their desires,
and are neither testy nor morose, find old age
endurable.*

— Cicero

Cameron Longview was one of Raleigh's older continuous-care retirement communities. Located inside the Beltline on the west side of town, the campus consisted of several two- and three-story gray stone buildings set in a grove of huge live oaks.

And here on a rainy spring afternoon, it did indeed look more like a university campus than a modern retirement village, thought Ray McLamb. Duke, maybe. Or Oxford.

Although his wife seldom watched supposedly true-to-life cop shows set in New York or LA, she had been

addicted to the Inspector Morse series and she always
watched the reruns, as much for the architecture of
Oxford as for the stories. They lived in a comfortable
brick house with all the modern conveniences, yet she
yearned for multi-paned leaded windows set deeply
into thick stone walls.

Lillie would like this place, he thought.

The buildings were connected by covered walkways
and their graceful wrought-iron columns were corded
with wisteria vines that dripped huge purple clusters.
Sturdy teak benches offered comfortable seating shel-
tered from spring rain or summer sun.

According to the brochure the deputies had picked
up at the main office, Cameron Longview offered one-
and two-bedroom garden apartments for independent
living, efficiency apartments for assisted living, and
hospital rooms for skilled nursing care when the need
arose. As Ray navigated the drive that wound between
the buildings, Tub read aloud from the brochure.

"Sumptuous cuisine. Evening cocktails on the terrace
overlooking the garden. Cultural events. Aquatic and fit-
ness center. On-site hospital facility. Adult day care."

"If you have to get old, this is the place to do it."
With a touch of sadness, he thought, *Sorry, Lillie. Our
retirement fund'll never stretch this far.*

"Bet it costs a fortune," Tub Greene said, echoing
Ray's thoughts. "Where does a retired preacher get the
money for a place like this? Don't you have to buy
your apartment and then pay a monthly charge?"

"Maybe he has a wealthy son or something."

* * *

The curving roadways widened in various places, permitting those who could still drive to park near the entrances of their quarters. Ray eased the cruiser to a stop beneath tall rain-drenched oaks next to a small porch where an old man with stooped shoulders waited for them, alerted by the staff member who had given them directions.

"Come in, come in!" he called, urging them out of the rain as they splashed across the wet grass. "You'd be surprised how many people get lost trying to find me. But here you are!"

His long narrow face was made longer by a hairline that had receded to the crown of his head. The white hair across the top was so thin that his scalp shone through and he wore round rimless bifocals. Ray noticed a slight tremor in his hands when they shook.

Once inside and the introductions were over, he said, "I just made a fresh pitcher of lemonade. Let me get y'all some."

As Snaveley pottered with glasses, napkins, and a plate of oatmeal cookies—"They bake them fresh for us every day," he said—Ray reflected that the small room did have the cozy ambience of an Oxford don's study: oak desk and sturdy captain's chairs, floor-to-ceiling bookcases, a couch and wing chair upholstered in soft mellow colors. The rain that beat against the leaded panes of the tall mullioned windows only added to the coziness.

"I don't think we've met before," he told Ray, "but what about you, Deputy Greene? Any of your people ever attend Bethany?"

Tub shook his head.

Ray did not take offense. Things were slowly changing, but as Martin Luther King once observed: "The most segregated hour of Christian America is eleven o'clock on a Sunday morning." All those years and it was still true. If any of his family had sat in the Bethany congregation back when Snaveley was pastor, the old man would surely have remembered.

"Now how can I help you young fellows?" Snaveley asked.

Ray took a bite of the cookie. It was moist and chewy, studded with plump raisins. "We're trying to get a fix on who was in Rachel Morton's room last Wednesday and when they left."

"Our alibis?" The word seemed to amuse him.

"Well, take you, for instance," Ray said. "Mrs. Byrd says you and some others walked out of the hospital together?"

He nodded.

"So that alibis them, but then you went back into the hospital?"

"To use the restroom. Yes."

"Did you see anyone you knew when you came back out?"

"As a matter of fact, I did. At the next urinal. Marvin Galloway. We served on a church council together about twenty years ago. His granddaughter had just had a baby boy and he and his wife were on their way up to see her."

Tub jotted down Galloway's name. Snaveley thought he lived in Dobbs, but wasn't sure.

"Did you see anyone from Mrs. Morton's room when you went out to your car?"

"No, I'm sorry. Galloway's the only one I saw. Shocking to think that Rachel Morton was smothered like that so near to the natural end of her life."

"Can you think of any reason she was?" Ray asked.

"Not a thing. She was a fine woman. Of course, I hadn't seen much of her these last few years. Weddings and funerals, I'm afraid."

"We're thinking that perhaps someone was afraid she was going to say something damaging."

Snaveley frowned. "I doubt that. As I recall, Rachel loved to talk and tell stories, but never mean ones, and if there was anything embarrassing about her stories, she never gave enough details for you to figure out who she meant."

"We've heard that, too," Ray said, "but some of the things she talked about last week were things her family didn't recognize. I've got a list of them here. Maybe you could help us with them. How long were you there?"

"Twenty-six years."

"Not her church," said Ray. "In her room."

"Oh, sorry. I arrived a little after five and was there until the drink got spilled on the bed and we all left. Perhaps six thirty?"

Ray smoothed out one of the sheets Mayleen had given them. "She said that someone had signed what sounds like a promissory note, but that he never paid the debt. She mentioned that two or three times."

"A promissory note? No, that doesn't ring a bell."

"What about a cowbird egg?"

Snaveley's long face lit up with a gentle smile. "Human nature being what it is, that could apply to at least half a dozen families I've known over the years, but please don't ask me for names."

"Were any of them in Mrs. Morton's room that afternoon?"

He thought for a moment, then shook his head. "Not that I know of, but a lot of the people were strangers to me."

"She kept going back to that fire," Ray said.

"And the drowning," Tub added as he reached for a third cookie.

"Rachel's brothers? Yes, that happened before she married and moved her membership to Bethany, so I never knew those boys, but it did prey on her mind at times."

"Like the house that caught fire?"

"Such a tragedy. And so hard on Rachel because she had been over just that morning to take Jannie some tangerines. It was her family custom to buy a crate of them every Christmas and share them out. And then to look out her back window and see the house on fire? By the time she and her husband and the other neighbors got there, it was too late. Nobody could get through those flames. Heart pine, you know. Light-wood. Fat with resin. Might as well've been drenched in kerosene. Once heart pine starts burning, you can't put it out, and the nearest fire department was seven miles away."

Using both hands to steady the glass, the old man took a sip of his lemonade and carefully set it back on the tray. "Nearly killed her brother, too. Richard Howell. Rachel was the one called him. He blamed himself something awful that she was living in that firetrap. Kept saying he should have forgotten about medical school. Should have dropped out and got a job that would've helped Jannie and the girls live in a safe house. Thought he'd been selfish."

"Why?" asked Tub. "He didn't have anything to do with her husband leaving her, did he?"

"No, but people aren't always logical."

"What about the man who hit a woman?" asked Ray.

"Excuse me?"

"She said that some deacons put the fear of God in a man for hitting his wife."

Blank-faced, Snaveley said, "I didn't hear her say that, but then there were so many people in the room, I must have missed a lot. Did she give more details?"

"That was all. Did anything like that happen when you were her preacher? Did the deacons ever take someone to task for beating up on his wife?"

"You must remember that I left Bethany years ago. Have you spoken to her current minister? He was there, I believe."

"Not yet," said Ray.

The old man carefully lifted the glass pitcher with trembling hands and turned to Tub. "More lemonade, young man?"

As he poured, Ray put the first paper back in his pocket and took out the form Mayleen had devised.

"Sir, if you would, just put a check mark next to all the people you're sure were there when you were."

Snaveley set the pitcher back on the tray and wiped his damp hands on a napkin before taking the form. Minutes later, he handed it back with only four non-family names checked off.

"Like I said, I really didn't know many of them. Her minister, Richard Howell, and the Byrds, of course. Sam and Kitty. Hadn't seen them in a while so I mostly talked to them." His eyes went to the picture of a white-haired woman on his desk. "Kitty Byrd became a very dear friend of my late wife. Like us, they never had children either."

"No kids?" Tub was surprised. "But how—?" He broke off in confusion.

Snaveley looked at him over the top of his glasses. "How what, young man?"

"I'm sorry, sir, I don't mean to be nosy, but this looks like an expensive place to live and if you were a preacher and you don't have kids—"

He looked to Ray for help, but the older deputy kept a bland face and waited to see how Tub was going to get out of it.

Fortunately, Furman Snaveley chose to be amused.

"You're wondering how I could possibly afford Cameron Longview?"

Embarrassed, Tub nodded.

"Simple, Deputy Greene. I can't. It's by the generosity of Dr. Howell."

He leaned back in his chair, took off his glasses, and rubbed the bridge of his nose where they seemed to pinch him. "Richard credits me with keeping him sane in those dark days after the fire. I did nothing more than my pastoral duties, really, but I made him stay with my wife and me that Christmas. We took long walks together and I let him talk all the poison out of his system. Richard had always been a rather self-centered young man up until then. He wanted what he wanted and didn't seem to care who got hurt in the process. He felt entitled and I'm afraid his grandmother spoiled him after his parents died. Doted on him, in fact. Not that she didn't love Jannie, too, but he was the male. He was bright and he was ambitious and in her eyes he could do no wrong, an opinion he fully shared, and he didn't hide his light under a bushel either. If he made all A's in his high-school classes, he'd be sure you heard about it. Same with his scholarships and academic honors. He did the work, so he wanted the glory, and his grandmother certainly gave it to him. After the fire, he blamed himself for that, too. Thought that was why Jannie married so young, that she got tired of the comparisons."

He held his glasses up to the light, polished away a smudge, and put them back on. "His grief was so deep, he was ready to chuck it all and go dig ditches in Africa or something, but I was able to help him see how much good he could do in the world if he applied his talents to serving others, and you see how he's done that—the burn unit at the hospital, the pediatric wing, the scholarships he's funded, all in their memory. 'I'm like King Midas,' he told me once. 'I used to worship money. Now everything I touch turns to gold, but when it might have saved Jannie and her babies, I had nothing.'

"After I retired, my wife needed a couple of expensive operations and they wiped out our savings." He shook his head sadly. "Wouldn't it be the Christian thing to make medical care affordable for everyone?" He sighed. "She died anyhow and I was living on Social Security in a little apartment over in Boylan Heights, back of the prison. Richard came to see me. He'd heard about her death. When he saw that apartment...well, two weeks later, he brought me here. Wouldn't let me say no. Jannie's death was a tragedy, but at least some good came of it. It changed a selfish, self-centered boy into a generous philanthropist."

He smiled. "Not that he's a complete saint, mind you. He still likes recognition and praise, but he's certainly earned it, don't you think?"

And yet—? Furman Snaveley pushed aside the small troubling aspect that had suddenly occurred to him and said, "I'm sorry there aren't more cookies, but what about another glass of lemonade?"

* * *

"Thanks for coming in, Miss Collins," Mayleen said.

She had seen Amanda Collins when assembling the DVD from videos and snapshots taken last Wednesday, but the eighteen-year-old freshman was even prettier in person. Only five two, but her petite blonde beauty filled the room. Major Bryant and the others kept referring to cowbird eggs and she got the analogy, but Mayleen was country born and bred and she knew that cowbirds are plain and nondescript. This girl, with her long blonde hair, was like a small neat canary.

"No problem," Amanda said as she took the chair next to Mayleen's desk. "I was coming home today anyhow. My last exam was at ten o'clock this morning, so I'm finished until summer school starts next week."

She touched the screen of her phone and read the message that popped up. "Oops! My roommate says I left a pair of sandals in our room. Let me just tell her to keep them or toss them. Oh, and I need to let my dad know I'm running a little late."

She tapped the screen a few more times, then put the phone on mute and slid it into her purse, an expensive little green leather case with a long narrow strap. It matched the simple green-striped knit top she wore over plain white cotton slacks. They were equally expensive and equally understated.

"Sorry," she said, "but you know how dads worry."

"Sure," said Mayleen, whose own dad hadn't cared enough to come to her wedding and who would probably make comments about half-breeds when he heard about the baby.

Again, she explained about the need for cross-checking alibis and gave Amanda the form she had devised.

"I'm sorry," the girl said again, "but I really didn't know any of these people, just Miss Rachel. See, what happened was, my car was burning oil, so I drove it down to the dealership in Fayetteville and Dad was going to drive me back to school."

"Meredith College, right?"

"Yes, ma'am. I sort of wanted to go to Appalachian, but Dad talked me into staying closer to home for my first year and he was right. I would've been so homesick way off there in the mountains."

Her smile was rueful. "I guess I really am a daddy's girl. And with Mom and Talmadge both gone, he would've been homesick for me as well, so this lets us do it gradually."

"Talmadge?"

"My brother. He's a musician. Lives in Glasgow so we don't get to see much of him except when Dad has business there."

"You must miss him," Mayleen said sympathetically.

"Dad does." A shadow passed over that pretty face. "He's sixteen years older and we were never very close. Actually, he thinks I'm a spoiled brat and I think he's a jerk."

She looked down at the paper in her hand. "I'm really no help here. Dad and I were about to leave when somebody spilled a drink on poor Miss Rachel and we all cleared out. He stopped to talk to somebody out in the vestibule for a few minutes—a Dr. Howell?—and then he wanted to go downstairs to ask somebody's opinion about who the governor's going to back to replace our state representative." Her tone turned indulgent. "Dad's a political junkie, and since I didn't know any of those people I told him I'd meet him back at the car. He swore he'd only be a few minutes, but it was more like half an hour. We didn't hear about Miss Rachel till the next day."

"How did y'all know her?"

"My school was near Dad's work and he drove me back and forth, so we passed by her vegetable stand on our way home. He grew up on a farm and he loved to sit and talk to her. He liked for me to hear her, too. Dad's always been big on family and heritage and since all my own grandparents were gone, I guess he thought Miss Rachel could give me an idea of what his mother had been like." She twisted a strand of bright gold hair into a tight coil and her blue eyes were sad. "She was so sweet to me. Fed me strawberries in the spring, then sent me blueberries and watermelons in the summer. It was a real shock when Dad told me what had happened."

"You say you saw Dr. Howell out in the vestibule. Did he go downstairs with your dad?"

She shook her head and that coil of bright hair slowly unwound itself. "No, ma'am. A nurse came to ask him something and he went down the other hall with her."

The *ma'am*s were starting to make Mayleen feel ancient. "Did you see anyone from the hospice room when you were leaving?"

"I saw a woman in the restroom across the hall, but like I said, I didn't know any of them. Just Miss Rachel. Well, I had met her son and daughter back when I was a kid, but I think they went downstairs when the others did. I just sat in the car and waited for Dad. My friends and I were texting back and forth."

"What about this man?" Mayleen showed her a picture of Furman Snaveley.

Amanda Collins shook her head. "Sorry. I'm afraid I was looking at my screen the whole time. You know how it is."

Dwight returned from Cotton Grove as Amanda Collins was leaving. Ray McLamb and Tub Greene rolled in a few minutes later so that the four of them were able to bring each other up to date on what they'd learned from their interviews.

Most interesting to the three deputies was to hear that Billy Thornton had probably cut the rope swing and caused Jacob Knott to fall to his death.

"I'll talk to the DA tomorrow," Dwight said, "but I'm pretty sure he'll agree that it would be pointless to arrest a man who can't remember what he had for breakfast."

"So Rachel Morton's death had nothing to do with her brother's?" asked Tub, trying to get it straight in his head.

"Doesn't look like it. Did you two get an alibi for that preacher?"

Ray shook his head. "He confirms that the Byrds left immediately after the drink was spilled, but he did go back inside to use the facilities. He gave us the name of a man who was at the next urinal and we'll go talk to him tomorrow if you like, but that guy went upstairs to meet his first great-grandson and Snaveley says he went out to his car without seeing anyone he recognized.

"We asked him about those other things on the list. He couldn't tell us about a debt or a wife-beater. He's known some cases where fathers were raising kids that weren't theirs, but he wouldn't name names."

"Tell him about Dr. Howell," Tub said.

"He's the one paying for Snaveley's cushy retirement place," said Ray, and repeated everything that the old man had told them about Richard Howell's crushing guilt after his sister's death.

"You ever gonna tell us why Snaveley's in the running?" asked Mayleen.

"I'm not trying to shut y'all out," Dwight said, "but it's something embarrassing that happened forty or fifty years ago and no point in repeating it till it's relevant. If you can't definitely alibi him and nobody else looks good for it, then we'll zero in on him. In the meantime, do we have alibis for Howell and Collins?"

"Judge Knott and her cousin Sally Crenshaw alibi Collins," said Mayleen, "and she saw his daughter leave." She gave them the details. "As for Howell, both

Mrs. Crenshaw and the Collins girl say he never went down to the family room because a nurse snagged him at the top of the stairs and they went over to the other side of the hospital."

"Write it all up," Dwight told them, "and let's keep checking all the alibis."

"What about family?" asked Ray. "I don't mean to be out of line, but—" He gave a hands-out shrug.

"No, you're right, Ray. Everyone's a suspect. Except that they all were down in the family room, according to my wife. Some of the kids left early, but none of them drove away alone."

He turned to leave, then remembered the other cases they were working. "That flash drive you got from one of the break-in victims. Any luck with that picture?"

"Not yet, Boss. I gave copies to the uniforms and they're canvassing the Black Creek area."

CHAPTER
25

*Premeditated wrongs are often the result of ap-
prehension, the aggressor fearing that he will
be the victim if he does not strike the first blow.*

— Cicero

Rain was still falling when I left court on Wednesday afternoon. As soon as I got home, Dwight and I drove over to the homeplace. Dwight had given me the bare bones of his interview with Billy Thornton and the response he'd gotten with the music I'd downloaded (who knew Bing Crosby ever sang country?), but over at the homeplace, he fleshed out the story of Jacob's death for Daddy, who listened grimly.

"Billy cut the rope so he could have Letha to himself?"

"I'm afraid so, Mr. Kezzie."

"Now he's senile and Letha's dead."

"Yessir."

"And you're sure none of their people had anything to do with killing Rachel?"

"The only one with a link to either of them that we can find was that orderly I told you about. Letha's grandson. He says he didn't know she had any connection to Miss Rachel and I believe him. Besides, at least four different witnesses saw him delivering dinner trays in a hall at the other end of the hospital during the relevant time."

"Well, I'm real sorry nobody's gonna go to prison for what they done to Jacob, but I sure hope it ain't gonna be another sixty years before we know what happened to Rachel."

"It won't," Dwight said firmly. "Back then, you thought Jacob's death was an accident. We know for a fact that this is murder."

Daddy stood up and reached for the straw Panama he wears from April to October. "I appreciate y'all coming and telling me, Dwight, Deb'rah. Now I reckon I better go let Sister know."

"Want me to come with you?" I asked.

"Naw. I expect her and me'll want to do some long remembering about Jacob and Jedidiah."

"It's supposed to keep raining till morning," I argued.

"I been driving in rain for seventy years," he said harshly. "*And* at night."

"Daddy—"

He cut off my apology with a softened tone. "Don't worry, daughter. If it's dark and raining real hard, I'll just stay the night with her."

I stood on tiptoes to kiss his leathery cheek, then

Dwight and I walked out with him and we hurried through the rain to our trucks. Dwight turned his toward a lane that would lead back to our house, while Daddy headed for the road toward Fuquay.

"It's okay," Dwight said as the windshield wipers slapped back and forth. "He's got the eyesight of a hawk."

"Hawks don't fly at night," I said bleakly. "Or in the rain."

"He'll be fine, honey. Seth'll let us know when it's time to start hiding his keys."

"You think?"

"I know. Somebody follows him home at night about twice a month."

That surprised me. "They do?"

He reached over and squeezed my hand. "You're not the only one living out here that worries about him."

Thursday and Friday passed uneventfully. Uneventfully for Dwight, anyhow. His deputies were out canvassing every name on the master list. Mayleen had drawn up a large chart to cross-reference who was where after Lois Boone left Aunt Rachel. Black lines had been drawn through the names that had at least two separate confirmations but it was slow work.

And no luck, so far, on that photo that one of the break-in victims had given Ray McLamb.

As for me, the rains finally stopped on Thursday, the sun came out, and on Friday, Portland sent a message up to my courtroom urgently asking me to come to her office during my lunch break. "Salads on the deck," she'd written.

When I got there, she and a clerk were in the process of sorting through fifteen years' worth of client files, deciding which she and Avery would take with them and which would go into storage.

Like Lee & Stephenson, Brewer & Brewer occupied a remodeled house. Theirs was plain vanilla brick, though, vintage 1960, and more than a block away from the courthouse.

"Found a buyer yet?" I asked as Portland took two clear plastic containers from the refrigerator in the kitchen and we went out to the shady back deck, which was furnished with white patio furniture. The air was still humid and it frizzled her short dark hair into tight little curls all over her head.

"One strong nibble," she said. "Joyce Mitchell and her partners are interested."

Normally this would merit a good ten minutes dissecting Joyce and her law practice and which rung they occupied in the local bar's pecking order, but Portland seemed distracted. She had brought out silverware but forgot drinks and napkins.

I fetched the pitcher of iced tea. "What's up? Avery's not joining us?"

He often did when we had lunch on the deck. Dwight, too, if he could get away.

"He had to go to Charlotte. I don't want to tell him anyhow. In fact, I really shouldn't even be talking to you about this, but my head's going to explode if I don't tell somebody."

I didn't remind her that we've always trusted each other with our deepest secrets, even up to the point of technically breaching attorney-client confidentiality if it was something troubling. Instead, I snapped the lid off my salad and drizzled raspberry vinaigrette over the baby spinach, blue cheese, walnuts, and dried cranberries. "Tell me what?"

"Tuesday night. Remember I said that Mrs. McElveen's rewriting her will because her niece, the one that stayed with her after her car accident, had died?"

I nodded.

"And you remember how Avery said if Mrs. McElveen had executed a durable power of attorney for financial management, her niece didn't have to die for her to keep control?"

"So?"

"So he was right, even though that's not what he meant. She probably wouldn't have died."

"Huh?"

"I think Mrs. McElveen killed her."

"What?"

"Shh," Portland said. "Keep your voice down. The whole neighborhood doesn't have to know and certainly not our clerks."

"She killed her caregiver? Her own niece? She told you this?"

"Not in those words, but yes. I think so."

"Think?" My voice was rising again. I couldn't help

it. This was one of the leading citizens of Dobbs. This was Laurel Foster McElveen, a woman who sat on half the important boards in town.

"You remember how she seemed to be losing it? Stopped going to board meetings? Quit going to therapy for her legs? Acted depressed? Drifting in a fog?"

I nodded.

"Then the niece died."

"I remember."

"When I saw Mrs. McElveen after the funeral last week, she was back in the land of the living. Cogent, sharp, ready to whip this town into shape. And the first thing she wanted to do was rewrite her will, disinherit the remaining nieces and a nephew."

"Nothing odd about that," I said.

"Right. But when Avery said what he did, it got me thinking. Because she told me last week that her niece had wanted her to sign an irrevocable POA and that if Evelyn hadn't died so *fortuitously*, she might have done it because she'd almost lost her ability to concentrate and make decisions."

"Fortuitously?" I asked, trying to spear a walnut with my fork.

"Fortuitously."

"Okay, not the term most people would use for the death of a niece, Por, but hardly grounds to suspect murder."

Portland brushed away a curious yellow jacket that had buzzed over to land on a melon cube in her fruit salad. "I know, I know. But there was something about the way she said it. Her niece did have heart problems. In fact, she was due to get a stent put in next month, which is probably why her doctor signed the death certificate without an autopsy. Her mother died young, too. Heart attack for both of them, Mrs. McElveen said. Today, though, she asked if you can tell someone's been poisoned once the body was cremated, and I told her no. You can't, can you?"

"I don't think so."

"So then I flat-out asked her if she thought her niece had been murdered, and guess what she said?"

"You're fired?"

Portland didn't smile. "No, she said it was probably an unintentional suicide. 'Because'—and I quote— 'surely it isn't murder if someone switches drinks with the person who poured them.'"

I nearly choked on my salad. "She *didn't*!"

"She did. So what do I do now, Deborah? Even if I wanted to violate attorney-client privilege and told Dwight, what could he do?"

I was stumped. There are hundreds of substances that can cloud a person's cognitive powers, thousands that can kill someone with a weak heart, but unless it's something commonly used, like ethanol or a heavy metal, testing for an unknown is like trying to catch lightning bugs blindfolded. And that's if you have a body.

"Cremated?" I asked.

"Cremated," Portland said. "*And* the ashes are going to be scattered tomorrow."

"Wow!" I said. "That's fast."

We batted it around for another twenty minutes while finishing lunch, but in the end, there was really nothing that could be done. Even if Dwight were to get another judge to sign a search warrant and turn Mrs. McElveen's house inside out, even if he were to find the poison, if poison it was and not a prescription for something as innocuous as sleeping pills or allergy medicine, there would be no way to prove anything without a body.

"You going to keep her on as a client?" I asked.

"Why not? Do you know how much we bill her for every year? Thank God she's never asked us over for drinks."

CHAPTER
26

In order to give pleasure to the audience, the actor need not finish the play...nor need the wise man remain on the stage till the closing plaudit.

— Cicero

At breakfast on Saturday morning, I asked Dwight if I could still borrow his truck that day.

He looked at me blankly.

"Girls' day out. Will's auction," I reminded him. "Mrs. Lattimore's estate sale. That end table I liked."

"But we're building the pond shed today. Can't you stick it in the trunk of your car? Haywood thinks we need another roll of tarpaper and I forgot to figure in the overhang when I ordered tin for the roof."

"There will be at least four other trucks here today if you need to run to a lumber yard or building supply place," I said. "Barbara and April saw some things on Will's website that they're interested in and if they buy, we'll need a truck to get everything home."

Reluctantly, he handed over his keys. Married almost two years and this would be the first time I'd driven his truck when he wasn't in it.

April and Barbara both laughed when I told them about the pained expression on Dwight's face as I left. "Like he was saying goodbye to a faithful horse he never really expects to see again," I said.

"Andrew's just as bad," said April, who was squinched in the middle between us with her feet on the hump because her legs were shorter than Barbara's. "He keeps saying that old truck of his is a work mule, but let me put the tiniest little dent in the fender?"

"Zach doesn't have a truck," Barbara said, "but don't ask to borrow any of his power tools."

"Well, that's sorta how I feel about *my* power tools," said April, who may teach language skills at the local middle school but could hire out tomorrow as a skilled carpenter.

She had her eye on that stained glass panel Will had mentioned, while Barbara said she was just along for the ride, "Although Karen asked me to try to get that Rebecca pitcher by Nell Cole Graves if it goes for under three hundred."

Karen is married to Adam, Zach's twin, and they live in California, but she's been collecting Seagrove pottery ever since Mother gave her a Jugtown vase the first Christmas after they were married and still living in a singlewide at the far side of the farm while they were getting their degrees in computer engineering at

State. (Their current home has five bedrooms and an infinity pool, but Karen hasn't gotten above her raising. Adam? That's another story.)

The parking lot at Will's was crowded and the street out front was lined with cars, one of which was a limo with tinted windows and a Maryland license plate. A hefty uniformed chauffeur sat behind the steering wheel in a visored black cap and mirror sunglasses. It was not the only car with out-of-state plates, but it was certainly the most expensive. Although it wasn't that hot here at nine o'clock in the morning, the chauffeur had the motor running for the air conditioning.

The auction wasn't due to start till ten, but like so many others, we had come early so that we could examine the offerings and decide what we wanted to spend.

Will's major Lattimore sale would be next Saturday when her more valuable antiques and collectibles would go on the block. Today was to prime the pump, he said. "If they know I consider this stuff the odds and ends, it'll whet their appetites for what's to come."

This was the first auction I'd been to since the old warehouse burned and I was impressed by how professional he'd become. It was a long way from flea markets and hauling trash. For starters, he and his staff all wore identical dark blue golf shirts with a Knott Auctions logo embroidered on the pocket. Four wooden church pews had cushions of the same blue, and folding metal chairs had been spray-painted that color, too. From the setup, they seemed to be expecting about two hundred people. The walls were reclaimed 1960s paneling that had been painted white to make a background for pictures, mirrors, and other decorative wall ornaments.

The catalog consisted of ten or twelve sheets of copy paper stapled at the corner, with thumbnail descriptions of each lot. After we had registered at the front desk and procured numbered paddles so we could bid, April immediately zeroed in on the wall that held the stained glass.

"Look at that beveled mirror, Barbara," she said, pulling out her tape measure. "Isn't that exactly what you've been looking for to brighten up the back hall by Emma's room?"

While they went off to measure the mirror, I wandered over to look at the displays on the counters that lined two sides of the auction room. Items were grouped on numbered trays. Lot #31, for instance, consisted of a china wash basin, pitcher, and shaving mirror, circa 1900, while Lot #32 was a dozen mismatched brass candlesticks of varying heights and no date. I paused at a locked glass case that held good-quality costume jewelry and saw three women eyeing some Celtic-looking brooches made of glass and small chunky stones. Lot #26.

One of the women waved a vigilant staff member over and asked to see the pieces up close to verify that everything was intact and without repairs. It was Jody Munger, one of the women who had sat on last week's jury and had clearly been unimpressed with the plaintiff's Hummel expert.

"Hey, Judge," she said as she unlocked the case and took out the brooches. "You collect Miracle pins, too?"

"Is that what they are?"

The first woman opened a loose-leaf notebook with plastic sleeves that held colored pictures of costume jewelry, and she compared what looked like a dagger-shaped pin of yellow and brown stones to one of the pictures. I heard her murmur to her friends, "Nineteen-sixties."

When she realized that I had overheard, she snapped the notebook shut and handed the brooch back to Jody before walking away with the other two, their heads close together.

"Are they valuable?" I asked.

Jody smiled as she returned the brooch to its tray and locked the case. "Not especially. Once in a while, a Miracle piece might bring a hundred dollars, but these you could buy on eBay for no more than fifteen to thirty each. She's afraid you might be a collector who would run up the price."

"Not me," I said. "I've never collected anything."

"Really? No Hummel figurines or hobnail milk glass?"

I shook my head, laughing. "No Barbie dolls or baseball cards either."

"You're lucky. Once the collecting fever hits, reason can fly out the window. So what are you here for to-day?"

I described the end table that had interested me.

She pointed toward the front. "Furniture's over in

the left corner. I'd come show you, but I can't leave my post. We'd like to think that none of the customers have sticky fingers, but you'd be surprised."

I shook my head. "Nothing in that line surprises me anymore."

I made my way through the growing crowd to where Will was. As I approached, another man got to him at the same time. Will reached out and put an arm around me. "Hey, baby sister. You ever meet Rusty here? Rusty, this is my sister Deborah."

The man's thick hair was more gray than red now, but he had a redhead's florid coloring and offered me an easy handshake. "Glad to meet you, ma'am."

He wore a gold ring with a large diamond on the pinkie finger of his beefy right hand, and a gold chain flashed at the open collar of his golf shirt.

"Rusty's my competition, so don't feel you have to be nice to him," said Will, talking trash with a smile.

"Rusty Alexander?" I asked. "Alexander Auctions over in Widdington?"

A pleased smile spread across his broad face. "You've heard of us?"

I nodded. "Oh yes. I didn't realize that auctioneers attended other people's auctions."

"Like your brother says, gotta keep up with the competition. You're getting a nice crowd, bo. I even saw a limo outside. Maryland plates."

"Limo?" asked Will. "Whoa! I didn't know I had any limo owners on my mailing list. I must be moving up. Wonder what he's here for?"

The other man's eyes narrowed. "You ever hear of a man named Dawson Bridges? From Baltimore?"

"Dawson Bridges?" Will rolled that name over his tongue, then shook his head. "He one of your clients?"

"We've done business before but I've never met him. He always phones in his bids. Just wondered if that's him."

"What's his interest?"

Rusty hesitated. "He's a big gun enthusiast. I see you have one on the block today."

As he walked away through the crowd, I almost told Will he was probably lying. But then Will was probably lying, too, so I asked where the end table was and went over to look at it. As he'd said, it was a nice piece but no antique. According to the description in the catalog, it was a circa-1940 reproduction of a Louis XVI table, mahogany with brass drawer pull and tapered fluted legs. No nicks or dings, and the wood was mellow from years of furniture polish. Perfect to sit beside the lounge chair in our bedroom. The drawer opened and closed smoothly and would hold my manicure set and cotton balls for when I wanted to watch a video and do my nails while Dwight and Cal watched a ball game in the living room.

At a few minutes before ten, people started finding seats. As the crush around the front entrance thinned, the door opened and the uniformed chauffeur I'd seen earlier maneuvered a wheelchair through the double doors. A small cylinder of oxygen was attached to the rear of the chair and the old man in the chair wore a nasal cannula that was barely visible beneath a broad-brimmed summer hat that obscured his face. A nurse in white slacks and a crisp white lab coat followed. The old man in the chair reached out with his cane and hooked the arm of a staff member. Evidently he was asking where a certain item was, because the staffer pointed to a nearby case. Immediately, the old man's chauffeur pushed him over.

April and Barbara were signaling me to join them in one of the front pews, but I saw Rusty Alexander drifting over to that area. Curious, I drifted over, too. Someone in the Lattimore line must have been a sportsman, because I saw a bundle of fishing rods, a twelve-gauge shotgun, a rusty bear trap, a couple of old duck decoys, a rabbit box made of unpainted wood, and a mounted deer head with an eight-point rack. The shotguns were locked inside the glass case, the deer head hung on the wall, the bear trap, decoys, and rabbit box had been left atop the counter, which meant, I was coming to learn, that they were of only nominal value, decorative items to furnish someone's fishing lodge or hunting camp. I wasn't sure what the old man was most interested in, but he did look at the underside of both decoys and he examined the eyes with a pocket magnifier.

Through the loudspeaker at the podium, Will announced that the auction was about to begin and asked that everyone take a seat.

The old man placed the decoys back where he'd found them, and as he was wheeled away, Rusty

Alexander stepped forward and took a look at the decoy undersides himself.

"What are you looking for?" I asked.

He smiled, turned them over, and held them out to me. "Tell me what you see."

Both had been hunted over in the past because they were pitted with shotgun pellets. One was a weathered green and worn on the bottom, the other was in better condition with well-defined black feathers, a white spot on its head, and touches of orange on its white bill. On that one, initials had been scratched in near the tail.

"HN?"

"Yeah, that's what I see, too."

"Who's HN?" asked a familiar voice, and I turned to see my cousin Sally. Today she wore the newsboy cap and its fringe of black curls with short white shorts that showed off her remarkably shapely legs.

Her question was directed at me, but Rusty Alexander answered. "I collect decoys, but I never heard of an HN. Y'all interested in them?"

"Not me," I said, but Sally shrugged. "I've got a place at Crenshaw's Lake that I'm redecorating. These would look good over the bar if they don't go too high."

"Don't get your hopes up," he said. "See that old guy in the wheelchair? I'm not sure, but if he's Dawson Bridges, these are what he drove down from Maryland for."

"Really?" said Sally.

Before she could question him further, he walked

away and we turned our attention to the front, where Will stood at the podium.

"Welcome to today's auction," he said. "You must have a paddle to bid. Everybody have a catalog?"

Several hands shot up and staff members quickly passed out extra copies. I slipped into a pew in the second row beside Barbara and April, who had saved me a seat.

"As most of you know," Will continued, "everything up for sale today came from the Lattimore house over in Cotton Grove. The house was built in eighteen-seventy by Aaron Lattimore, a prominent businessman of the day, and has remained in the family ever since. The Lattimores had money and they had taste, as you can see by what's here." A sweep of his arm took in the walls and cabinets. "Although the Lattimores kept pretty good records of their major purchases over the years, these lesser items are undocumented, so let me make it crystal clear that everything is being sold 'as is.' We've tried to identify makers and age where we could, but it's caveat emptor and all sales are final. Are you ready?"

Happy murmurs of anticipation arose around me.

"Lot number one," Will said. "Solid brass floor lamp. Probably made in the nineteen-thirties. Who'll give me five?"

"Five!" cried a voice from somewhere in the back.

"Ten!" said a woman in front of me, and Will immediately went into his auctioneer mode, chanting the prices as he urged them on, flirting with the woman on the front row.

"Ten, ten, who'll give me fifteen?"

"Fifteen," said a man behind me.

"Now it's twenty over there. Can you go twenty-five? Do I hear twenty-five? Twenty-five? Thank you, sir! Do I hear thirty? Thirty? Thank you, ma'am. I've got thirty here on the front row, do I hear thirty-five? Thirty-five, sir? Can you go thirty-five? He's shaking his head. All in? All done? *Sold* to the little lady here for thirty dollars. What's your number, darlin'?"

Flushed with success, the woman held up her paddle and Will repeated her number for the two staff members at the desk who were keeping track of who bought what and for how much.

With so many items to get through, Will kept things moving briskly and did not waste a lot of time trying to cajole more bids once it was clear that the interested parties had reached their limits.

Several people competed for the stained glass panel, but once the bid passed a hundred, the field narrowed to April and two others. She persisted and it was hers for two-twenty.

Karen was luckier. Barbara was able to get her the signed Rebecca pitcher for seventy-five. Unfortunately, the beveled mirror Barbara herself wanted went for twice what she was willing to pay, although she did wind up winning an assortment of badly tarnished sterling silver picture frames, all with their glass missing.

"No prob," said April. "Picture frames come in standard sizes, so go to a dollar store, throw away the plastic frames, and you've got your glass."

The woman who collected Miracle pins got three of them for forty dollars and looked happy, but her friend lost out on a small bronze reproduction of a Roman god that some long-dead Lattimore must have picked up in Italy.

A bidding war broke out between two dealers over a 1928 Seth Thomas mantel clock. The clock was pretty and it did chime, but the catalog clearly stated that the glass front and one of the hands were replacements, something Will felt compelled to repeat aloud when the bidding passed six hundred. It went for eight-fifty.

To my complete and utter surprise, I got the end table for fifty-five. Sally was the only one who offered a bid on the deer head, and the old rabbit box was hers for another five dollars as well, which encouraged her to go after the two decoys.

Before the bidding could start on them, a staffer in one of those blue shirts handed Will a flat plastic bag with a small slip of torn paper inside. Will looked at it, then said, "Ladies and gentlemen, one of my staff has just reminded me that we found this receipt stuck in one of the Lattimore account books and it will go to whoever takes the decoys. I can't guarantee that this receipt is for these ducks, but it's dated December 9, 1898. The top's torn, so best I can tell it's from Hancock Hardware, Morehead City." He held it up and read aloud, "*One box twelve-gauge shells, $1.25. 2 decoys, $1.50. Total, $2.75.*"

He smiled at the crowd. "Now let's see if we can't get more than a dollar-fifty for these two ducks."

Rusty Alexander hadn't been kidding when he told Sally not to get her hopes up. No messing around with five-dollar increments. I was astonished to hear an opening bid of five hundred dollars, and it was fifty dollars a bid after that. Soon it was by hundreds and Will was looking equally astonished. When it passed three thousand, everyone was twisting around in their seats to see who was bidding.

After what Rusty Alexander had said, I was not surprised to see that he was one of the bidders, and I had to look closely to see the almost imperceptible nod from the old man in the wheelchair, but what surprised me most was to see that the third determined bidder was Ned O'Donnell, one of our superior court judges.

Ned hung in till the twenty-thousand mark. At twenty-seven, the old man straightened up in his chair as if he sensed he'd won. Rusty Alexander hesitated as Will chanted, "All in? All done? Final call—"

"Twenty-eight!" Alexander shouted.

As if annoyed, the old man prodded his chauffeur with his cane and was quickly wheeled out the door to his limo.

"Sold!" Will said, looking slightly dazed. "All yours, Rusty."

The crowd erupted in spontaneous applause. As the entourage from Maryland passed, I took a second look at his nurse. Amazing how much it changed a young woman's appearance to forgo lipstick, put her hair in a severe bun, and add oversize horn-rimmed glasses. Kaitlyn Lancaster?

And that stocky man in a chauffeur's uniform with visored cap and mirrored sunglasses? I could see only his back now as they went through the door, but I had heard a familiar squeak when he passed. With the cuffs of his black pants falling across his instep, his black socks and black leather sandals could almost pass for dress shoes.

I searched the crowd with my eyes. Near the back, Marillyn Mulholland beamed at JoAnn Bonner and her aunt, and Sally had a cat-who-ate-the-canary grin on her face.

After all that, it was hard to get the crowd to settle down, and Barbara scored a charming three-drawer oak chest for peanuts.

When Will brought his hammer down on the final lot, it was a quarter past one and I was more than ready for lunch. Barbara and April went off to pay and collect their booty and I made my way over to Will, who was talking to Judge O'Donnell. I got there in time to hear Will say, "What'd I miss, Judge? I don't know decoys, but I looked online and I couldn't find any collectible decoy carver in eastern North Carolina with the initials HN."

"That's because it wasn't HN," said Ned. "It was HW. A carver named Hanley Willis used to sign his ducks like that—slanting uprights with a crossbar between the first two. Mostly he carved redheads. We know of a couple of pintails, one ruddy duck, and one green-winged teal, but this is the only known example of a Hanley Willis drake surf scoter. When I saw the picture of those initials and saw that speck of white in the eyes, I was really hoping nobody else would notice. Especially not ol' Rusty there, but I should've known it was too good to be true. Don't feel bad, Knott. He may have gotten a bargain, but you got a fair price for a piece that hasn't been market tested."

As he walked away, I glared at Will. "And what would you have done if Ned had outbid Alexander?"

"What do you mean?" he asked, all wide-eyed innocence.

"You know damn well what I mean. That was old Spencer Lancaster in that wheelchair, not some Maryland decoy collector."

Will shrugged. "I told him to keep bidding till I rubbed my nose. If Rusty dropped out first, he'd have kept on bidding. I know better than to try to con a judge." He hugged me with a big grin on his face. "You either, honey."

CHAPTER
27

...he may be old in body, but will never be so in mind.

— Cicero

We stopped for lunch at a grill on the edge of Dobbs, so it was 2:30 before we got back to the farm. April and I dropped Barbara and the oak chest she'd scored off at her house, then drove on over to the pond, where Andrew and some of my other brothers were. I hadn't been down to the site since last weekend when it was nothing but a concrete slab. Now the shelter was nearly finished.

"Wow!" said April. "Look how much they got done."

Not only was it completely framed in pressure-treated 2x4s, there were waist-high walls on three sides, a full wall at the back, and a low-pitched roof covered with sheets of tin. A first coat of stain had been applied to all the wood. As soon as it dried and a second coat was added, they would hang the double screen doors at the front and screen in the sides to make a shady, mosquito-proof place to gather on summer afternoons and evenings.

Annie Sue or Reese must have stopped by after I left, because electrical outlets had been roughed in on all four sides and wires dangled from the ceiling where a fan would eventually go.

Dwight and Andrew were cutting strips of molding for the screens when we drove down the slope but Dwight paused and walked over to where I'd parked beside Andrew's truck. I nudged April. "He's making sure I didn't bust the headlights or dent the fenders."

She swung down from the cab. "You gonna tell him about the taillight?"

"Tell him what?" Dwight asked.

Even though we were both laughing, he still stepped around to the back to check. "I see you got your table."

"And I got my stained glass," April told Andrew.

He and Dwight shifted her panel into the back of his truck.

"Y'all eat?" April asked.

"Yeah, Dwight bought us dinner at the barbecue house."

"Least I could do with all the free work I'm getting," said Dwight.

April looked longingly at the saws and hammers. "Hope you left something for me to do."

"I don't suppose you want to miter the molding for us?"

"Sure. Just let me go change out of this dress and fetch my miter saw."

Cal had waved to me when I arrived, but he and Mary Pat and Jake were busy watching Haywood. As April drove off, I walked over to watch, too.

"He's making us slingshots," Cal explained as Haywood finished attaching rubber strips cut from an old inner tube to the last of three Y-shaped limbs off a hickory tree.

"Y'all didn't have no leather laying around, so I had to make the patches outen duck tape," he told me, giving the finished slingshot an experimental pull.

The kids had set up a row of scrap 2x4s some yards away.

"Let's see if I've still got an eye," Haywood said. He put a small rock in the patch, then pulled back, sighting through the tips of the Y. When he released it, one of the scrap pieces immediately flipped over.

Homemade slingshots are a farm kid's first weapon and soon the three of them were firing away at the targets.

"Now listen here," Haywood said sternly before he turned them loose and armed. "You got to pay attention where you're aiming and mind what's behind that. Don't never aim at another person and watch out for windows and trucks. You can shoot at all the tree rats and crows you want, but not any songbirds or lizards or frogs."

"What about snakes?" Mary Pat asked.

"Oh yeah!" Cal exclaimed. "Guess what, Mom?

Bandit found a copperhead in the garden and we chopped it in two."

"You're sure it was a copperhead and not a corn snake?" I'm not crazy about any snake, but I don't believe in killing harmless ones.

"No, Aunt Deb'rah," Mary Pat said earnestly. "It was a copperhead, all right. It had a triangular head. Uncle Dwight saw it, too."

Dwight nodded. "It was a copperhead."

"What'd you do with him?" asked Haywood, and I saw Andrew try to hide a grin.

"We buried him," said Jake.

"*How* did you bury him? Which way was his head facing?"

Cal shrugged.

"Why?" asked Mary Pat. "What difference does that make?"

"What difference?" Haywood looked outraged. "Deb'rah, you telling me these young'uns don't know about burying snakes? What kind of mama you call yourself?"

He turned back to the wide-eyed children. "You better make sure he's facing west, because if you buried him facing east"—he shook his head—"soon as he sees the sun come up, he's gonna crawl right out of the ground and come looking for who killed him."

Startled, Cal looked up at me. "Is that true, Mom?"

"I never had one come crawling for me," I said with a straight face and complete honesty, "but I always made sure I buried them facing west myself."

"Get the hoe," said Mary Pat, and the three of them took off toward the garden while Haywood sat back laughing.

"First time me and Herman killed a snake, Robert and Frank like to've scared us to death telling us that. We was already in bed and I reckon we lay awake half the night thinking it was coming for us. Next day, we dug it up and by pure chance, his head was facing west. Was you there, Andrew?"

"Probably, but I don't remember," said our brother.

"Anyhow, Robert and Frank said that proved it. Iffen it'd been the other way, they said we'd be dead."

"All I know is if Cal has nightmares tonight," Dwight told me, "you're the one getting up with him."

"Right after I call Haywood and wake him up," I promised.

Nevertheless, by the time I took Mary Pat and Jake home, the kids knew that we'd been teasing them, although six-year-old Jake was still glad they'd made sure that copperhead was reburied in the correct position, just in case.

After Cal was asleep, Dwight put on the DVD Mayleen had assembled and stretched out on the couch to watch it again with his head in my lap. That couch is one of the few things he brought from his apartment and I love it. A rich brown leather and a full ninety inches long, it's really the best piece in our living room, which is furnished in family castoffs for the most part. I keep thinking I should let Barbara and April redecorate, but in truth,

I've pretty much decided that we value comfort over beauty and the couch is very comfortable. All three of us fit on it. On Sundays when we don't go to church, Dwight and Cal can lie at one end and I can curl up with some of my casework at the other end and nobody's crowded.

"I keep thinking we've missed something," Dwight said. He fast-forwarded through the still photos to play the parts where we could hear Aunt Rachel actually speaking.

Once again, we listened as she wept over Jacob's death and for the death of Richard Howell's sister and nieces. We heard her concern over unpaid debts and domestic violence and her amusement that someone didn't realize he was parenting another's child.

"You haven't found the answers to any of these questions?" I asked.

He touched the pause button. "Promise you won't repeat any of this? Not even to Portland?"

This wasn't the first time either of us had extracted such a promise since we'd married, and of course I'd made him promise to keep it to himself when I told him how Will and the Designated Daughters had scammed Rusty Alexander that morning.

"The domestic violence was Furman Snaveley."

"The preacher? And he reformed after the deacons talked to him?"

"I gather they used a rather forceful argument, but yes, he learned to control his temper and changed his ways for good. We still haven't fully confirmed his whereabouts during the time Miss Rachel was left alone, but I'd be surprised if it was him."

"Who got the cowbird egg?"

"That was Jim Collins."

"Oh? So that pretty little blonde that was with him is his goldfinch and I'm one of their alibis, right?"

Dwight nodded.

"I'm glad he's been ruled out. He's a staunch Democrat."

"I've arrested a lot of Democrats," he reminded me with a big yawn as he pressed the play button on the remote.

By the time Aunt Rachel got to unpaid debts for the third time and how some little boy ate all the chocolates in two Easter baskets, he was gone. I caught the remote as it slid from his fingers and heard her laughter over bathing suits that turned transparent in water. Hazel Upchurch, Jay-Jay had said, but neither she nor her husband had been at the hospital that day.

Aunt Rachel had mentioned Annie Ruth several times and how Daddy's first wife worried about someone who needed her help, someone who'd made her a promise that he didn't keep.

And nowhere in all that she'd rambled on about was there anything that could make a normal person want to shut her mouth for good.

Unless...? Daddy's first wife. Wasn't she always called Annie Ruth? Like Herman's daughter was always called Annie Sue? What if—?

But Dwight roused up about then, and all the nebulous what ifs went flying.

CHAPTER
28

The consciousness of a well-spent life and a memory rich in good deeds afford supreme happiness.

— Cicero

First thing after church on Sunday morning, the calls started coming in. Even though high school was still in session, our college kids were home for the summer and the cousins thought we ought to christen the pond shed before farm work or summer jobs took them off in different directions. They know that I'm always up for a spontaneous party and that they can invite their friends. Annie Sue and Reese had told us they were going to finish the wiring that morning. The whole family was in on the secret of the neon pig sign I'd bought from Will and they wanted to be there when Dwight first saw it.

The weather was warm enough to drag out the picnic tables and lawn chairs and to fire up the cooker. While my poor oblivious husband ran over to NutriGood for enough chickens, I took a few pounds of link sausage out of the freezer. Seth and Minnie donated a cooler full of soft drinks. Doris and Isabel volunteered vegetables, April brought one of her amazing fruit salads, and Barbara said she'd bring munchables and paper plates. Over the years, flea markets and garage sales have provided us with dozens of knives and forks and spoons that we keep in a communal basket that Daddy brought over with him when he came. Beats flimsy plastic hands down.

Early arrivals helped Cal lay out a horseshoe pitch, although once the others saw Cal's new slingshot, Haywood had to draft Robert and Andrew to help him make extras. Drink cans and more scrap 2x4s were balanced on the sawhorses for target practice and they used the coarse gravel spilled around the edges of the slab for ammunition. Who knew Minnie was the Annie Oakley of slingshots?

Cal was in a ferment of excitement because he'd talked me out of waiting till Father's Day for the unveiling. Annie Sue and Reese managed to walk the pig sign in to that back wall with the rest of the neon without Dwight noticing, because he was busy basting the chickens. My sisters-in-law kept him distracted while the signs were tested to make sure they worked, then Reese covered them with a tarp till sundown.

Someone must have called over to Dobbs, because Will and Amy showed up with Herman and Nadine in their backseat, along with ice cream and some cheap champagne.

"Hey, I'm not breaking a bottle of Dom Pérignon on a shack," he said when I called him on it.

Herman can walk a few steps if assisted and he transferred from the car to Isabel's golf cart. He had brought his guitar and I saw Daddy's fiddle case on the seat of his truck, so there would be music later. Several of us had been in for swims and the deck railing held an assortment of damp towels drying in the late afternoon sun.

By the time the chickens and sausages came off the grill a little after five, everyone had heard how Jacob died and that Dwight and his people were no closer to learning why Aunt Rachel had been smothered. Doris, Bel, and Nadine had persuaded themselves that we might never know what innocuous remark had triggered her murder, but that reminded them of an article in the day's *News & Observer*.

Dr. Richard Howell had delivered the commencement address at one of the local universities, which had also awarded him an honorary doctorate for his generous donations to pediatric units in the area.

"I reckon he'll go to his grave mourning them two little baby girls burning up like that," said Doris.

"Such a good man," said Bel.

For some reason, Amy, who was standing nearby, rolled her eyes at that, but said nothing, and no one else seemed to have noticed.

Nadine insisted on saying grace, then lines formed

on either side of the serving table. I had made a huge bowl of potato salad with potatoes scratched out of our garden. The bowl is about seventeen inches in diameter, a wedding gift from Pam and Vernon Owens over at Jugtown, who know what a big family I have. I saw Barbara eyeing it with interest.

"Thou shalt not covet," I told her.

"Not for me," she said. "For Karen."

I laughed. "Karen saw it at the wedding and it almost went home in her suitcase."

With so many teenage appetites, not to mention Haywood's, the food evaporated like dew on a July morning. Dwight had saved me a drumstick and there were lots of salads and vegetables left, so I filled my plate and took it over to one of the quilted moving pads we spread on the grass whenever we run out of lawn chairs.

As the late afternoon wound down toward sunset, Daddy rosined his bow and began to play a bluegrass classic.

"Rachel always liked that one," he said and played it through again while the rest of us remembered how she used to enjoy our monthly get-togethers at the barbecue house.

As one old favorite melted into another and the mood began to lighten, I was not surprised when Haywood and Isabel joined in on fiddle and banjo, nor that Will had brought his guitar, but it delighted me to see Reese pull out his harmonica and tell Cal to run get his. As long as he was going up to the house, I asked him to bring my guitar down for Stevie, who's better with it than I am. Cal's a little shy about playing in front of others because he misses the right chord three tries out of five, but Reese is teaching him and the others tolerate it because he blows very softly. Emma and Ruth both play piano and both were once again swearing they were going to learn to play something more portable.

"How 'bout a piccolo?" Lee teased.

"Or a recorder?" said Annie Sue, who doesn't play an instrument but sings like an angel.

A.K. hadn't brought his drums, of course, but he and Jane Ann were beating time with wood blocks from the scrap pile, and Annie Sue shared out small plastic boxes of screws and wire nuts from the bowels of her truck. They almost sounded like castanets or tambourines when the others shook them. Daddy looked pleased when they all finished "Gingham Dresses" on the same beat. "Y'all get any better and we might have to go to Nashville. Try out for the Grand Ole Opry."

"The Knott Family Players," said Haywood. "We ought to make us a YouTube video."

For some reason, the idea that Haywood could use a computer or even knew about YouTube tickled Will and Zach, which offended Haywood so much he put down his fiddle and declared it was time for cake and ice cream.

While the Knott Family Players took a break, I wound up beside Amy, and not by chance. Curiosity's an itch I always have to scratch.

"What've you got against Richard Howell?" I asked her quietly.

She looked surprised. "Me? Nothing. Why?"

I shrugged. "You rolled your eyes when Bel said he was such a good man."

"I did?"

"You did."

"Well—" She hesitated. "No, Bel's right, Deborah. Dr. Howell *is* a good man."

"But?"

Again that hesitation. "I don't know. It's just that he likes for everyone to know what a good man he is. God knows I'm not religious but you remember how in the Bible Jesus said to do your good deeds and your praying in secret?"

(Religious or not, anyone who's spent the first twelve years of life in a Southern Baptist Sunday school never ever quite forgets the lessons learned.)

"But didn't he also say not to hide your light under a bushel?" I murmured. "Let it shine?"

"Jesus didn't have to tell Richard Howell that," she said. "He likes his name in the paper and he likes his name shining on any bronze plaque. The Anne Peterson Howell Pediatrics Wing at the hospital. The Janice Howell Mayer Memorial Burn Unit. I walk past those plaques every day. Then there's the Emily Celeste and Mary Beth Mayer Memorial Scholarships out at the community college, and let us not forget the Anne Peterson Howell fountain in front of the hospital."

She gave me a rueful smile. "Petty of me, isn't it?

But he just strikes me as someone who's always working on his obituary, making sure the world's going to remember who he was and what he did."

"Anne Peterson Howell," I said. "Was that his grandmother?"

Amy nodded.

Before I could ask if she'd been kin to that Peterson from the Makely area who ran for lieutenant governor last time, Cal came running up, his eyes shining with mischief.

"Annie Sue wants to know if we're ready to show Dad the signs."

"Sure," I said. For once, I had my cell phone in my pocket and I turned it on as Cal and I took Dwight by the hand and led him over to the pond shed. When Reese threw the switch and that neon pig started trotting, I was ready.

The look on Dwight's face is preserved for the ages.

CHAPTER
29

Nothing which comes in the course of nature can seem evil.

— Cicero

Monday morning was Memorial Day, a holiday for the courts as well, so I changed the sheets on our beds, did two loads of laundry, and made a chocolate cake while Cal cleaned the bathrooms and Dwight finished cutting the grass. After lunch we collected Mary Pat and Jake and drove over to Dobbs for the Memorial Day parade. Everyone who's ever worn a service uniform is expected to march.

Dwight feels a little self-conscious about it since he was never in active combat, but it's easier to march than argue with Bo Poole, who considers participation in all such events good public relations. I myself look upon the day as a chance to get out and shake hands with the voting public, and I did plenty of that while finding an open spot along the sidewalk where the children could sit on the curb to watch.

With several sharp blasts from his brass whistle, a high-strutting drum major started things off, followed by a flag-spinning color guard. The county's last World War I vet died years ago and our last World War II vet is now in a wheelchair, but he led the veterans in a white golf cart that was decorated with red, white, and blue bunting and driven by two grandsons who had served in Iraq. Next came troops of Scouts from around the county, then more marching high-school bands with cheerleaders who twirled and tossed (and didn't always catch) their batons. Shriners cavorted in their little red cars and the town's two fire engines preceded a float lavishly adorned with azalea blossoms and beauty queens. The current Miss Colleton County sat on a gilt throne borrowed from the Possum Creek Players Theatre. Seated slightly lower amid the flowers were Miss Cotton Grove, Miss Dobbs, Miss Pleasants Crossroads, and Little Miss Black Creek. All had perfected the Queen Elizabeth wave that looks like someone screwing in an overhead lightbulb.

Bringing up the rear were a dozen horses and riders, including two of my nieces, and a lone mule whose banner reminded us that Benson's sixty-third annual Mule Day celebration would be held in September. Lest anyone think that mules don't belong in a Memorial Day parade, there are plenty of mule enthusiasts to remind us that mules have pulled cannons and carried supplies and ammunition in most of our wars. And they're still doing it in Afghanistan.

At the end, we spectators fell in behind and followed the parade to the war memorials on the courthouse lawn for a solemn service of remembrance that ended with a lone bugler blowing taps. I wasn't the only one with tears in my eyes by the time he finished.

After that, though, it became a street festival with food vendors and craft booths and various catch-me-eye amusements. Cal and his cousins darted off with some school friends while Dwight and I went around to the crowded steps on the shady side of the courthouse and found space at the far end. After standing for so long, I was ready to sit.

Minnie came by a few minutes later. She had helped Seth and the girls with the horses and looked tired. "Any room for one more?" she asked plaintively.

"Absolutely." I scooted over so that she could sit between Dwight and me, accidentally bumping the leg of someone behind me in the process. "Sorry," I said.

"No problem, Judge," said a genial male voice.

I turned and looked up into the homely face of Jim Collins, whom I hadn't noticed before. His big nose and bald head were both red from too much sun.

After congratulating Minnie again on my successful campaign last fall, he immediately began to banter with her. "She won by such a wide margin, why don't you run her for the state legislature?"

"Good luck on that," said Minnie. "I can't even get her to think about the superior court."

I let them enjoy themselves for a few minutes, then said, "Y'all just go ahead and pretend I'm not here, 'cause I'm perfectly happy where I am. Besides, if I moved up to superior court, Dwight and I might never have another normal conversation."

"Who?"

"My husband."

Dwight put out his hand. "Dwight Bryant, Mr. Collins."

"Yes, of course. I forgot that you two were married, Major. How goes the investigation?"

"Slowly," he admitted. "Lots of people may have had the opportunity, but we just can't settle on a motive. And that reminds me, Minnie, Jessie seems to have left a few minutes after the aide came down to the family room. Did she leave alone?"

"Are you thinking for one minute that one of our children—?"

Before she could get too huffy, I reminded her that he had to account for everyone and she lowered her maternal hackles. "You're right. Sorry, Dwight. Jess went home with Emma and Barbara."

"What about you, Mr. Collins?" Dwight asked easily. "You left around that time, too."

"Did I? Let me think. Oh yes, I walked out to the parking lot with Buzz Crenshaw and he stopped to speak to my daughter, who was waiting for me in the car. You know kids these days. She'd been without her cell phone for at least a half hour up in Miss Rachel's room and she really didn't know anyone except Sally and Jay-Jay."

"Did either of you see Mr. Snaveley or Dr. Howell after you left the hospice room?"

Both of them shook their heads.

"What about some of the things that Miss Rachel kept going back to? We know what happened at the creek with Jacob, but what about that debt someone didn't pay? Or the wife-beater?"

Minnie immediately reminded Dwight that she'd already told him no on both counts. Collins looked thoughtful as he again shook his head.

The conversation strayed into other paths as children and their parents passed by. Some high school band members who had taken off their jackets this warm day converged on the other end of the steps with ice cream cones and raucous laughter. The boys pushed and shoved, showing off for the girls, who giggled and flirted.

Eventually, Minnie said it was time for her to go meet Seth, and Dwight wanted to check up on the kids. I was too lazy to move and Collins didn't seem to be in a hurry either.

I had tucked several small bottles of water in my straw tote and I offered one to him.

He uncapped the bottle and moved down to sit beside me. With no one else nearby, he said, "He knows, doesn't he? You both know."

"Know what?"

"Don't play games, Judge. Rachel Morton mentioned cowbirds and goldfinches more than once, yet your husband didn't ask me about that."

"I'm sorry. Yes, he knows. But only because he pushed the person who told him. And told him reluctantly. I don't think you have to worry about it going any further."

He sighed. "Thanks for that. Amanda would be appalled to learn she was a cowbird egg. She adored her mother and I think it's safe to say she loves me, so it would hurt like hell for her to know Mavis had an affair. We always told her she was our bonus baby, a gift from God after we'd given up hope of having another child. She may not be mine biologically, but she's got my brains and she's got my drive. She's going to summer school so she can graduate in three years and she'll be running Mediway in another ten."

He took a swallow of water, then carefully screwed the cap back on. "I probably should have told her long ago, but Mavis was so ashamed and before she died, she made me promise I wouldn't. Anyhow, it was my fault more than hers. Mediway was just taking off and I was working sixteen-hour days. On and off planes to Boston, Chicago, or San Diego at least twice a week. Our son was fifteen and already in a band."

He turned the plastic bottle in his hands between his knees and did not look at me. "It was my assistant. My right-hand man. Holding down the fort for me." He gave a bitter laugh. "Or so I thought."

The silence built between us except for the crackling of the thin empty bottle as he drained it, crushed it flat, and continued turning it over and over.

"I'll take that," I said, reaching out for it.

He looked at the crushed bottle blankly, as if he'd forgotten it was there.

"Thanks." He stood up to leave, a short homely man with a bald head and a big nose, but he met my eyes squarely and there was dignity in his face. "Thanks," he said again and walked away in the crowd.

I was glad that he'd had no opportunity to sneak back to Aunt Rachel's room, but keeping his daughter's conception a secret from her sure would have made a strong motive.

When Dwight and the children came back, Cal's face was painted like Spider-Man and he had bought me a stretchy elastic bracelet with blue beads that he slipped onto my wrist with a proud smile.

Maybe not the child of my body, but damned if he's not the child of my heart.

CHAPTER
30

The third [question of duty] is the conflict be-
tween the honorable and that which appears to
be expedient.

— Cicero

Next morning, Dwight rode into Dobbs with me after leaving his truck at Jimmy White's to get a leaky
water hose and frayed fan belt looked after.

Whites have been keeping our family's vehicles going ever since Jimmy's daddy quit running whiskey for
my daddy and went to running his own garage, which
Jimmy expanded to a two-bay operation when he took
over the business. The all-white county commissioners wanted to zone the garage out of existence when
the first housing development went up in the neighborhood, but John Claude and I managed to get him
grandfathered in. Before that, though, when we realized how gentrified things might become, we advised
Jimmy to buy a couple of adjoining acres so that there

would be room to add another bay and a salvage yard if his son James decided to carry on the work, which he has.

Between berms and evergreen shrubbery, most newcomers don't even realize there's a garage and junkyard back there in the trees behind his house until they start asking around for a good mechanic. The only indication is a small sign at the entrance drive, because word of mouth gives them as much business as they can comfortably handle.

Dwight's official workday begins a full hour before mine, so I had time to talk my way into Ellis Glover's office early and go hunting through the will books. Twenty minutes later, I found the one I was looking for. It was straightforward and exactly as I'd heard last week, and it even named the attorney who had drawn it up, a name I could run past John Claude, who's been practicing law long enough to know every firm in the district.

"Louis Royster?" he said. "I think he died at least twenty years ago."

"Who would have taken over his practice?"

"His daughter, of course. Patricia Hawkins."

"Pat Hawkins is his daughter? But Royster practiced in Makely and Pat's here in Dobbs."

"So is her ex-husband," John Claude said dryly.

Sometimes you just get lucky. Gray haired and nearing retirement, Pat considers herself one of my mentors. She recommended me to the then-DA when I first passed the bar and needed to get my feet wet before joining Lee & Stephenson. She had been an active supporter when I decided to run for judge and we have stayed good friends. Indeed, we had hugged each other warmly when we met at the bar association dinner only last week, so I didn't hesitate to call her office.

"It's not just idle curiosity," I told her when her secretary put me through and I had explained what I wanted and why. "You know how Dwight gets if he thinks I'm not minding my own business, so I don't want to say anything about this if there's nothing there."

"I do still have all of my dad's files," Pat said, "but of course that one's been inactive for years and I honestly doubt if there's any smoking gun in it."

"You don't still represent him, do you?"

She gave a sour laugh. "You kidding? I'm too small-town for him." She named a large law firm in Raleigh, then said, "I'll have one of my clerks root out that file."

"Thanks, Pat. I'll leave my phone on."

"Don't thank me yet, honey. I'm not promising you a look if anything's there," she warned.

After the long weekend, I knew that first appearances would be a busy session. Happily, Julie Walsh, one of the more organized and efficient ADAs, was there that morning for the State.

It was the usual mixed bag: five D&Ds after the weekend brawls, two cases of domestic violence—one male on female, the other female on male—a hit-and-run (not fatal, thank goodness), four drug possessions, etc., etc.

Some of the etceteras charged with felonies waived their probable cause hearings and were ready to proceed directly to trial. For those, I advised them of their right to an attorney, then set their dates to appear in superior court and their bonds, as appropriate.

Making her first appearance was Valerie Rhodes, 18, white, and accused of deliberately ramming a 2012 Toyota Camry owned by her sister and occupied at the time by Helen Barefoot and Randall Nehring shortly before midnight Saturday night. Miss Rhodes was charged with two counts of felony assault and one count of malicious property damage.

Seated on the front row behind the prosecution were Mr. Nehring and Miss Barefoot, she in a neck brace, he with a cast on his right arm, a black eye, and bruises on his face. Also present were his wife, an attorney for Miss Rhodes, and assorted parents.

According to the prosecution, a Dobbs police officer had been called out to a disturbance at a side street that dead-ended behind a defunct grocery store, a site that's showed up in my courtroom more than once. It's popular with couples who can't or won't spring for a motel room and who have no convenient bed elsewhere.

When he arrived on the scene, the officer saw that a Honda Civic driven by Miss Rhodes had rammed into the Camry, which sustained damages approximating $1500. He found the occupants of the Camry in a state of partial undress and saw Miss Rhodes hitting Mr. Nehring with her cheerleader baton.

I wondered if she'd been in yesterday's parade, but didn't ask.

The officer had called for an ambulance to convey Mr. Nehring and Miss Barefoot to the hospital and he had placed Miss Rhodes under arrest. A magistrate had set her bond, which was immediately met so that she didn't have to stay in jail.

Even though a first appearance is not really the time for it, I allowed Mrs. Nehring to speak.

She looked almost as young as her sister. Same long brown hair, a similarly pretty oval face and earnest brown eyes. "Please, Your Honor, Val's only eighteen. She shouldn't have done this, but she did it for me. I knew that Randy was cheating, and when she saw how much I was hurting, she wanted to hurt him back. The Camry's in my name, not Randy's, and I don't want to press charges, okay?"

I know how impulsive eighteen-year-olds can be. Hell, wasn't I only a month or two past my own nineteenth birthday when I stabbed a man with a rusty knife because he called me Debbie one time too often? And he was only annoying me, not hurting someone I loved.

I looked over at Julie Walsh. "Madame DA, it appears that the State might have a problem with the maliciousness of this offense. Are you sure you want to go forward on it?"

She agreed that the State could offer no evidence

at this time on this misdemeanor and took a voluntary dismissal of the property damage charge.

I turned back to Valerie Rhodes, who sat beside her attorney and looked scared. "I'm afraid the felony assaults stand unless Mr. Nehring and Miss Barefoot want to drop them?"

Miss Barefoot looked incredulous. "Is she kidding?"

"Absolutely not!" said Randy Nehring. (And how appropriate is *that* for a nickname?)

"Very well," I said. "As to the misdemeanor, the State has taken a voluntary dismissal. However, with regard to the felony assault, I will set a probable cause date on that for June fourth, and between now and then, the State and your defense attorney can talk about it. As a judge, I have no opinion on this at all."

At her attorney's request, I left Miss Rhodes's bond where it was. She was no flight risk.

The combatants stood to leave, and I had a feeling that Mrs. Nehring would soon be back in someone else's court to begin divorce proceedings.

Last on the morning calendar came Glenn Judd, 41, and Henry Wegman, 53, both white, both charged with felony larceny and conspiracy to obtain property by false pretenses. It was the old roofing scam with a twist.

As laid out by the prosecution, Judd and Wegman had knocked on the Cotton Grove door of two elderly sisters during last week's rains and told them that they'd been passing by and noticed that the porch roof was leaking. When the women walked out onto the porch, there was indeed a wet place where water had run down the front wall from a spot where the porch ceiling joined the main house, although no new water seemed to be running down at the moment despite the falling rain. The men painted a picture of rot and water damage and offered to take care of it right then and there since they had just finished another job and had their ladders and a bucket of tar on the truck.

The sisters agreed and after Judd and Wegman were up on the roof for twenty minutes, they came down and explained that they normally charged $3500, but since they were already out, it would be only $2500.

The sisters paid with cash on hand, but a few days later, it finally occurred to them that a rainy day is not the time to tar a leak; and even if it were, should a twenty-minute job warrant such a high price? They then called their nephew, who came over, went up on the roof, and could see no evidence of fresh tar. In any event, he had overseen the installation of a new roof only two years earlier. He reported the incident to the local police, who were sympathetic but had no way to help because the sisters could furnish neither a name nor a license plate number.

As I listened, I wondered if the nephew knew my cousin Sally. Clearly, this man was his aunts' designated daughter.

Happily for the ladies, Judd and Wegman were greedy enough and stupid enough to come back on Friday for a second bite of the apple. This time, they offered to reroof the whole house for only $5000. While one of the sisters offered homemade cookies to seal the deal, the other called their nephew, who immediately called the Cotton Grove police, who responded in time to make the arrest.

The two men glumly waived a PC hearing so I bound them over to superior court and set their bonds at $5000 each.

This was not a sexy case, it would not make headlines. Indeed, it would barely merit a mention in the county's local paper, but like the way Rusty Alexander cheated Miss Jones, these consumer fraud cases hurt people and do as much real damage to their lives as if they'd been robbed at gunpoint. Over and over again, I see the elderly, the naïve, and the retirees with Alzheimer's or other dementia issues lose their life savings and retirement accounts. Nurses, teachers, military retirees, and the disabled—no one's off-limits for these bottom-feeders.

I have a lot of issues with our current DA, but one thing about him: he does not allow any plea bargaining in cases like this. These two were definitely going to see the inside of a jail.

Pat hadn't called by noon, so I went downstairs, planning to eat lunch with Dwight in his office. I had made us both tuna salads with lettuce from his cold frame.

When I got there, though, Mayleen told me that they finally had a lead in those Black Creek break-ins. "Whoever stole one of the phones took a picture with it," she said and explained how the owner had talked the person who'd bought it into giving him a jump drive with all the pictures. "Tub Greene got an ID on the two strangers and guess what? A girl took that picture."

She said that the break-ins now looked to be the work of three girls in that neighborhood and that they had even burgled their own homes to throw off suspicion. "One of them told Tub it was to get money for college. That they didn't want to wind up with a huge debt at the end of four years."

"Boy, are they in for an education," I said, shaking my head.

Mayleen laughed.

I got my salad out of their fridge and as I passed back through the squad room, I spotted the chart Mayleen had drawn up to show who was where when Aunt Rachel died. Most of the names had lines through them, indicating their elimination.

"Still haven't found anyone to vouch for Dr. Howell?" I asked.

"Ray's out checking right now," she said. "The Collins girl said he went off down a hall with a nurse, but the nurse's father had a heart attack late that night and she flew out to Iowa to be with him, so we haven't talked to her yet. There was a medical emergency on that hall about then and there was too much coming and going for anyone to be certain. Hard to think that Dr. Howell really needs an alibi, though, isn't it? With all the good he does?"

* * *

On the way back to my own office, I ran into Sally
coming out of the clerk of the court's office. She wore
the springy blonde wig today, curls flying in every direction as she shook her head at me in exasperation as
if I had personally written the probate laws for North
Carolina.

"You ever settle someone's estate?"

"No," I said.

"Well, you better make sure Uncle Kezzie has a detailed will. Twelve children and God knows how many
grandkids, right? I just have the one brother and he's a
sweetheart, but we still have to agree on every single
detail, because Mama didn't leave a will and Jay-Jay's
got the business sense of a grasshopper."

I laughed. "So how much of a cut did Will take on
that Hanley Willis decoy?"

She joined my laughter, her blonde curls bouncing.
"Wasn't that a hoot? Wouldn't you love to be there
when that cheating Rusty Alexander realizes it's a
fake? We're hoping he'll take it up to Maryland to brag
on it in front of the real Dawson Bridges."

She told me how she'd gone down to the Waterfowl Museum at Harkers Island to get authentic details and how Will had shot a few lead pellets into
the doctored decoy to make it look as if it had been
hunted over a hundred years ago. The initials, the
white dot in the eyes, the feathering details, and the
final "weathering" were done by a friend of his who
did period restorations—something I really didn't

want to know too much about even though Will does make a point of saying on his website and in all his ads that everything is sold "as is" with no guarantees as to provenance.

"Lucky that he found an old bill of sale among the Lattimore papers," I said.

"Oh, honey!" she giggled. "Luck had nothing to do with it. That was Marillyn Mulholland."

Her face sobered, though, as she told me that Will had turned all the money over to JoAnn Bonner and her aunt except for the restorer's fee. "It compensates for the tea service, but it's not nearly enough to save the house. They've decided not to even try. They've emptied the house and the bank has foreclosed on it." She gave me a defiant look. "And we did check under all the floorboards, but we couldn't find the Tiffany jewels. The bank will probably sell it for scrap and some lucky contractor may wind up with a quick quarter million."

As she turned to go, I caught hold of her sleeve. "Sally, you said that Aunt Rachel wasn't close to Annie Ruth?"

"So?"

"But she kept talking about an Annie. Was that Richard Howell's grandmother?"

She nodded. "Why?"

"No reason," I lied. "Just wondered."

Midway through my afternoon session, Pat Hawkins sent me a text asking me to drop by when I could.

While Julie Walsh thumbed through her shucks, I unobtrusively texted Pat to expect me around five.

When I called Dwight after adjournment, he said, "I'm still down in Black Creek, so don't wait for me. I'll get somebody to drop me at Jimmy's."

There was no need to rush, but I still went out the side door of the courthouse, cut through the parking lot and down the alley to Pat's on the next street over.

Her secretary showed me into her office, where a single sheet of paper lay facedown on the desk before her.

"I've gone over all my dad's dealings with the Howell family, Deborah. He handled the sale of old Mr. Howell's feed store. It sold back then for twenty-eight thousand and there was approximately twenty-five thousand left when he died, which his wife, Richard's grandmother, inherited." She leaned back with her elbows on the arms of her chair and tented her index fingers against her chin.

"This is not for public consumption, Deborah. I don't have to remind you of attorney-client privilege, even though most of this doesn't fall into that realm."

I nodded.

"Dad kept pretty complete notes on all his clients, and reading between the lines of this paper, I'm thinking she used some of the money for Jannie's wedding and part for Howell's tuition at Carolina for his undergraduate degree. Can you believe that board and tuition at Carolina was way less than a thousand a year? He got a small grant from Duke when he was accepted into medical school, but Duke wasn't Carolina when it came to tuition and board. It probably was going to take most of the rest of whatever was left out of that twenty-eight thousand to get him through the next four years, so Dad thought she went ahead and gave him the money, but she brought Dad a sealed envelope and directed him to keep it with her will, which left everything to be shared equally between Howell and his sister. Here's what Dad wrote about that."

She slid the paper over to me and pointed to the handwritten notes on the second half of the page:

Earlier, Mrs. H. told me that she had asked her grandson to sign a promissory note to repay the loan to her estate as soon as he was qualified to practice medicine and I assumed that was what was in the envelope although she did not say so. Upon her death, I gave him the envelope. He had been practicing medicine for almost a year when his sister died. If he ever gave her a share of the money, I am not aware of it.

"So that was what Aunt Rachel meant about unpaid debts," I said and repeated some of the other things Aunt Rachel had said. "She must have told Aunt Rachel, and Aunt Rachel would have known that he never repaid it. Maybe his sister wouldn't have died if she'd been able to afford a better house and maybe that's the real reason why he's felt so guilty all these years. One of the neighbors told Dwight that

Howell always wanted what he wanted and felt entitled."

Pat nodded. "I'm willing to bet that he's the boy who ate all the chocolates in both those Easter baskets you told me about."

"He really seems to like having the whole world think good of him," I said. "But if Aunt Rachel had kept talking, she might have added enough for everyone to know who she was talking about."

Pat looked thoughtful. "Sound like a motive for murder to you?"

"*And* he doesn't have an alibi," I said.

CHAPTER
31

I approve of gravity in old age, so it be not excessive.

— Cicero

Dwight got home shortly after me. Jimmy White had to replace both the water hose and the fan belt, and he'd changed the oil as long as the truck was up on the lift. Dwight's faithful horse was now good for another few thousand miles.

We ate an early supper, then carried our drinks down to our new screened-in pond shed so that Cal could go swimming. He's part fish and we try not to be too overly protective, but we never let him go swimming by himself. As he and Bandit and one of Seth's dogs played in the water, Dwight and I positioned our chairs where we could watch, and I listened while he told me about the teenage girls who thought they could build a college fund by robbing half the houses in their neighborhood.

"If it hadn't been for that cell phone picture, they'd still be at it," he said. "Girls seem to be a little smarter than boys when they turn to crime. They'd babysat in some of the houses and had a good idea of where things were. We think they pooled their information about which houses were empty during the day."

"Nobody ever caught them on a security camera?" I asked as Cal tried a wobbly jackknife dive off the end of the pier.

"Twice, but they were smart about that, too—hoodies to cover their hair, scarves over their faces, latex gloves. We thought they were boys. They didn't tell any of their friends, they didn't trash the houses or leave fingerprints, and they only stole stuff that was easy to pawn or sell. Laptops, iPods, cell phones, and jewelry."

"How old are these girls?"

"Two are fifteen, the other's sixteen, a high school junior."

"Minors," I said.

"And already lawyered up. In fact, the girl who let slip that they were saving for college? Now she says she was talking about her babysitting earnings."

"All middle class, all pretty, all white, and all hoping to draw a middle-aged male judge with teenage daughters?" I asked cynically.

"Middle class and pretty, but more like the UN. One white, one Latina, and one Asian American. I don't know about the judge."

He sipped his beer—a light ale he'd brewed last month—in gloomy silence.

"Speaking of college funds," I said, and told him
what I'd learned about Dr. Richard Howell and how the
Annie of Aunt Rachel's worried comments wasn't Annie Ruth but Annie Howell. I described the promissory
note Howell's grandmother had told Pat Hawkins's father about and the debt that was never repaid. I also
repeated Amy's assessment of his almost pathological
need to be revered for all his good works. Indeed, I
laid everything out for him like Cal showing us all the
goodies that Santa had left in his Christmas stocking.

"Interesting," Dwight said, "but—"

"Pat Hawkins thinks he might kill to keep that reputation, *and* he doesn't have an alibi."

Dwight shook his head. "Except that he does."

"*What?*"

"The nurse that came up to him on the landing? Ray
talked to her late this afternoon. She's back from Iowa
and she's quite sure that he was with a patient during
the relevant time. She even gave Ray the names of the
patient's parents and it all checks out. Sorry, shug."

I felt like a balloon with all the air let out. "So
Richard Howell gets to keep his untarnished reputation?"

"That's up to you and Pat," Dwight said. "I know
how you feel about hypocrites and people who think
they're entitled to take what they want, and I'm sure if
you told Amy, it would be around the hospital in ten
seconds flat."

"It would, wouldn't it?" I said, momentarily
tempted.

Hey, I can be as petty and mean-spirited as anybody else. I've never put myself up for sainthood like Howell has. Besides, it would give some long-overdue justice to Jannie Mayer and her two little girls.

Or would it?

Right now, they are innocent victims of fate in the eyes of all who know the public story. Telling the private story would turn them into victims of greed. Still innocent, but somehow diminished. Weigh that against all the good Howell had done to make up for his youthful selfishness. I'd be a hypocrite myself if I tried to deny that good. The pediatric wing, the burn unit, all the health workers that continue to be educated? Their names are in bronze and they are not forgotten. So if Richard Howell wants to pat himself on the back for all he's done, if he wants to be remembered as a generous philanthropist, so what?

I sighed and Dwight smiled. He knows me well enough to know that my sigh meant I was going to keep my mouth shut about what I knew. Pat Hawkins would never go public either. While it could be argued that technically she had not breached her father's attorney-client privilege for me, it still wasn't something she would want known.

Cal finished his swim, wrapped himself in a towel, and came inside with us to sit cross-legged atop a wooden picnic table and play Angry Birds on Dwight's cell phone.

"So who does that leave?" I asked.

"We're still cross-checking alibis," he said. "There

are several left with opportunity, but we've run out of motives. Obvious motives, anyhow. We still haven't verified the Reverend Snaveley's alibi, for instance, and there are three or four others."

We batted it around for a few more minutes as he drained his beer glass and I finished my soft drink.

"Any homework, honey?" I asked Cal, whose summer vacation wouldn't start for another two weeks.

"Just a little," he said, intent on the small screen in his hands.

"Better go take a shower and get on it," I said.

"In a minute. I just have to get one more—"

Dwight waited two beats, then held out his hand for the phone. "Minute's up, buddy."

"Awww, man!" Reluctantly, he handed it over and let the screen door slam behind him a little harder than he needed as he trudged up the slope to the house and homework.

I smiled at Dwight. "Awww, man, you spoil everybody's fun."

"I reckon you both'll get over it," he said.

Cal came to the back door as we neared the house. "Aunt Zell's on the phone, Mom. She wants to talk to you."

"I hate to ask you, honey," Aunt Zell said, "but my ox is in the ditch. Ash has gone fishing down at the coast and tonight's the last visitation for one of my UDC friends over in Widdington. You know what my night vision's like these days. I'll be so glad when these cataracts are ripe enough to harvest. Portland was going to drive me, but Carolyn had her DPT shot yesterday and she's running a little fever so—"

"Of course I'll take you," I said. "I'll be over as soon as I can change."

Which is how I wound up in a Widdington funeral home that night, looking down into the casket of a sweet-faced old woman and offering condolences to her children and grandchildren, none of whom I'd ever met before. A Confederate flag stood with the state and national flags and yes, it has negative connotations to most people.

Aunt Zell recognizes that. "All my life it's distressed me that the KKK used it for hate and bigotry," she said as we drove back to Dobbs that night. "But my great-grandfather and two of his brothers fought and died under that flag even though they never owned a single slave. South Carolina dragged us into that awful war, and we lost more than twice as many men as any other state, four times more than South Carolina. How can I not honor them?"

I patted her hand, remembering how the memorial service at the courthouse last Monday included our Confederate dead along with the casualties from all the other wars.

Aunt Zell sighed as the memory of one old UDC member called up the memory of another. "Tell me about Olive Jones's daughter, Deborah. Such a shame about her silver tea service."

I swore her to secrecy and she listened with amusement when she heard how Sally and Will had managed to get back most of the money Rusty Alexander had cheated Frances Jones out of. "Will she be able to keep the house?"

"I'm afraid not. She's about decided that's not a bad thing, though. The house needs so much work and the neighborhood's gone down a lot in the last few years. She's moved in with her niece. They seem very fond of each other. It's just too bad that they couldn't find her mother's jewelry."

"Jewelry?"

"She told us that her mother owned some very expensive pieces from Tiffany."

"Oh, she did," said Aunt Zell. "I've never quite understood why someone would spend that much money on things that really aren't appropriate for daily wear, but I must admit they were quite lovely. Her engagement ring! A huge square diamond surrounded by more diamonds almost as big as the one in the engagement ring Ash gave me. And there was a necklace. Pearls and emeralds and more diamonds. She wore that to the banquet the year she was state president of the UDC, but my stars! What that necklace must have cost! I suppose Carlton sold it after she died?"

"Not according to their daughter. In fact, she says he hid the necklace and the ring and at least one pair of very valuable earrings somewhere in the house. Sally and some friends helped them search the place right down to the floorboards before Frances had to turn the keys over to the bank, but they never found the jewelry."

By now we were approaching Dobbs in full darkness and Aunt Zell said, "Did they know about the secret hiding place in the mantelpiece?"

"It was empty."

"What about the one behind it?"

"Behind what?" I asked as we turned into her street.

"It was a double secret," she said. "Olive showed it to me after one of our meetings. I had told her about Ash's grandmother's desk. You've seen it. Remember? Even after you open the secret cubbyhole, there's another space behind that. She swore me to secrecy because Carlton didn't want anyone to know, but surely their daughter knew?"

"I don't think so, Aunt Zell. Do you remember how it worked?"

"Oh yes. You press one of the rosettes to open the first one, then you have to reach inside and press two other places at the same time and another little door swings up. Carlton's father hid gold coins in it when President Roosevelt took us off the gold standard and made it illegal to own them unless they were rare and worth more to collectors than face value. Carlton still had two or three of them when Olive showed me that secret compartment."

Sitting in Aunt Zell's driveway, I said, "Feel like a little breaking and entering?"

"Oh, Deborah, I don't think we should do that. Can't we call the bank tomorrow and ask Roger Junior to let us into the house?"

Roger Junior, the son of one of the bank's founders,

is in his sixties and, as I recalled, a by-the-book businessman.

"What if he says no? What if he decides that everything still in the house now belongs to the bank? What
he doesn't know won't hurt him. Besides, we can be
in and out in five minutes if you can remember how to
open that compartment."

"Can't I just tell you how it works?"

"Sure," I said. "And then when I can't get it open,
we'll just forget about it and Frances Jones can go on
welfare."

To my surprise, she giggled. "You sounded just like
Sue, then. She could always manipulate me into doing
things against my better judgment. You have to promise not to ever tell Ash."

"Only if you promise never to tell Dwight."

"And you also have to promise not to scratch up
Ash's crowbar. You know how he is about his tools."

"Crowbar?"

"Well how else are we going to get in? I'm too old
to crawl through a window and you're not dressed for
it either," she said tartly.

"Credit card," I said blithely. "They do it all the time
on TV."

"I'll get the crowbar," she said. "Wait here."

The Jones house was located on a side street that had
seen better days. Fortunately, there didn't seem to be
much traffic and we saw no one out on the sidewalks.
All the same, I parked around the next corner. No point

in advertising our presence. The lawns were deep, but one was strewn with large plastic play sets, another had a car up on cement blocks, while a third looked as if no one had cut the grass or pruned the shrubs in years. I took a small flashlight from the glove compartment as we got out of the car and Aunt Zell slid the crowbar up the sleeve of her jacket and let the curved part rest in her hand.

"Have you done this before?" I asked.

"With your mother," she murmured.

She led me to a large two-story buff-colored brick house with hipped roof dormers in the attic and a simple portico floored with flagstones. Like the surrounding houses, it was set back from the street amid oaks and magnolias. The front entrance was a pair of French doors that did not yield to my credit card and we decided that if we were going to use the crowbar, perhaps we should pick a side entrance where bushes would screen us from the street.

"I don't understand it," I said ten minutes later. "It looks so easy on television. The guy slides his credit card down the door frame and he's in like Flynn."

"Hey, Judge!" said a voice behind us.

Aunt Zell and I both jumped. I turned to see in the shadows a black teenager smiling at me in happy friendliness.

"Marcus?" I said. "Marcus Williams?"

"Yes, ma'am."

This man-child had stood in front of me more than once in the last two years. Light-fingered and the bane of convenience stores, but unfailingly polite and with an inner core of sweetness that always melted my heart. He reminded me so much of some of my nephews that I could never throw the book at him. Besides, he always promised that he was going to stop doing whatever it was that had brought him into my court that day, and so far it was never the exact same infraction.

"Can I help y'all?" he asked now.

"We need to get inside," I said, "and I forgot to get a key."

"I thought the bank owned this house now."

"They do."

"And they said it was okay for you to go in?"

"I'm a judge, Marcus. Do you really think—?"

He held up his hands in protest. "Hey, I'm just asking."

"What are you doing here anyhow?"

"I live here. You parked your car in front of my house and I sorta like to know what goes on around here. I've got two little sisters."

I suddenly remembered that he'd shoplifted a couple of preteen dresses from the local Walmart.

"So you want me to do that for you?"

He took my credit card and after a few deft movements, the knob turned in his hand and the door opened. I could have hugged him.

"I'll keep a watch out for y'all," he said.

Before I could tell him not to bother and send him on his way, Aunt Zell said, "Thank you, Marcus. That's very kind of you."

"They turned the lights off day before yesterday, but I guess the bank told you that."

I gave him a sharp look. "Have you been in this house before?"

"Well, sure, Judge. Miss Jones used to watch my sisters. Their school lets out about an hour before mine does."

"No, I mean since Miss Jones left."

"Well...I might've walked through. Just to see if they forgot anything," he said sheepishly.

It took Aunt Zell a few minutes to orient herself. "Everything's so different without furniture."

I gave her the flashlight and she set it shining around the walls and windows. I immediately grabbed it back. "Not the windows, Aunt Zell!"

"Oops!" she said. "I wasn't thinking. This was the dining room, I believe, and across the hall should be the living room."

It was. She went straight to the fireplace and pressed one of the carved rosettes in the surround. Immediately, I heard a click and a little door popped open. She shone the light into the cavity. "Empty. Now as best I recall..."

She put her hand inside and a moment later exclaimed, "Oh, my stars! There *is* something here. Hold the light, honey."

While I watched, she pulled out several small velvet pouches.

"You take a look, Deborah. Make sure I didn't miss anything."

Even shining the light directly into that second cavity, I couldn't see anything else.

"*Psssst!*" Marcus was signaling us from the hallway. "Hey, Judge! A police car just pulled up out front!"

"Oh dear," said Aunt Zell and rushed toward the side door. "Hurry, Deborah!"

I gave one final sweep with my hand and my fingers closed around two small heavy objects. I quickly shut both little openings and followed Aunt Zell and Marcus into the dining room just as a strong flashlight beam at those French doors lit up the hall from the portico. Another half second and I'd have been caught in that light.

"Hurry, hurry!" Marcus urged. He shoved me through the side door and locked it behind him before pushing us past the overgrown shrubbery into the next yard and on into the yard after that. Somewhere a dog barked and I heard the crackle of the cruiser's radio.

"Bet it was old man Walker called them on us," Marcus said when he felt it was safe to talk. "He's scared of his own shadow."

Two minutes later, we cut through his backyard and out to my car.

"Thank you, Marcus," I said. "That could have been awkward."

He grinned. "And you a judge? With permission to be there?"

"Oh dear!" said Aunt Zell. "Ash's crowbar! I left it inside."

"I'll buy you another one," I told her.

"But he'll know!" she protested. "It'll be the wrong size or a different brand."

"Well, if you really want me to go back and get it," I said.

Marcus was laughing so hard even Aunt Zell saw the humor.

"No, no," she said. "I'll just pretend I don't have a clue. Maybe he'll think he misplaced it himself."

We were halfway back to her house and she had just said for the second time what a nice young man Marcus was when it finally struck me. "Oh, *shit*!"

"Deborah?"

"Sorry, Aunt Zell. I just remembered that Marcus didn't give me back my credit card."

"Never mind, dear. Wait until tomorrow to cancel it and I'll take care of any charges he puts on it. A workman is worthy of his hire, don't you think?"

Next day, I tapped at Aunt Zell's kitchen door about five minutes after I recessed at noon. She had called Sally and invited her and the current Designated Daughters to come for lunch and I wanted to be there for the presentation. Unfortunately, Marillyn Mulholland's mother-in-law had taken a turn for the worse and she was unable to attend, but the others arrived on schedule. I helped Aunt Zell serve lunch in the garden, which was wheelchair-accessible, something the house itself wasn't.

"So far, the stairs and steps aren't a problem," she

said, "but Ash and I will have to think about adding ramps if we stay here, and they can be so ugly."

Sally knew something was up but she hadn't figured out what it was. The others were unsuspicious and thought Aunt Zell had invited them because she was one of the earlier Daughters herself. Frances Jones remembered her from her mother's UDC days and felt compelled to tell her how she'd lost the Georgian tea service.

"But Deborah tells me that you-all managed to avenge it with a duck decoy."

"Yes, but I can't really justify spending that money to get the set back."

Aunt Zell smiled. "Deborah?"

I laid two gold coins on the table. "Maybe these will help?"

Wide-eyed, Frances reached out a timid finger. "Are these my grandfather's twenty-dollar gold coins? Where on earth—?"

Aunt Zell handed her the little velvet bags.

"Mama's ring?" Frances whispered. "Mama's earrings?" Crying now, she opened the last bag and the ornate necklace slid onto the tablecloth. Sunlight caught the facets of emeralds and diamonds with gleaming pearls. "Where were they? We looked everywhere."

Aunt Zell explained about the second secret compartment. No one thought to question how she got into the house and retrieved them, but Sally's Botoxed lips stretched into an evil grin. "Well, damn!" she said to me. "Not so tight-assed after all."

* * *

Back at the courthouse, I zipped up my robe and hurried into the courtroom.

"All rise," said the bailiff. "This court is now back in session, the Honorable Deborah Knott present and presiding."

As I took my seat, I saw a crowbar on the bench before me.

"Mr. Overby?" I said.

"Some kid came by with it, ma'am," said the bailiff. "Said for me to give you this, too."

He handed me a return envelope for some charity or other. The charity's name and address had been crossed out and my name printed above it. Inside was my credit card and a note: "*You owe me one Not Guilty.*"

CHAPTER
32

Rashness belongs to youth; prudence to old age.

— Cicero

I took pains with my makeup and dressed more carefully than usual on Thursday morning, because I was taking a day of personal leave. I'd been invited to speak in Raleigh at a luncheon sponsored by an association of local trial lawyers. I spoke the truth when I told Jim Collins that I was happy in district court, but I figure it doesn't hurt to keep my options open, not to mention build a few bridges I might want to cross someday.

Aiming for a look that was professional but not uptight, I settled on a cropped green jacket with three-quarter sleeves over a dark blue sleeveless shift. Navy heels and a shiny yellow clutch bag just big enough to hold the essentials and the notes for my talk. While hunting for a particular lipstick, I upended one of the purses I'd used last week and when I did, a pearl fell out, the one I'd found in the bathroom when Amanda Collins's necklace broke. I had totally forgotten about it.

Jim Collins had said that she was in summer school at Meredith College, which was very near where I'd be speaking. Why not run by and return it to her after lunch? I tucked it into the little pocket of my purse so that I could find it again, reviewed my notes, then headed for Raleigh an hour earlier than I really needed to. Nothing said I couldn't check out the shoe sale the Belk store in Garner was holding, since it was right on my way.

And a very nice sale it was. I found a perfect pair of taupe sandals to go with some of my summer outfits. Leather straps, cork wedge heels, and only thirty dollars.

Lunch was chicken salad with fresh fruit slices, washed down with iced tea. My talk—"10 Things a Defense Attorney Can Do to Annoy a District Court Judge"—was meant to be funny, and the laughter and applause it got were quite gratifying. I didn't realize, though, that Chief Justice Sarah Parker was in the room until I was halfway through my talk.

(Yikes! Do I sound snarky or is she amused?)

To my relief, her laughter at number six seemed genuine and I could breathe again.

Meredith is a liberal-arts women's college on the west side of Raleigh just inside the Beltline. Originally chartered by the Southern Baptist Convention, it shed those historic ties when the Convention turned more conservative back in the nineties and began to emphasize male supremacy. A lot of students did not take kindly to an injunction to "submit graciously" to a husband and they did not want to keep silent in church.

A helpful clerk in the administration building told me that Amanda Collins lived in Stringfield, a residence hall across from the library. A student leaving the building held the door for me and no one asked to see my ID, so I went on up to the first floor and knocked on the open door.

From the boxes stacked on the second bed, I gathered that she must have just moved in and hadn't yet unpacked everything.

Wearing white shorts and a maroon T-shirt, she sat cross-legged on one of the beds with a thick textbook on her lap and earphones plugged into the iPod on her desk. Her blonde hair was pulled back in a ponytail and she was barefooted. Until I knocked again, louder this time, she didn't realize I was there. Upon seeing me, she gave a friendly smile as she pulled off the earphones. "Can I help you? If you're looking for Laurel, she won't get here till Sunday."

"No, I was looking for you," I said, opening my purse. "I'm Deborah Knott and I have one of your pearls."

I held it out to her and she was both surprised and pleased. "Of course! You're the one who helped me pick them up. Thank you! As soon as I got to the car and counted them, I realized one was missing. I went back up to that room and looked everywhere but I couldn't find it. Where was it?"

"It bounced into the bathroom. Behind the waste-basket," I said. "I tried to catch you, but you'd already gone."

She seemed so happy to get it back that I said, "Didn't you say they were your mother's?"

Amanda nodded. "It was an add-a-pearl necklace from her grandmother. She started it when Mom was born so that she'd have pearls to wear on her wedding day. I can't tell you how much it means to have them all. I may go and get them restrung tomorrow."

As I turned to go, her words suddenly registered.

"You came back to the third floor?"

"Yes, I—"

I watched her eyes fill with horror as she realized what I was asking and all the color drained from her face.

"*You?*" I was stunned. "*You* killed Aunt Rachel?"

"No! No, I didn't. I *didn't*!" Her textbook fell to the floor as she scooted farther away from me until her back was against the headboard next to the wall. "I *didn't*!"

But we both knew she did.

"*Why?*" I asked. "What did she ever do to you?"

She was crying now, huge racking sobs that seemed to come from a deep well of shame and grief. "She kept talking about it and I didn't want Dad to know."

"To know what?"

"That he's not my real father," she sobbed. "That Mom had an affair with some damn cowbird."

"What?"

"My brother. My *half* brother," she said bitterly. "Before he left for Scotland. Something he said made me take a good look at us. Mom was dead, but her pictures...And Dad. All of them have dark hair, and just look at mine."

She gave her head an angry jerk and that blonde ponytail brushed her fair cheek as more tears spilled from those blue eyes. "We were studying DNA in my science class and I sent samples from Dad and me to a lab I found online. No kinship. It would just kill him to think Mom had an affair. They loved each other so much. I don't know what happened. Maybe she was raped or something. But Miss Rachel...she was already off life support. She was going to die any minute anyhow. Wasn't she? Everybody said so."

She was sniffling through her sobs and patting her pockets. I spotted a box of tissues and handed them to her. She blew her nose and looked at me helplessly.

"But what if she didn't? What if she woke up and started talking about me again? Then everyone would know and Dad—!"

There was such a heaviness in my chest that I had to take deep breaths before I could speak.

"He knows, Amanda. He's known from the beginning."

"He *knows*?"

"Your mother made him promise not to tell you."

It was too much for the girl to bear. She rolled over onto her stomach and buried her head in the pillows, her whole body racked with hopeless grief.

I walked out into the hall and called Dwight.

And I stayed with Amanda until he came.

CHAPTER
33

*I have known many old men who have made no
complaint.*

— Cicero

We told the family immediately, of course.

By the end of the week, their surprise and anger was
somewhat tempered by sympathy for Jim Collins, who
was devastated and heartbroken over what Amanda
had done. When talking to Dwight the night she was
arrested, Collins castigated himself over and over for
not breaking his promise to his late wife. "It's my fault.
All my fault. If only I'd told her. Why didn't I *tell* her?
She knew I loved her. Telling her the truth wouldn't
have changed that."

While waiting with her for Dwight to come,
Amanda had told me everything.

"I was worried about Dad," she said, her face
blotched from crying, "but honest, the reason I went

back upstairs—the *only* reason—was to try and find that last pearl. I came up through the new part of the hospital because I didn't want to run into any of the others and there must have been some sort of emergency going on because the third-floor hallway was full of people. But when I got to the hospice hall, it was empty."

She had gone into the room across from Aunt Rachel's and searched the floor, all the time thinking how devastated her dad would be if Aunt Rachel woke up and started harping on goldfinches and cowbirds again, perhaps this time with details that everyone, including him, would recognize.

"I kept hoping she would just go on and die and never wake up again. Then I saw her aide leave the room and go down the hall to the elevator. She didn't see me and I thought if I could just...just...you know, help her stop breathing? But as soon as I put the pillow over her face and mashed down, it felt so awful—*I* felt so awful—that I stopped. It was too late, though. She was gone that quick."

Shivering with shock, still tearful and scared, Amanda told me how she'd stuck the blood-spotted pillow case in her purse and pushed the pillow itself under the lowered bed, hoping it wouldn't be noticed. After that, she'd scurried back downstairs, dumping the pillow case on the way, then out to the car before Collins returned.

"I thought she was cleared," said Dwight, who had eliminated her as a suspect early on. "You told me she left and others saw her waiting in the car. And there was Ray and Tub trying to see if poor old Furman Snaveley, eighty-seven years old, could get upstairs and back again when all the time it was a teenager racing up and down."

Upon advice of the criminal attorney Collins had retained, Amanda was going to plead guilty to voluntary manslaughter and throw herself on the mercy of the court. If the court accepts her plea, there will be an active prison sentence, but she'll have plenty of time to get her life back on track. Hell, she may even wind up running Mediway a few years from now as Collins had hoped.

Jay-Jay was saddened by the whole situation but Sally, who has her own record of youthful rashness, was taking it more in stride. "I hate like the devil that she broke Mama's nose, Deborah. I really hate that, even though Dr. Singh says she probably didn't suffer. If she'd done it for money or out of spite...? But she didn't, did she? She did it because she loved her parents. If I've learned anything from the Daughters, it's how much you'll do for people you love.

"Look at little Katie Lancaster. She bitches about ol' Spencer, but she's the only one in the whole damn family who puts up with him. She bathes him and cooks for him, cuts his toenails, and gets him clean underwear if he doesn't make it to the bathroom in time. She sees that he takes his meds and listens when he tells her the same story for the fifty-third time. Oh, they'll pay her for his care, but don't ask them to come take Spencer off her hands for an afternoon or evening."

While I did not feel compelled to share with her the time I stabbed Allen Stancil, I did tell about Valerie Rhodes, who was so upset over her sister's humiliated misery that she'd smashed into the car where her brother-in-law and his girlfriend were getting it on.

"There you go," Sally said.

A couple of mornings later, I was enjoying a few quiet moments on our back porch with Bandit snoozing at my feet. Dwight and Cal had already left and I had gone out with a cup of coffee to skim through the paper and see what new rollbacks our current legislature had enacted in its determination to undo all the progress the state's made in the last fifty years. Not too long ago, we led the area in education, jobs, civil rights, and quality of life. Now we seem to be competing with Alabama and Mississippi to see who can dive to the bottom first. Voting rights curtailed, social programs cut, oversight authorities with no power, our aquifers threatened by undisclosed fracking chemicals, women told what they can or can't do with their bodies. Our safety nets have been shredded and we've become the butt of jokes on talk shows.

Depressing.

I was ready to chuck the paper when Bandit suddenly roused up and started wagging his tail. A moment later, I heard the rattle of Daddy's old truck and watched as he pulled up in the drive and got out.

"Maidie sent you some bushes," he said, taking several potted plants out of the back.

His housekeeper had rooted us a couple of snowball bushes, a purple hydrangea, and a gardenia from bushes Mother had first planted around the homeplace. Maidie has the greenest thumb of anyone on the farm and over the years, cuttings from Mother's original plantings have flourished in the dooryards of all my brothers, including Adam's. Karen takes rooted cuttings back to California every time she's here.

He set the pots on the back steps and came on up on the porch when I opened the screen door and offered him coffee. I even brought him an ashtray. He's cut back a lot on the cigarettes, but he'll never quit completely and we've all stopped nagging him. "If they ain't killed him by now," says Doris, another smoker who'll reach for a cigarette on her deathbed, "quitting at his age ain't gonna help."

"You not working today?" he asked as he lit up, using one of the wooden kitchen matches he tucks into his cigarette packs. That whiff of sulfur always carries me right back to childhood. Some of my earliest, sweetest memories have the smell of sulfur and cigarette smoke embedded in them.

"I don't have to be there till later this morning." I sensed something was on his mind, but I knew he'd tell me in his own good time.

For a while, we sat and watched the bluebirds go in and out of the box on the other side of the screen. A pair of wrens had nested in one of my hanging baskets and every time one of the adults flew up to perch on the rim with a beakful of insects, we could hear the nestlings' loud peeps.

"Sounds like they'll be flying in a couple of days," Daddy said.

We couldn't see the towhee that was scratching in the mulch beneath the birdhouse, but we could hear his low distinctive call. Out among the pines, jays and crows were going at it in a loud, raucous slinging match. Both will rob eggs from other nests, so it's an ongoing battle. It's never completely quiet in the country. No, we don't have taxis, buses, or endless sirens. Our background noises are more subdued, but they're there. Birds, frogs, cicadas, crickets, the wind through the trees, an occasional rooster crow, or the distant lovesick shriek of Zach's solitary peacock. Somewhere on the far side of the farm, I could hear a tractor working the fields.

For a few minutes, we sat and listened without talking, then Daddy said, "What's gonna happen with that girl?"

"Amanda Collins?"

He nodded.

"No trial," I said. "She'll plead guilty to voluntary manslaughter and go straight to sentencing."

"How much time's she likely to get?"

"Voluntary manslaughter? No priors, no aggravating circumstances? At least three years, but no more than four. I guess that doesn't seem like much to you, balanced against Aunt Rachel's life?"

He didn't answer, just took another drag on his cigarette and looked out across the yard to where it slopes to the pond. We sat in silence for several minutes as the wrens came and went and the towhee continued to scratch for insects.

"Rachel won't never mean-minded," he said at last. "I reckon she'd say that's about right."

He stood to go.

"What about you, Daddy?" I asked as he opened the screen door and started down the steps to his truck.

"I know what prison's like, shug. Remember? But it ain't gonna bring Rachel back, is it?"

Judge Deborah Knott finds herself wrapped
up in a murder investigation that may
reveal mysterious details of her
deceased mother's past...

Turn the page for a preview of

Long Upon the Land

1943

She first notices him because he always sits at a table off to the side of the USO club and he usually sits alone. For some reason, he reminds her of her father, the only person in Dobbs that she misses. Not her mother, not the friends she had gone to school with, and certainly not the boys who joined up as soon as they turned eighteen and who think she is counting the days till they return.

KEEP UP THEIR MORALE the posters urge; and to do her part, she writes weekly letters that give them news from home yet promise nothing, no matter what they might think. If they survive the war—and one has already died in the Battle of Corregidor—they will come back and become doctors, lawyers, or bankers like their fathers before them. They will be good men, pillars of the community, and they will live in big houses and buy their wives fur coats or take them to Europe every three or four years once things settle down after the war, but she never plans to become one of those wives herself. Turn into her mother? Devote her life to maintaining a perfect home, to keeping up appearances?

No—NO—*NO*!

She drops out of Saint Mary's after one semester. "It's a debutante school!"

"So?" says her mother. Ever since Sue and Zell were toddlers, Mrs. Stephenson has dreamed of seeing her daughters make their debut together, and she will never forgive the Germans for a war that has canceled all debutante balls for the duration.

"You keep saying what you don't want," her bewildered father says. "What is it you *do* want, honey?"

"I don't know," Sue cries. "I don't *know*! I just want to live a real life," which is the closest she can come to articulating this nameless yearning to be needed, to make a difference.

"Do you want to teach?" he asks.

In his world, teaching is the most popular choice for women who do not immediately marry.

"What about music?"

The organist at their church is a woman, a woman so pale and timid that he immediately searches for a more vigorous alternative and thinks of Margaret Mitchell, a distant cousin. "Or perhaps you could write?"

She is honest enough to know she has no true artistic

talents. No desire to pour out her soul on paper and no deep interest in classical music. After years of piano lessons, she mostly plays Cole Porter and Irving Berlin by ear, while that one lackluster semester at St. Mary's only confirms that she is bright but no intellectual.

In eighth grade, a fiery and dramatic teacher reads them Wordsworth's stirring call to action—*"Life is real! Life is earnest! And the grave is not its goal."* That's when a restlessness first takes root in her soul, a sense of time inexorably passing, a feeling that there is a life she is meant to lead, things she is meant to do, things that have nothing to do with the war, although it is the war that has let her mother be persuaded that they could contribute to the national cause. Mrs. Stephenson feels vaguely guilty that she has no sons to send to battle, which is why she finally allows Sue and Zell to go to Goldsboro in their stead.

Sue has pushed Zell to come with her, but she has no illusions that her job here at the airfield is vital to winning the war. Clerk-typists are at the bottom of the paper-pushing totem pole, and there is an endless stream of paper that must be pushed. Anybody who knows the alphabet can file. What raises her up an extra pay grade is her typing speed and accuracy. In the department where she and Zell work, every document requires four carbon copies. Make an error on the top sheet and each has to be carefully corrected with two separate erasers while all nine sheets—one bond, four carbons, and four onionskins—are still in the machine so as not to lose the alignment. Most of the girls in the typing pool average two errors a page; she averages one error per three pages and her slender fingers hit the keys so squarely and with such force that the fourth copy is almost as legible as the first.

The material itself is boring, though—reports and requisitions that are as dull as the deeds and depositions she types for her father in the summer when she fills in for vacationing clerks at his law firm.

After three months in Goldsboro, she tells her sister, "Let's go to Washington. That's where all the fun is."

"*Washington?* Don't be a goop, Sue. Mother barely agreed to Goldsboro and it's only sixty miles from home. She'd never let us go three hundred miles away. Never in a million years."

"We don't need her permission."

"Yes, we do," Zell says logically. "I do anyhow." Zell is bookish. She shares none of Sue's troubling doubts and looks forward to becoming Mrs. Ashley Smith when Ash comes safely home. "Please stay here. I couldn't stand it if you went and left me behind."

"Who's leaving you behind?" asks Beulah Ogburn, who shares the top floor of the boardinghouse with her brother and the two Stephenson sisters.

"Sue wants to go to Washington."

"What's in Washington?"

"Life!" says Sue. "Excitement! People! Bright lights!"

"With blackouts?"

Sue gives an impatient wave of her hand. "You

know what I mean, Beulah. Don't you ever get tired of J.C. bird-dogging us?"

J.C. is their self-appointed chaperone and protector. A slight deafness has kept him out of the army, so he too works at the airbase. Night shift in the machine shop. He'd rather be farming, but he adores his sister and figures she'll be ready to go home as soon as he's saved enough money to buy a tractor.

The next day Beulah brings them a flyer calling for volunteers at the USO club. "They need girls to entertain the boys who'll soon be going overseas."

"Entertain how?" growls J.C.

Beulah reads the flyer. "Serve them coffee and doughnuts. Dance with them. Or just talk to them." Beulah is outgoing and gregarious and her feet were made for dancing.

J.C. disapproves, of course, especially as it means they'll be going out at night while he's working. Sue laughs at him. "Zell will chaperone us, J.C. She's practically an old married woman."

And indeed Zell would be quite happy to continue their quiet nights, reading a library book and writing long letters to Ash, but she's a good sport and Sue can talk her into almost anything. "At least it isn't Washington," she writes Ash.

They are popular additions to the club. Zell is a sympathetic ear for homesick young farm boys learning to fly, Sue augments the jukebox's outdated selections on the piano, and Beulah can convince the most uncoordinated left-footer that he's Fred Astaire. Like Sue, Beulah writes chatty letters to her brother's best friend, a boy who plans to marry her as soon as the war was over. "Not going to happen," says Beulah. "Footloose and fancy free. That's me!"

(Except that she will go and fall head over heels in love with a boy from Nebraska who will be killed in action so that she winds up marrying J.C.'s best friend after all, but that's in the unknowable future. Right now, it's laughter and fizzy ginger ale and Friday night movies.)

But Captain Walter Raynesford McIntyre, US Army Air Corps, has the same sad eyes as her father, and she wonders if he is unhappily married, too.

"He's too old for you," her sister Zell says the first time Sue meets him away from the USO club. "Besides, he's probably married."

"He's only thirty-four," she says. "And he's not married. I had someone take a look at his personnel file."

They go to a small club at the edge of the airfield. He drinks bourbon on the rocks and she pours a little into her ginger ale. They talk about the war at first, then she tells him about Dobbs with its small-town social constrictions and suffocating standards. In return, he tells her about growing up in New Bern, down toward the coast. New Bern may be bigger, he says, but its people are just as small-minded and Raynesfords lead the pack, so he understands her frustration at not knowing what she wants from life.

Unlike most adults, he does not suggest possibilities.

"You'll know when you see it," he says. "I did." There's sadness in his voice and bitterness, too.

He's a flight instructor and she thinks he means that he wants to join the action, that he chafes at being kept stateside.

When he lights her cigarette, she takes the lighter from his hand. It's a brass Zippo with his initials engraved inside a frame composed of a vaguely familiar design.

"Greek keys," he says. "They're supposed to symbolize the flow of life...or love."

"Did your girlfriend give it to you?"

He slips the lighter back into his pocket without answering. The sadness is back in his eyes and such a No Trespassing look on his face that she jumps to her feet as the jukebox plays a popular fox-trot. "Let's dance!"

She falls a little in love with him and he's sensitive enough to realize it. Nevertheless, it's two months before he tells her about Leslie's suicide and the dreams the two of them had of making a life together. He continues to badger his superiors—"I'm not a penguin, for God's sake. Let me fly!"—and orders finally come through. The night before he leaves for Europe, they drive out to the river to watch the moon rise. She drinks too much and starts crying because she's sure he won't come back.

He swears that he will and gives her his lighter to

hold for him until he does. "But if I don't, promise me that you won't be afraid to break the rules if they get in your way. We only get one life, Sue. Don't waste it playing safe. Promise me that you'll have the life Leslie and I didn't get to have."

Her tears glisten in the moonlight and she holds the lighter between her two hands as if swearing on a Bible.

"I promise," she whispers.

Now there are diversities of gifts.
                                    —*I Corinthians 12:4*

I almost forgot," my brother Will said. He pulled a small, brightly wrapped box from his pocket. "Got another birthday present for you."

"Aw, you didn't need to do that," I said. "The trellis was more than enough."

Will's an auctioneer and does estate appraisals, too. Somewhere or other, in his ramblings around the state, he had found a beautiful wrought-iron trellis that someone had scrapped. All it needed was a good sandblasting to get rid of the rust, and Dwight had gladly taken it to a body shop in Dobbs. He and Will said it was a birthday present for me and yes, I would enjoy its beauty once it was in place, but we both knew who was the more enthusiastic gardener. This trellis was seven feet tall with graceful leaves and bunches of iron grapes, and once it was set in holes filled with concrete, it would support the scuppernong vine that Dwight had already begun to root from one over at the homeplace.

When he's not digging trees out of the woods or transplanting flowering bushes to turn what once was a tobacco field into his own Garden of Eden, Dwight is Sheriff Bo Poole's second in command. I'm a district court judge and I should have been prepping for the heavy workweek coming up. Our benighted state assembly keeps slashing the court's budget, so in addition to my usual workload, I'd been asked to take a day out of my rotation and hear a case down in New Bern next week. Since the trellis was ostensibly for me, though, it was only fair that I help set it in place. Besides, helping Dwight erect a trellis was a lot more fun than reading depositions. But first Will and I had to wait while Dwight and another brother ran down the farm's posthole diggers. Seth thought Andrew might have been the last to use them when he expanded his dog run a few weeks earlier.

Our son Cal and his Bryant cousins never miss a chance to ride in the truck bed, so they'd gone along, too.

We had wrestled the massive weight from the back of Will's van, and while we waited for the posthole diggers, I took the little package Will had handed me and tore off the paper. Inside was a flip-top Marlboro box and inside that was something small and hard, wrapped in white tissue paper that fell away as my fingers fumbled with it.

A brass Zippo lighter.

I stared at it in surprise and my eyes filled with involuntary tears.

"Will?"

He gave a self-conscious shrug and his own eyes seemed to glisten for a moment. "Adam and Zach never smoked. You quit almost before you started and I quit last year. I thought you might want to keep it."

I could almost see our mother's strong, slender fingers closed around it, cupping it in her hands to light a cigarette. She was never a chain-smoker—four or five a day was her limit, but I never saw her use a match. This lighter was always in her pocket, the brass smooth and golden. The engraved initials were almost worn off from the constant turning in her fingers whenever she was in deep thought. We should have hated it. After all, she died of lung cancer when I was eighteen. But it was so much a part of her that all the boys wanted it after her death. Not just her sons but her stepsons, too. Indeed Andrew was almost ready to fight the others until Seth stepped in and decreed that Will, as her oldest son, should be the one to have it.

It might have amused me had I been around at the time, because I was the only one who knew whose initials—W.R.M.—were engraved on the case inside a frame of Greek keys. By then, though, I was in such deep denial, so angry at the world, at my whole family, and at Mother for dying that I eloped with a sweet-talking car jockey, a man I almost killed with a rusty butcher knife, and didn't come home for a few years.

· The first time I saw the lighter in Will's hands, I almost lost it, but for once I'd kept my mouth shut.

Now I opened the lid and flicked the little wheel with my thumb. It sparked, but the wick didn't catch fire.

"Must be out of fluid," Will said and reached to take it back. "Who was Leslie?"

"Who?"

He pulled the lighter apart to show three lines of engraving on the inner casing: *11/11/1934—Happy 25th.* Below that was the name *Leslie* followed by four notes on a bar of music: *C, G, E, A,* a mixture of half notes and quarter notes.

"I never saw this," I said. "Mother told me that the man who gave it to her was a flight instructor at the airbase over in Goldsboro. I forget what the W stood for, but I think the R was a family name—Raynor, or something like that. His last name was McIntyre, though, and she called him Mac."

"Was he her boyfriend?"

I shook my head. "She said she could have liked him, but he was carrying a torch for someone who committed suicide."

"This Leslie?"

"Maybe. Mother never mentioned the woman's name."

"It would go with that scrap of music." Will hummed the notes and I recognized one of the old songs she used to play on the piano she had brought out to the farm with her when she and Daddy married. *"Let's Fall in Love."* When she was feeling sentimental or flirting with him or making up with him after one of their infrequent spats, this was the song she always played. What he used to play, too. I suddenly realized that he hadn't played it since she died. Not that I ever heard, anyhow.

I looked at the date again. "He would've been in his early thirties when Mother met him."

"So why'd he give her a lighter his girlfriend had given him?" asked Will.

"I think she was supposed to hold it for him as a sort of guarantee that he'd come home safely from the war. Only he didn't."

"So she *did* like him."

"Not the way you mean. But she did say he changed her life."

"How?"

I shrugged. "It was one of those things she started to tell me, but then Aunt Zell or somebody came to sit with her for a while and we never got back to it."

There had been a terrible urgency about Mother's last summer. She had been too busy living to keep a diary and it was as if she felt that her life would be completely lost if there was no one who knew her stories. So between bouts of nausea and diarrhea, she told those stories to me.

Most of them, anyhow.

Only later did I realize how much she had left unsaid. On the other hand, I'd be lying if I said I remembered all the details and nuances of the things that she *did* tell me.

"Would Daddy know?"

"We could ask him, but..." I didn't have to finish the sentence.

Will nodded. "Yeah," he said.

Daddy's never been one to talk about his feelings, but we know how deep the hurt goes. He'll smile with the rest of us when we talk about her—the house parties that lasted for days, the way she could play any song she'd ever heard, the time she lured his best looper away from the barn with better wages than he'd been paying, the way she teased that she fell in love with his eight little boys before she fell in love with him. But we knew not to probe deeper than those lighthearted family legends and anecdotes. Mother probably would have told me about their courtship had I been mature enough to ask, but I was as self-centered as any teenager back then. More interested in whether to go to a ball game with the team captain or with the coach's son.

The boys were all off starting their own lives that summer. College. New jobs. Marriage. Having babies. And all of them were unnerved by her losing battle with death. Daddy was in such fierce denial that he drove himself to exhaustion with farm work from first light to last dark. Even though Mother was dying, I couldn't help feeling sorry for myself. It seemed monstrously wrong that her day-to-day care fell squarely on me. I was supposed to be looking forward to college, not mired in bedpans and soiled bed linens and torn between grief and guilt.

I know now that those last two months were a gift,

and more than once I've wished that I'd listened closer or asked more questions, but she and Daddy were so right together that it never occurred to me to wonder how she could have married a roughneck bootlegger who barely finished grade school and who had eight little boys to boot.

She was a privileged town girl. Had it not been for the war, she would have made her debut in Raleigh wearing long white gloves and a virginal white ball gown.

He grew up in rural poverty, the son of a small-time moonshiner.

Her father was a prominent attorney whose associates tried to get him to run for governor.

His father had died in a car crash while running from a bunch of revenuers.

She had studied Latin in high school.

He spoke the Queen's English—Queen Anne's English, as filtered through three hundred years of informal usage.

She was forever correcting our grammar. Although she never completely broke the older ones from using double negatives, none of us could get away with saying *ain't* in her hearing.

"It's not fair," Adam once grumbled. "Daddy says *ain't* all the time and you never correct him."

"When you're the man your daddy is, you can say whatever you like," she told him. "Till then, you're fixing to go to bed without your supper if you keep arguing about it."

* * *

At the sound of a motor, we looked up toward the house, but when the truck came into sight, it was Daddy's, not Dwight's.

"Speak of the devil and up he jumps," Will said with a grin.

I slid the lighter into a pocket of my jeans and went forward to greet him.

Without cutting his motor, he yelled, "Call the rescue truck! Somebody's been hurt bad and I'm scared to try and move him."

I patted my pockets, but of course I didn't have my phone on me.

Will already had his out, though, punching in 911. "Where is he, Daddy?"

"Down in the bottom, where Black Gum Branch cuts back from the creek. Somebody's smashed his head like a rotten melon. Where's Dwight?" He threw the truck in reverse and I scrambled to catch up with him.

"Wait! I'll come with you. Is he bleeding? Should we bring some ice?"

"Might help," he agreed and slowed to a stop by my back door.

I darted inside, scooped up some clean dishtowels by the refrigerator, emptied the whole bin of ice into a large plastic bag, grabbed my phone from the kitchen counter, and was back out to the truck in only seconds.

Will roared up in his van. "The ambulance is on its I'll go get Dwight," he said and dug off toward 's house.

"Who is it?" I asked as we fishtailed through the sandy lanes that led down to Possum Creek.

"He was throwed down with his face in the dirt," he said grimly. "I won't sure if I should move his head, but I turned him so he could breathe. Leastways, I think he was breathing."

The farm is crisscrossed by lanes, some of which lead out to a couple of nearby roads that also cross the farm or serve as boundary lines.

"I was on my way to the food store," Daddy said by way of explanation, but I knew it was only a partial explanation.

A lane might be less direct from Point A (his back door) to Point B (his destination) than the road, but the lanes let him check up on parts of the farm he might not have visited recently. Most farmers still walk or ride their boundaries regularly, keeping an eye on crops, on fences, on drainage ditches that might need cleaning, or for a dozen other reasons. As a boy, he could have walked the family's hundred acres in an hour, but over the years, he and I and my brothers have added so much land to the original holding that wheels were a necessity. He's never cared much for what he calls "stuff," but let an acre of land come up for sale anywhere near the farm and he's right there with an offer, cash in hand. Last time my brother Seth totted up all the non-contiguous bits and pieces, too, we were surprised to realize that together we own close to twenty-five hundred acres.

We had been driving along the northern edge of Possum Creek. Now, as we neared the turn by the branch, Daddy put the truck in four-wheel drive and edged off the lane into the field.

"I probably already messed up any good tracks for how he got here," he said as he stopped and cut off the motor, "but you never know."

Mindful of his words, I was careful to step only on unmarked sand when I hopped out with my ice and hurried over to the body lying on the far side of the lane. Another two feet closer to the branch and he would have been hidden by a thick tangle of weeds and vines.

Blood had matted his hair and drawn flies and yellow jackets. I flapped them away with my dishtowel and gently laid the bag of ice on the wound, which was still oozing blood. Oozing meant his heart was still beating, didn't it? Or was it only gravity because Daddy had turned his head minutes ago? When I pressed my fingers against the side of his neck, I couldn't feel a pulse and I couldn't tell if he was still breathing. It's been years since I'd taken a CPR course, but Daddy helped me move him onto his back and I started compressing his chest.

When Daddy relieved me, I used my phone to take pictures of the ground around the man where some tire tracks lay. No footprints and it looked like someone had used a dead branch to sweep the sand smooth. I walked a few more paces down the lane past where Daddy had stopped the first time and took more pictures.

Before I could kneel to take over again, Daddy sat back on his heels. "He's gone, shug. Ain't nothing more we can do."

We heard the sirens then and Dwight's truck barreled through the lane, a blue light clamped to the roof of the cab. One of our local rescue trucks followed and Will was close behind.

Three EMTs hurried over to the man who lay motionless on his back, his eyes closed and bluebottle flies circling his head.